A WAGON TRAIN LEGACY

Also by W. C. Augustine

Atlas Rising Series

Atlas Rising
For the Common Good
USA 2.0

Shades of Green

A
WAGON TRAIN

LEGACY

W.C. AUGUSTINE

A Wagon Train Legacy

Published by Atlas Rising Publishing.

Cover and interior design by Carol Davis, www.tolgraphics.com

Published and printed in the United States of America
Library of Congress Cataloging-in-Publication Data is available upon request.

ISBN: 978-0-9864355-4-6
1.Fiction, General
2. Family

Forward

My intent in writing this book was to bring a family history to life in an interesting, imaginary story without exceeding the bounds of known family legacy. The main characters are fictional, although often reality can be more interesting than fiction.

The historical flashbacks are to real places and situations my ancestors experienced. My fourth great grandfather did indeed travel to Russia in Napoleon's army, and the family immigrated to America for the reasons described. In America, they moved several times, finally moving to avoid swamp fever in Indiana.

As a pioneer in Iowa, family legend has him killing an Indian. Whether it was an act of bravery to save his family, or the unwarranted murder of an indigenous person, I do not know. My fictional account is what could have happened, although I know he moved because of the incident.

The Wyoming hanging of a former wagon train traveler is fictional, as was his brother's move to Missouri. My third great grandfather, the wagon train captain, did have a general merchandise store in two California gold mining camps, and legend has it that his wife, Dorothy, was the only woman in camp one winter. They did briefly move to pre-civil war Missouri where, being Methodist abolitionists, they were run out.

The wagon trail log of my ancestor's fourth wagon train trip at the end of the book is real. It was not found as described in the book but given to me by my grandfather as was the pocket watch of my ancestor.

CHAPTER I

"I've got a present for you," Clark Adams declared while reaching in front of his fiancée, Sarah Conners, and pulling a bag from the glove compartment of his Porsche.

"What is it? You promised you wouldn't buy me more jewelry after this gorgeous ring until we were married."

Her eyes involuntarily fell to the three-quarter carat diamond on her finger as they did with any mention of her engagement ring. The ring glistened in the light from the light pole in her apartment parking lot. The need for a manicure touch-up crossed her mind while ignoring what might be in the bag. Her fingers should look as luxurious as the ring.

Sarah had moved from her parent's home in a Chicago suburb to a studio apartment in West Des Moines ten months previously. Moving to Des Moines was an opportunity to escape unpleasant memories of her father's early death and years of caring for her suffering mother. The apartment manager was pushing her to decide whether to renew her lease. She hadn't decided.

As Clark pulled the bag from the glove compartment, his hand brushed her exposed knee sliding her sundress hem higher. She felt herself flinch from the poorly disguised accident. Again, the thought crossed her mind, *was it normal to flinch from the touch of the man you were to marry?*

He pulled two boxes from the bag. One had obviously been opened.

"I've been Covid tested twice. I feel fine; why another test?" she asked.

"These aren't Covid tests. They are DNA sample kits for Background USA. I've already put oral drool in my tube. Now it is your turn."

"But why? We haven't discussed this."

"Don't you want to know where you came from? Both our families have legends of ancestors on a wagon train. And I'd like to validate my mother's contention that our family had indigenous American blood; it would be advantageous to my legal career."

"I don't know, let me think about it."

"What is it? Are you afraid your ancestors owned slaves or perhaps sold liquor and guns to the Indians? Perhaps, you are afraid that mine will validate the rumor that I'm also a descendant of two presidents whose name I carry?

"That's not funny."

"I think if we're to be married we should know more about each other. Wouldn't it be neat if our ancestors traveled on the same trail?"

"I'll think about it." She brushed her sun dress hem lower and reached for the door handle.

"We can talk about it inside."

"No, not tonight," she placed one hand on his shoulder as her right hand opened the door.

"Come on, we'll soon be married." He pleaded.

"We'll have plenty time then, and thank you for the pizza," she said leaning toward him and giving him a good night kiss which he unsuccessfully tried to extend.

He remained in the car intently watching her walk to the apartment complex entry door. She looked great in the white sundress with roses spread upon. Disappointment fell over him as she swiped her card at the door. Would she turn and wave as she entered the door; perhaps change her mind? She could feel his eyes on her and avoided turning.

Sarah was a junior in college when Clark invited her to his fraternity dance. It was their first of only three dates while in college. To his disappointment she dated two other boys off and on and always seemed busy when he asked her out. Although they attended the same university, they ran in different circles.

For five years after graduation with a degree in library science, Sarah only worked part time at various metro libraries. Caring for her invalid mother was nearly a full time job. When her mother passed, she remembered that Clark's mother was director of library services in Des Moines. A call to Clark, followed by an interview with his mother, Andrea, landed her a library job in Des Moines. Given the source of her job, it was difficult to avoid accepting Clark's date requests. They soon became an item.

Within a year Sarah was assistant director in one of the city's libraries. Andrea had taken Sarah under her wing as her son wooed her. The more she become acquainted with Clark, the more Sarah found him to be, as they say, a chip off the block. In this case, the block still controlled the chip.

Andrea invited Sarah ride with her to a small town library in Oskaloosa. She would be training outlying library personnel on non-binary gender inclusivity. Sarah suspected she'd been invited because she had not shown interest in the subject. She was wrong.

"Sarah, as Mildred is retiring I want you to apply for assistant city library director."

Sarah was stunned. "Why me? It is flattering, but others have much more experience."

"Yes, but they will not be my daughter-in-law. Clark is an up and coming lawyer in his firm. Married to an advancing city employee would seem appropriate."

"What about meritocracy, Jeanie for instance, she has been with the library for years, and I still must go to her for advice?"

"Jeanie is not on my list. If I don't choose you, I'll pick Marcia."

"But she's been with the library less time than I."

"Yes, but I must consider diversity, both race and sexual proclivities."

Sarah agreed to submit her application.

The library in Oskaloosa was a red brick Carnegie donated structure which had been modernized. It had a homey feel as did the town square. Although the staff was personable, Sarah could sense they reluctantly tolerated the gender lecture.

On the ride back to Des Moines, Andrea commented on the town's history. "Isn't it great to have a town in our state named Oskaloosa for a native American princess in a county named Mahaska for an indigenous chief?

Sarah ignored the comment and asked, "Will you recommend any of your staff for the director vacancy in Oskaloosa?

"No, neither do I wish to lose anyone or encourage anyone to submit themselves to small town mentality."

The comment vibrated in Sarah's head as she attempted sleep that night.

The next morning Sarah met a neighbor, Taylor, at a coffee shop. It had become routine as they shared a day off work. Over time they had become comfortable confiding in each other.

"There is a vacancy for director in a small town library, I'm considering applying for it."

"Why? Taylor purposely asked the open question.

"I had a good feel about the town."

"And?"

"Given our differences, I'm not sure working under a mother-in-law will be good for anyone."

"Yeah, bingo; you figured that out? What about the differences with your fiancé? Long term, how will you patch those over?

"He's actually not a bad guy."

"Not a bad guy, is that why you have dated other guys off and on between episodes with him? I have never seen any fire in your eyes for him."

"Fire may be overrated."

"With his family, your cultural and political differences, you must harbor a strong fire for him to overcome what will inevitably cause friction."

"I could do worse."

"Yeah, we could get coffee from a home brewed pot also."

Sleep came ever harder for Sarah that night.

Sarah found herself elated when her director application was followed by a request for an interview. Two weeks later on her day off she drove her 10-year-old Toyota to Oskaloosa for an interview.

"That is a beautiful statue of Chief Mahaska standing in the town square, particularly with the Napoleonic pose," Sarah said honestly but hoping to score points with the library board president.

"Well, there is a twist to that pose. He has his hand in his tunic because of necessity. It seems the chief was staying at the Willard Hotel in Washington during treaty negotiations and an occupant heard a woman screaming in the chief's room. The man burst the door open to find the chief beating his squaw as was common among Indians. The embarrassed chief jumped from the two story window and broke his shoulder."

She continued, "You don't, of course, in these politically correct times, always speak the truth publicly. We let visitors form their own opinion."

Sarah enjoyed the lack of pretense on the part of the library board president. It was refreshing. Nevertheless, she thought the likely futile interview would be a good experience. Her hope of acquiring a comfortable job somewhere accelerated. She tried to tamp down her enthusiasm for fear of disappointment on her drive back to Des Moines.

Before returning to her apartment, she stopped at a convenience store on the East side of Des Moines. In the dairy section a chill climbed her spine as an ill clad man's lewd, predatory gaze assessed her body. She vowed to avoid the store in the future. With orange juice and milk in a basket she reluctantly entered the cashier line behind the man who appeared nervous. "You're next," the cashier prodded him. The man scanned the premises for other customers. Sarah also did hoping to see others; she did not.

Suddenly, he pulled an oversized knife from his jacket. "Keep one hand above the counter and lay all the bills in a bag and hand it to me," he demanded.

Sarah froze. Running to the door seemed the prudent thing to do, but it would draw attention to her. Twice he quickly glanced over his shoulder at her.

She felt herself jump when a man behind her exited the candy aisle and hollered, "Put the knife down and hands away from your body."

The would-be thief turned to see a man holding a pistol pointed at the burglar.

"Now!" I said continued the man with the gun.

The thief complied and the cashier called 911.

Not another word was spoken as the cashier remained on the phone, the knife laid on the floor and the gun remained pointed at the disarmed man. Sarah could feel and smell her failing deodorant.

The cashier looked at the man with the gun, "The police are at the door. They want you to put your gun on the floor."

He complied. The police handcuffed the burglar and picked up the brave citizen's gun from the floor.

Four uniformed police officers and three detectives were soon on the scene. Sarah was told to stay. Detectives interviewed the cashier, Sarah, and the hero. Their stories were the same. She could hear a detective asking the man if he had a concealed gun permit. He did not.

"Why are you handcuffing him?" Sarah asked.

"He has no permit."

"Well, he saved the day. No leniency?"

"Sorry miss, if I had my way, I'd give him a medal, but I have no choice if I wish to keep my job."

She approached the man and hugged him, "Thank you for what you did, do you have a lawyer?"

"No, doubt if I can afford one."

Back at her apartment Sarah called Clark. "What about the pizza place tonight, it is my turn to buy?"

"How about I bring a frozen pizza to your place, and we toss it in the oven?"

"Yes, I know how that will turn out. Joe's pizza is better."

After ordering pizza, Clark led her to a corner booth. She sat facing the door in the middle of the bench hoping to remain alone. "Aren't you going to scoot over and make room for me?" he asked.

She reluctantly complied.

"Did you get results from Background USA on your DNA submission?"

"Yes, it didn't amount to much."

"Surely you learned something, did it confirm part of your family lived in Springfield, Missouri?"

"I didn't learn much. It was a waste of money."

"I'm surprised you haven't asked me to submit my DNA again, since you bought the tests. Aren't you still curious whether our mutual family rumors about wagon trains are but myths?"

He changed the subject. "Mother says you may be the new assistant director, I think that will be wonderful."

"We'll see."

He was taken back by her short non-committal answer and changed the subject again. "Tell me about your convenience store ordeal."

Sarah went into detail about the attempted robbery and what she considered the fortuitous presence of a hero.

"Did you fear for your own safety?"

"Absolutely, a woman can intuitively feel the perverted intensions of a man. I have a favor to ask. The man who stopped the crime was arrested for not having a carry permit. He said he couldn't afford a lawyer."

"The court will appoint him one."

"Yeah, what kind of lawyer will that be? Can you or someone in your firm take his defense?"

"We do very few pro bono cases and those we do are targeted toward enhancing our social standing."

"Well, he is a minority."

"Yes, but we can't be seen defending someone carrying a gun."

"You mean you only defend politically correct clients."

"I wouldn't say it that way."

"You often talk about fairness. We both know if the guy were well-heeled and could afford a good attorney, he'd get off. That man did more to defend our community than any of your regular clients."

"Whoa, whoa; I didn't make the system, although it is good to hear you speak up for the downtrodden once."

"What a statement coming from a hypocrite. Excuse me, I need to use the restroom."

When Sarah returned she slid in the booth opposite Clark. Further conversation was confined to the condition of the mushroom, sausage, green pepper pizza they had ordered.

Coolness in the air convinced Clark to avoid seeking an invitation to her apartment. She gave him a quick peck on the lips as she left the car. Walking to the door, it struck Sarah that he never thanked her for buying dinner the few times she did, although she always thanked him.

Sarah was finalizing an order for new library books when Clark's mother stopped at her desk. "Come to my office as soon as the board member standing by the newspaper rack leaves. I need to talk to you."

The library budget limited the month's purchase to fifty books. Seventy had been submitted for purchase. Two were easy culls. *Man-Boy Erotic Relationships* and *The Unwarranted Stigma of Underage Attraction* Sarah easily culled although Clark's mother had recommended them. Feeling courageous, Sarah would deal with the consequences if they arose, she thought as her phone rang.

It was a 673 phone prefix, an Oskaloosa number. She softly said a prayer before answering.

"Hi, this is Beverly from the Oskaloosa library board."

"Oh, so glad to hear from you. You have a beautiful library; did I tell you that?"

"Yes, you did, and we have decided to offer you the job of director with a six month probation period."

"'*Oh my God, I thank you*,' she thought, but didn't verbalize it out of learned habit to avoid such declarations and simply said, "I accept."

When they finished discussing details, Clark's mother was standing in the office doorway waiting with a stern look. "I'm ready for you."

Sarah had hardly sat down when Clark's mother announced, "You will be the new assistant director."

Sarah was stunned.

"Aren't you going to say anything?"

"How about the others? What will they say?"

"Why should you worry? It will be good for both you and Clark's career."

The director's phone rang, before she lifted it she said, "I went out on a limb with a board member to get you the job. Come back before closing and we'll do the paperwork."

It was closing time when Sarah meekly stepped into Andrea's office. "About time you came to thank me."

"I don't think I can accept the promotion. I accepted the job in Oskaloosa."

"You what? What is wrong with you?"

"I think I'd be more comfortable there."

"What about Clark? It is an hour and a half drive. How will that work? He may not tolerate you working there."

"We'll work something out."

"I'm sure Clark will be upset. Do you have any idea what kind of catch he is? You chance losing him and this position, for what?"

"I'm sorry to have disappointed you," Sarah said as she left the office. Suddenly her steps felt lighter.

It was after 7:00 when the front door buzzer squawked. Sarah was only surprised it had taken as long and knew who it was.

"It's me. We need to talk," Clark said.

Sarah didn't reply, just buzzed him in.

A Wagon Train Legacy

When he reached her studio, the door was cracked, and she was sitting on a chair leaving the settee for him.

"Do you have any idea what you are doing?" he said before sitting.

"I think so."

"You insulted my mother who was thinking of your future."

"My future or yours?"

"I'll ignore that. Three hours a day you will be commuting. Will there be any time left for us?

"If us is meant to be, we'll work it out."

"Do you think my mother will have the job waiting for you once you dispense with this rebel streak?"

"I don't have any illusions."

"Meet me at Joe's tomorrow evening. Hopefully by then you will have rethought this and come to your senses."

Abruptly, he got up, glared at her, and left without attempting to kiss her. She was relieved as she didn't know how she would have accepted a kiss at the moment. She couldn't help but wonder what the anger in him was contemplating. Her mind fell back to Beverly's tale of Chief Mahaska beating his wife. *What had changed in a hundred and fifty years?*

Clark had ordered their favorite when she arrived. Sitting at their usual back booth, he scooted toward the wall to make room for her. She chose to sit across from him. Her slight was noticed making it harder for him to control his anger, but he did.

"I'm willing to forget about last night and this craziness. I'm sure you've come to your senses by now."

"Yes, I have."

When she reached in her right jacket pocket, he saw her left ring finger was barren. "What the hell," he exclaimed as she handed him his ring.

"I wish you the very best, Clark; but I believe this is the best for both of us."

"You are crazy. Do you know what a catch I am?"

"I'm sure you'll find a woman better suited to you."

"I'm sure I will. Sherry, a legal assistant in our office, has flirted with me for a year," he offered in hopes of igniting jealousy.

"Well, ask her out then."

"And what will you find, some bumpkin in a small town?

"You never know," Sarah replied. She met the pizza boy delivering a mushroom, sausage, green pepper pizza to the table as she left.

Chapter 2

Sarah left her West Des Moines studio three weeks before the apartment lease expired. The commute she could have dealt with for another few weeks, but Clark's continuous *checking on her,* as he called it, bordered on harassment. It was common for him to be waiting for her when she arrived home. Once he had their favorite pizza waiting for her in his car.

Although the three-hour daily commute had left Sarah no time to make friends in Oskaloosa outside the library, Beverly couldn't have been more supportive. As library board president and not a paid employee, Beverly spent many hours at the library as a volunteer.

Pay as director of the small town library was similar to what Sarah would have earned as assistant director in Des Moines. Beverly directed her to a friend who rented Sarah a one bedroom apartment in a three-plex that was over twice the size of her studio in Des Moines for less money. Not that pay was a consideration in her move but financially she was better off in Oskaloosa.

Beverly had not pressured her, but more than once she had invited Sarah to her church. Sarah hadn't attended a church for years. Clark considered most a cult of superstitious customs and hypocrisy. Sarah assumed his beliefs came from his mother, but she never brought the subject up. Once she challenged him that his atheism was as much a belief as belief in a higher power. After neither made headway in the discussion, they dropped the subject.

Free time on Sunday morning, and a desire to reappraise beliefs she had tucked under her sleeve as her relationship with Clark developed, caused Sarah to investigate Beverly's invitation. On a Sunday morning, first she wore a grey suit. Assessing it in the mirror she decided it was great for the business-like atmosphere of the library, but on this beautiful May morning she desired something cheerful. Her white sundress with pink roses fit the mood she was in.

The church was three blocks from her apartment. The walk was invigorating. The constant cooing of mourning doves did nothing to tamper her joy. Only something good could happen this day she was sure.

Andrew was a church greeter. He stood outside near the door welcoming people. His job was much more pleasant this day than a January day he could remember. After he helped an older couple in the church, he saw a lady on the sidewalk wearing a white dress with what looked like pink blotches on it. Closer he could see they were painted roses. A visitor, surely, as he had never seen her.

Sarah noticed the man standing at the church door as if he were waiting on her. He was wearing a light blue shirt with a yellow tie. As he held the door open and welcomed her, the wind caught a strand of hair and whisked it down his forehead as he made eye contact with her. It caused her to wonder what her hair looked like after the breezy walk. She felt his eyes on her again after she entered the vestibule.

Several people she didn't know greeted her as she entered the lovely church vestibule flushed with colors from the stained glass windows. Beverly pulled her husband away from a conversation with another couple. She greeted Sarah and introduced her husband. Now Sarah knew two people in the church.

Sarah, expecting to feel out of place, self-consciously sat alone at a left side pew toward the back of the church. It had been how long since she sat in a church, two, three, five years? In an unexplained way, she felt at home. After the choir sang their first song, Amanda, the choir leader,

A Wagon Train Legacy

asked the congregation to greet all church neighbors. Sarah sensed the greetings were genuine rather than curiosity inspired. Amanda then invited newcomers to fill out a card in a chair pocket and text a number on the card for a gift. Sarah put the card in her purse. She would think about it later.

Midweek Sarah ordered pizza to pick up. In the pizzeria parking lot, she saw Clark's toy, his car. She left the pizza place, she could scratch up a meal at home, but second thoughts got the better of her before she was home. After a U-turn she parked next to him and walked to his passenger car window. He rolled it down. "Hi, perhaps we can try the pizza here."

"How did you know I was coming here?"

"I guess we think alike."

"You don't have any business in this town. You are stalking me. I tried to break it off amicably, but you won't accept that, will you?"

"Can't blame a guy for trying," he replied while sniffling.

"Your spring allergy is acting up, I see."

"Yes, it is particularly bad this year, how 'bout a little sympathy?

Sarah ignored the play, "What happened to the legal assistant who was hitting on you?"

"Not my type."

"If we share the pizza inside, will you promise to never come here again? As soon as the question left Sarah's mouth she realized her mistake. But he was out of the car immediately.

"Understand this is our good-bye meal."

"Yeah, I hear that," he replied obviously ignoring it as they were seated.

"What will your firm think if a junior lawyer is slapped with a stalking charge?"

"You wouldn't."

"Tell me how you knew I'd be here."

"Like I said intuition."

Sarah noticed Andrew, the church greeter, enter the restaurant with a woman. His entry distracted her from grilling her ex. The couple were seated two booths away. Andrew noticed Sarah as he was seated facing her. He smiled. The woman he was with seemed upset.

Although Sarah could not hear their conversation, it was louder than normal and seemed agitated. Andrew caught Sarah's eyes more than once.

In order to distract herself from the couple, Sarah asked Clark, "You never told me what DNA disclosed about your family history. Is there any evidence of American Indian ancestry or that your family was on a wagon train?"

"Those ancestry tests are bogus, just a lure to get money. The government should do something to regulate them."

Normally Sarah would have challenged him on his desire for more big brother control of a business, but she didn't and asked, "How about your rumored family history in Springfield, MO, and native American ancestry?"

"I wouldn't believe anything that comes from that company."

As he answered her, she could see him trying to stifle an allergy sneeze. Suppression made it worst. He reached for a napkin and expelled into it loud enough to draw looks around the room. After an apology, he wrapped the soiled napkin in another.

Sarah had learned that stress only exasperated his allergy symptoms. His body language, and voice tone indicated stress. He wasn't used to losing, his mother saw to that. Although for him Sarah was more of a possession than a soulmate, losing her would not set well with his mother who had gone out of her way to help Sarah.

For Sarah his behavior indicated he had given her a deceptive answer about the ancestorial results. Confirmation of his mother's claim of indigenous blood he would be talking about.

It was clear Background USA had found something in Clark's family embarrassing or wrong about which he wouldn't talk. Clark attempted to make small talk while Sarah thought about his lie.

Suddenly, the voice of the woman with Andrew rose enough to silence everyone in the room. Clark turned to see what the commotion was about. As he did, Sarah wrapped a third napkin around the napkins in which he had sneezed and slid them from the table into her purse.

As the woman abruptly left Andrew's table, Clark turned back to Sarah. "We would never let a silly disagreement escalate like that, would we?"

She reached for the last piece of pizza and didn't answer. On the way out they walked past Andrew sitting alone. He smiled and said hi. Sarah returned the greeting but didn't introduce Clark.

"Who was that guy?" Clark asked in the parking lot.

"A greeter at the church."

"You're going to church, wow; guess you have changed. What other small town habits have you adopted?"

"No, actually I haven't changed, just righted myself," she replied, then made it as plain as possible this was their last encounter and if he bothered her she would contact a local lawyer.

Walking to her apartment from her car she saw Clark drive by. She would have to do something. She ducked behind another car and attempted to get his license number but failed.

With the door locked and bolted, she placed the napkins in a plastic sealed bag and refrigerated them. On Background USA website, she ordered a DNA test kit.

"I see you are in the library on your day off; I guess we hired a really dedicated director," said Beverly finding Sarah doing research in the community's historical section of the library.

"I'm amazed that a family settled here after the family patriarch led wagon trains to the west coast."

"Why would that amaze you?"

"People who traveled that direction usually stayed."

"You've met someone in that family who might be able to answer that question."

After receiving an inquisitive look from Sarah, Beverly continued, "Yes, you met him; he's a greeter at our church, Andrew."

"Is he a history buff?"

"Yes, and a descendant of a wagon train captain. He also carries the family name, Augustine. Why your interest in wagon trains?"

"My grandmother believed we had an ancestor who rode in a wagon train through the wilderness, but she had no evidence. I'm interested whether it was true or just family hearsay."

"Well contact Andrew Augustine and I'll leave you to your research now."

Later they left the library and Beverly took her to a local popular diner.

"I really like your necklace," Beverly said. "Have you had it long?"

"It was my grandmother's. Since I'm not working today, I hope it is alright that I wore it."

"Why wouldn't it be?"

"The library director in Des Moines, as did my supervisor in Chicagoland, said the gold cross was too large and might offend someone."

"You wear it anytime you desire. No one will complain."

As they ate salads, Sarah asked, "I don't want to sound nosy or carry gossip, but I saw Andrew in a pizza parlor last week with a lady, and they appeared to be having problems."

"Well, that is no secret. She's a banker from Madison. The national bank moved her to this location, and she makes no secret about not liking it here. They met when Molly became Andrew's banker. He has an extensive farm and livestock operation. They don't agree on much, but their relationship started downhill when she refused him a loan as his operation wasn't organic enough to suit her."

"Probably more than you wanted to know." Beverly added as Sarah seemed to digest the information.

"I have never seen her in church."

"Oh, she refuses to come, says it's an archaic custom. Rumor has it that they are finished as he asked for his ring back."

"They were engaged?"

"Not anymore. So how has your move gone? Are you having any problems?" asked Beverly as they ate.

"One problem may have followed me here."

This time it was an inquisitive look from Beverly that caused Sarah to continue. "My former boyfriend, well former fiancé actually, from Des Moines has been coming here and following me."

"Has he harassed you?"

"No but he seems to know where I am. He was waiting for me at a pizza parlor recently. How he knew I was headed there I do not know."

"Sheriff Murphy is a friend. I'll give him a heads-up. Stop in and explain the situation to him."

"Why not the police?"

"That department is filled with bureaucrat functionaries. As the sheriff is elected, he is in tune with the community."

"I'm Sarah Conners to see the sheriff," she told the department deputy receptionist.

"Go on in, he is expecting you."

"Beverly told me about you. I'm glad to meet the new library director," the sheriff said standing and offering Sarah a hand then a seat.

Sarah explained Clark's surveillance of her.

"Do you have his car plate number?"

"No, but he drives a yellow Porsche."

"I can get his plate number but probably not necessary, the car will kind of stick out around here."

"Does he have someone following me? How did he know I was picking up a pizza?"

"How long ago and how did you come to acquire your cell phone? The sheriff asked.

"A year ago, Clark got a special deal on two phones. He paid the bill on mine until we broke up, but I kept the phone and number."

"As the original owner of the account, I suspect he has access to your call log. He may have caught you ordering pizza from the place."

Before the day ended, Sarah had a new phone with her contact list transferred to her new phone.

It was nearly a month later when Beverly walked into Sarah's library office and said she had received a letter meant for Sarah. From her purse, she pulled a letter addressed to a fictitious man named Anthony Jones from Background USA.

Sarah had placed Clark's expelled mucus in a test tube and filled out the requisite information with Beverly's address.

"I hope your using my address doesn't cause me trouble," said Beverly.

"Don't worry, I'll never tell him about how I received the information."

Background USA's focus was matching the DNA from customers with others and gleaning databases of birth, marriage, and death records throughout the country. Technology allowed Background to piece information together that would have taken the most sophisticated researchers years a generation earlier. Accuracy was paramount to expanding their customer base and increasing sales. Often test results would show someone a second or third cousin to the customer which the customer already knew to be the case. The known relationships enhanced and validated Background's reputation.

The company's algorithms were designed to give the customer accurate ancestral information, not identify fraud or red flag identical DNA sent by different names.

Following a series of calls and text messages from Clark, Sarah blocked his number. She came to wish she had acquired a new number when she changed phones. The block didn't stop him from calling from his law office. And now he was sending her letters; it was all too much.

After reading Clark's ancestral report under the name of Anthony, she unblocked his number and text him.

Does the senior partner in your law firm know what happened to your great, great uncle in Wyoming??

CHAPTER 3

In the year 1849, near South Bend, Indiana, Nathanial Adams, Clark's third great grandfather, wished his younger sons well as the wagon train pulled out for California. He had paid their fare and staked them with a team of oxen, wagon, and provisions. It was the least he could do as they were abandoning any future inheritance from the farm.

Nathanial felt some guilt as he watched the wagons disappear from sight. He had taught his sons the game of poker. It was a harmless pastime of his. But his sons had taken it to another level. The latest fight in which they found themselves was not the first, just the most violent. James, the oldest had sustained a knife wound to the arm.

Martha Adams was bandaging her son when the sheriff knocked on the door. "I'm sorry your son is injured but the other man is in worse shape. I've warned them about playing poker. It is now against the law in this county."

"How did the fight start?" asked Nathanial after he escorted the sheriff outdoors.

"The others accused James and Thomas of cheating. Like I said it has happened before. If they are caught playing for money again, I will lock them up."

For Nathanial, it seemed prudent to send the brothers west where the population was sparse, towns scarce, and money for card games was nil.

In some ways Nathanial envied his sons heading out on an adventure. It had been his adventure to move from Connecticut to Indiana. The brothers also relished the unknown in front of them. Their older brother was nearly running the farm, making a future place for them uncertain.

Although the pioneers traveled to the frontier on wagon trains for many different reasons, they all wanted an opportunity to start new lives. Many of the pioneers were farmers. They went to Oregon, Texas, and other areas of the frontier for inexpensive land. Much land was available for homesteading. They sought rich, fertile land for crops and green pastures for cattle. Other people came to the frontier because they had heard stories that made the new lands sound like magical places. Some went to the frontier in order to prospect for gold, to hunt and trade fur pelts, and for many other quests for adventure.

The excursion was an expensive enterprise. It was estimated that the journey in 1840-1860 including fare, equipment, and provisions cost over $20,000 dollars in today's money. Nathanial provided his sons with what they would need for the trip.

The traveler would need a specially prepared wagon in addition to animals pulling the wagon. The canvas top would have to be waterproofed with linseed or animal oil and stretched over a framework of hoop-shaped slats. Although mainly made of wood, iron was used to reinforce the wagon at crucial points. However, iron was used sparingly in construction, because the added weight would slow down travel and exhaust the animals pulling the wagon. The front wheels of the wagon were smaller than the back wheels. This helped the wagon turn. Underneath the back wheels they carried a bucket full of grease which hung from the axle. Grease was used to lubricate the wheels.

The wagons generally were heavy, broad-wheeled covered freight carriers used extensively during the late 1700s and 1800s. They were called Conestoga Wagons or prairie schooners, because from a distance the Conestoga wagon looked like a ship sailing slowly across the green prairie ocean. The sailing however was anything but smooth.

Traveling in a wagon was not an easy trip. These wagons were rough riding as they rarely had springs above the axles to minimize the bumps. Fortunately, for the riders they traveled slowly. Nor did the wagons have brakes, which caused serious problems when traveling downhill. One solution was to use chains to lock at least one wheel. Another strategy was to cut down a tree and pull it behind the wagon to supply drag.

During the journey across Illinois, the new state of Iowa and the plains of what would become Nebraska, the two brothers' stash of goods in their wagon increased as others' on the trail diminished. Only when the load became noticeably difficult for the oxen, did they stop pilfering neighbors.

After four days of hard traveling, they stopped to graze the livestock and rest for a day near the North Platte River, in an area which would later become the town of Bridgeport. The river provided sweet tasting water to replenish their supplies. The wagon train captain advised travelers that women would have use of the river from two until four in the afternoon and men after five.

It was around three in the afternoon that most of the men were on the opposite side of the wagons from the river engaged in a shooting match. Hildegard, the sixteen year old daughter of the family whose wagon the Adams brothers followed on the trail, was at the river. Both brothers had their eyes on her. Often they had tried to start a conversation with her which she usually ignored with giggles. Her father often discouraged their flirtation with his protective eye.

Cautiously walking to the riverbank, they hid behind scrub brush. The dress Hildegard had been wearing that morning was hanging on a tree branch. A basket of washed clothes was near. Careful maneuvering allowed them to spot Hildegard in the water. She was wearing pantalets with a cotton undershirt straps over her shoulders. The wet fabric clung to her body leaving little to the imagination.

She started to turn in the water when the brothers heard someone behind them yell, "What on God's earth."

The wife of the man who served as pastor on the trip had circled around them. They skedaddled for their wagon with the woman following scolding them.

When they returned to their wagon, the wagon train captain was standing holding a fancy oil lantern that had disappeared from his wagon.

The wagon trail organizer, guide, and master who led the caravan down the trail was called captain. He held the same authority and responsibilities as a captain of a seagoing vessel. The journey was very much like an ocean crossing. The captain commanded the wagon train, maintained law and order on the journey, led the caravan down the trail and made any decisions that affected the whole caravan. He would marry people, settle disputes, and make decisions such as when and where they were going to camp for the night. When approaching a river, the captain would decide when and how they would cross. Captains were also in charge of waking up the members of the wagon train, deciding when they would stop for lunch, and making sure everything ran smoothly on the trail.

"You are no longer welcome on this train. I'm commandeering your oxen and wagon for these two mules. You have but a few minutes to be gone."

The brothers thought it prudent to be gone before news of their peeping tom exploits made it back to camp. They gathered a few personal items the mules could carry. But before they left, they saw the preacher's wife talking to the captain. The brothers quickly mounted the mules and took off as the captain's look sent daggers at them.

From a discreet distance they watched the wagon train pull out the next morning and followed it staying half a day behind. The trail meandered along the North Platte River heading west and northwest.

On the second day they were confronted by the wagon captain who had waited behind the train. "You boys are not to tag our train. Be gone. If I find you trailing again, I'll have two mules and you will be afoot."

Now stranded, they sought a settlement. In a trading post that would later become Douglas in Wyoming, they found a saloon and poker table. Two days later they had upgraded their mules for horses. They learned that gold had been found near the next trading post in Glenrock.

Men who easily acquired gold were less cautious and more frivolous in spending than men who labored for it. James and Thomas had developed a scheme. One brother would enter a poker game an hour before the other arrived. Four inches difference in height and different hair hues hid their relationship.

James was better with his hands or sleight of hands as it were. Courtesy at the table usually allowed the smaller stakes gambler, or loser the deal. The brothers had developed a sign system. An upturn of the right side of the mouth meant an ace was needed, left side a king, two movements of the Adam's apple a queen. A glance at the man on Thomas's left indicated a nine was needed to make a pair or three of a kind. Thomas won money while James dealt cards he had marked with scratches from his fingernail.

Suspicion of cheating seldom focused on the loser at the table. After a couple days figuratively picking the pockets of miners, the brothers moved on. They rotated between the new settlements of Casper, Glenrock, and Douglas. Careful to take days off before hitting the next settlement in their rotation, they hid excess cash under a rock on the trail.

In their time not gambling, more than once the brothers snatched unbranded horses from a passing wagon train in the middle of the night and sold them in a distant town. Their cache under the rock grew.

They ventured to a higher stakes table in Casper. A know-it-all peddler kept a constant conversation at the table. "As soon as I sell enough goods here, I'm buying a farm around Springfield, Missouri," said the peddler.

James found it shrewd to keep a conversation going drawing attention from other activities, particularly by keeping others talking. Talking people concentrated on what they were saying hoping to not appear stupid.

"Why Springfield?" James asked.

"Because the best farmland in the country is located there."

"How do you know that?"

"A survey from that fancy new Harvard school out east determined the combination of soils and climate made the area the future hub of the nation's agriculture."

The president of the town bank sat across the table from James. "Where did that last card come from?"

"What do you mean?" queried James.

"Are you cheating?"

"If I am I'm very bad at it," he answered glancing down drawing attention to his dwindling chips while one hand remained under the table.

There was silence at the table until the banker reached inside his frock for a pocket watch. His wife would be in a foul mood if he was home late.

An unsaid rule was that if someone reached for a gun after accusing you of cheating, shooting them was a slam-dunk self-defense. No one saw James draw his 1848 Colt five-shot baby dragoon he had purchased a week prior. From under the table the 31 caliber cartridge angled through the thin tabletop and struck the banker's frock just missing a pocket watch. The piece of lead traveled upward between two ribs and ended its journey in his right ventricle. A look of shock overtook the banker's face as blood pulsated from him. His wife's warning that only bad things happened in saloons, with whiskey and cards echoed in his head. His body quivered before rolling out of the chair.

The peddler bent over him and reached in the man's frock and only found a pocket watch. "He was unarmed."

"How was I do know?" said James as he glanced at Thomas and headed for the door. The sheriff hearing the gunshot blocked the door.

"All of you, let's sort this out in my office."

In the commotion Thomas gathered his earnings. As they walked to the sheriff's office, he fell behind and was soon out of town. The sheriff took statements from all and arrested James. He told the witnesses to remain available as the circuit judge would be in town the next day in his three week rotation.

A jury had previously been selected for whatever trials might be presented to the judge the next day. The judge seldom tolerated a trial lasting over an hour. The jury in the first trial found a defendant guilty of horse theft.

The judge sentenced him, "I have hanged horse thieves, but as you have never previously been charged you are reprimanded to the territorial prison for three years. Next case."

The sentence lifted James's spirit, he had no brushes with the law in the territory and the trouble in Ohio at that time was inaccessible three states away.

Next a fourteen year old boy was charged with stealing licorice sticks from a jar in the general store. He was sentenced to a month's work without pay for the store owner.

The jury was composed of many who only grudgingly tolerated a saloon in town and found gambling an evil distraction from the Protestant work ethic. Two jurors had been given loans by the banker. Upon their return of a guilty verdict James stood and yelled at the courtroom, "I thought he was drawing a gun. It was self-defense."

Matter-of-factly, the judge passed sentence. "You've been found guilty of murder. I have no choice with the sentence. Tomorrow morning at dawn you will be taken to the large oak tree near the trail west of town and hanged. May God have mercy on your soul."

That evening Thomas entered the livery stable hoping to pick up James' saddle bag and see what had happened to him. He was interrupted by a stable boy. "Did you hear the news. There will be a hanging tomorrow morning."

"Nervously, Thomas asked, "Who was it?"

"I don't know his name, but he shot our banker at a gambling table."

Thomas knocked before entering the sheriff's office. "Can I see the prisoner?"

"Why? Are you related or know him?"

Thomas stuttered a lie before saying, "I'm holding an IOU from him."

"Makes sense, he is a loser all the way around. Good luck collecting anything," the sheriff said as he unlocked the hallway to four cells.

James didn't get up when he saw his brother enter but just shook his head back and forth as if trying to expel his sentence.

Thomas scrambled for something to say, "I can't believe this is happening. If there was anything I could do…"

"Don't know what it would be unless you can shoot my way out of here."

Thomas ignored the gallows humor, "Hope you don't mind but I won't be there in the morning."

"Goodbye, brother."

Thomas didn't know how to reply. He found himself shaking his head. Whether it was a genetic family trait to ward off adversity or he was involuntarily mimicking his brother, he did not know.

He remembered their father's warning as they left Ohio, You boys will experience many unforeseen opportunities and challenges. Face them with dignity and always look forward, never back.

Thomas had tied his horse on a rail away from the stable in case a quick getaway was called for. He wouldn't risk gathering James horse and belongings at the stable.

On his way out of town, Thomas stopped at the undertaker and left money for a proper burial. Although the box would be pine, he was assured the marker would be fine limestone without an inscription as to how Thomas died. Unbeknownst to Thomas the burial fee included recording details of the death at the county recorder's office. Information of which Background USA had access nearly two centuries later.

Early the next morning, Thomas gathered their cache of winnings and pilfering from under a rock. Ten miles away, James, with his hands tied behind him, was mounted on a horse and led under a large oak tree. Thomas headed for Springfield. He would buy a nice farm and put the past behind him.

CHAPTER 4

Sarah expected an immediate response to her text indicating she knew something about how Clark's great, great grandfather died in Wyoming. She was wrong. It was hours later she received a text response from him.

>*What are you talking about?*

Clark was infuriated. He waited until he calmed down, but anger made texting on a small keyboard more difficult with his male-sized fingers. His mother would say small keys designed for females and youngsters were a deserved payback for centuries of discrimination against women. He thought BS but would never dare convey the thought to his mother.

>*Sarah: You know what I am referring to*

>*Clark: How did you get into my home?*

>*Sarah: I didn't; now leave me alone; and this will remain with only me*

Sarah was relieved when her last text ended the exchange. He evidently had the message. Confident he was finished harassing her, she didn't re-block his number.

Clark found the Background USA report locked in his desk where he had left it. Not only had Sarah or someone on her behalf gotten by the security desk and broke into his condominium, but also the desk and copied the report. After checking his security system and finding no break-ins or failures in the system, Clark contacted the security system provider.

"My security system has been breached and someone gained access to vital items from my home. I can't identify who or when from my end. I expect you to get me the information. When can you send someone?

"We can check everything remotely. I have your telephone number, what is your password?"

With the password, the security company called back in 30 minutes. "Sir, the system is 100 per cent operational and no one has entered your home except you."

"Someone has accessed something valuable in my home. At the least, I expect restitution from your company."

"With your monthly fee, we provide theft coverage. What is missing?"

"It is not missing but accessed."

"What was accessed?"

"I am a lawyer and that is confidential. If the information illegally accessed gets out, I will sue your company for damages."

"Then you should contact our legal department."

As library director, Sarah didn't punch a clock. The director normally would not work evenings, but Sarah usually worked until eight o'clock closing two nights a week. Beverly noticed and told her it was good for employee morale. For Sarah, it was two evenings a week she was not home alone.

At 7:00, she asked one of the two employees working late, "Are Tuesday evenings usually this slow?"

"It varies, but only three card holders are in the building at present."

Finding the death certificate of Clark's uncle stating, 'death by hanging after murder conviction,' in Clark's background report spurred Sarah's interest in nineteenth century death records the library might have.

Had anything like that happened in this community? Researching would familiarize her with the local history section of the library.

A man was sitting at a table in the section. His denim jacket was draped over the back of the chair in which he sat; his flannel shirt was worn. She walked to an area which contained nineteenth century material and sought a book that recorded deaths in Mahaska County. As she searched the shelf, she felt the man's eyes checking her out and discreetly turned and catching him in her peripheral vision. Accustomed to seeing Andrew wearing a tie at church, she glanced twice before recognizing him.

"Oh, Andrew, hi."

"Hello, I'm sorry I didn't know it was closing time."

"Sit still, it is not. What are you researching?" she asked walking toward him.

"Land transactions in the 1920s."

After asking the question, Sarah realized it was forward; people expected privacy in what they searched and she hoped to dispel her forwardness by volunteering, "I'm looking for death records from the 1800s."

As soon as she gave the reason for her search she realized how strange it must sound. Why was she doing it anyway? she asked herself. What craziness had brought her to this section in the evening?

"You'll find those on the higher shelf. May I help you get it?"

"No thanks, I can reach it. Funny I'm the director here and you are advising me where something can be found."

"I've spent a lot of time here."

Sarah reached for a book on a higher shelf and felt her skirt raise with her shoulders. She turned and noticed his eyes quickly moved to a book he held open as his face blushed. She would ignore it, men were men.

"Beverly tells me you are a history buff whose family has a wagon train history."

"Yes, does that interest you?"

"Certainly, my grandmother said we had ancestors who traveled in a wagon train."

"Have you investigated it?"

"No, we really should talk sometime, but my… it is closing time now."

"I'll see you in church Sunday," he said as he walked to the door.

"You certainly will," she answered as their eyes connected with a smile.

Andrew wanted to ask her if blue eyes on a redhead was as uncommon as he had heard. Sarah wanted to ask him if he was the only left-handed person in his family.

Sarah had no dinner plans Saturday evening. It was refrigerator cleanup time. She had two books of death records from the library at home, but she had lost interest in them, enough morbid reading. Perhaps something on TV.

As her key entered the door she could hear talking inside, it sounded like TV chatter. Did she leave the thing on; no, she hadn't turned it on that morning. A wave of fear hit her, but it was too late, she'd already unlocked the door and started to open it.

Cautiously she stepped in the room. The sofa and stuffed chairs were empty as a huckster bloviated on CNN. Turning toward the kitchen she saw Clark.

"Hope you don't mind; I'm eating leftover pizza. I got hungry waiting."

"What are you doing here? How did you get in?"

"Let's back up for a minute. How did you get access to my Background USA file? What else do you know?"

"I'm calling the police, I mean sheriff."

She held her cell phone and was prepared to dial the sheriff when he jumped up and grabbed it from her. "I want some answers first."

"You break-in, take my cell phone, are you going to beat me next?"

"No but can't say it hasn't crossed my mind. What else do you know about my family's past?"

"I know your great, great grandfather owned slaves in Missouri."

"Did you have someone hack into Background USA?"

"Why should I tell you anything?"

"If they leaked the information voluntarily or had it hacked, I will sue them for everything and end up owning the company."

"Would you really want all that publicity? What would your mother think?"

"She doesn't know anything about the Background report, and I want to keep it that way."

"Perhaps we could make a deal."

"You started this."

"No, you started this by following and harassing me," she retorted.

"That information can't get out. It would jeopardize my career and devastate my mother."

"Okay, how about a two for two. I never divulge your information and tell you how I acquired it, and you never try to contact me again and tell me how you got in here."

"How did you get the information?"

"Do we have a deal?"

"Yes. I picked the lock. It was easy."

"Understand if you try to contact me again, I will mail the ancestry report to your law firm and the Des Moines library."

"Okay, okay."

"Remember when we had pizza here and your allergy was acting up? I sent a sample of your sneeze to Background USA."

"That is fraud."

"Do you want me to keep the information to myself or not?"

He nodded his head.

"Good, now get the hell out of here and never come back."

"Give me a copy of the report and I'll be gone."

She handed it to him without telling he she'd copied it in the event she decided to mail copies. The next morning with the landlord's permission Sarah called a local locksmith and had them upgrade the lock and install a security system in her apartment.

Andrew hoped Sarah would be working until closing again on the following Tuesday. He was right. Fieldwork prevented him from arriving until an hour before closing. The receptionist noticed a warm smile exchanged between Andrew and Sarah beyond a normal customer greeting.

"You know him?" she asked.

"Yes, he's a greeter at the church I attend."

"Ah, hah."

"You are jumping to… never mind."

The speculation of the receptionist prevented Sarah from following Andrew to the community history section. She mustn't give the staff the wrong impression of her.

At 8:00, Sarah told the receptionist she could leave early, Sarah would lockup. The dismissal drew a coy smile from the lady. *Why must people always jump to nasty conclusions*, thought Sarah.

Andrew waited until 8:00 hoping Sarah would enter. She didn't and he headed for the exit to find Sarah alone.

"It is still early, how about stopping at the bar across the street for a cocktail?"

"No, thank you – I don't drink."

"Well how about hitting the coffee shop down the block?"

"It is too late for me to drink coffee."

"Then let's try the ice cream parlor on the other side of the square."

"You are certainly persistent, aren't you?"

"What is your favorite flavor? He followed up interpreting her comment as acceptance whether it was intended or not.

"Okay, okay, cherry nut; you hit my weak spot."

"I should have guessed; it's what makes your hair red, right?"

"Greeter, historian, jokester, and suave hopeful wooer, what else are you?"

"Dirt farmer, pig farmer and cattle feeder."

"Wow, is this how you pick up all women?"

Walking two blocks with a near stranger after dark Sarah would not have considered in other places, but she felt comfortable here. If Clark were crazy enough to show up he wouldn't mess with this toned man beside her. She had to ask, "Do you stay in shape by tossing hay bales?"

After a chuckle he answered, "Maybe my dad or grandfather did, but that doesn't happen today."

"Which of your usuals will it be tonight?" the server, behind a counter containing at least 20 two and a half gallon open containers of ice cream, asked with a playful smile, "Will it be cookies and cream or cherry nut tonight?"

Without asking Sarah, Andrew smiled at Melanie and said, "It'll be two scoops of cherry nut in two dishes."

"You mean one scoop in each dish," Melanie seemed to tease.

"No, you know me better than that."

"Missed seeing you in here the last couple of weeks," Melanie stated with a grin.

"Yeah, been kind of busy, farming and all."

Both with a two scoop dish of ice cream, Andrew headed for a corner booth before Sarah could suggest otherwise. He held out a hand inviting her to sit in the bench facing the door. She was relieved when he sat across from her instead of beside her.

"Is this your usual booth?"

"Not really, but when I do I usually sit where you are; Hickok complex, I guess."

"Wow, you know of Bill Hickok's obsession with seeing the front door, you are a history buff."

In the silence that followed, an unfamiliar feeling about Melanie's flirtation emerged inside Sarah that almost scared her. It also struck her that according to Melanie cherry nut was one of his favorites, he couldn't have called her and tipped her off. No, no; she needed to get crazy thoughts out of her mind.

"Was that your boyfriend I saw you with at the pizza parlor a few weeks ago?" Andrew asked.

"No longer, though he continues to pester me. But since you are bold with questions, your girlfriend didn't seem happy that evening."

"She wasn't very happy about me asking for my ring back."

To move the conversation from depressing subjects and to avoid discussion about what could be embarrassing romantic issues, Sarah asked more than stated, "I understand you have a done a great deal of research on your family's history."

"Yes, I have. It is a hobby of mine."

"We've shared the belief that each of us has an ancestor with a wagon train past, but my family has no proof, only folklore. Does yours have evidence?"

A WAGON TRAIN LEGACY

"I have much evidence, but what alludes me is a log of one of the trips. Family legend says one exists."

"Have you tried using Background USA?"

"Yes, I've thought about it but haven't. I'm skeptical about an entity having my DNA. Goodness knows in whose hand it may end up."

"Might your DNA help the FBI solve a crime?"

"Yeah, all the banks I've robbed. They are looking for me."

"Seriously, I feel the same way about someone having my DNA. The information could be sold to advertising agencies, or God forbid, wind up in the government's hand."

The booth was engulfed in silence as the realization struck them that they harbored similar concerns. Although neither mentioned it, they each noticed the person across the booth was also eating ice cream with their left hand. How much more did they have in common?

To break the silence, Sarah asked, "What else about your family background do you know?"

"Where would you like me to start."

"How about as far back as you have been able to determine."

"My fourth great grandfather, Michael, spelled Mikkel in German, immigrated from Württemberg, Germany in 1827. Passenger logs show they entered the port in Baltimore. Logs didn't list family members on the ship's manifest at the time, but we know he entered the country with his wife, Hannah, and five children."

"Was Württemberg a large city?"

"Actually, it was a Germanic territory in the southwest corner of what now is Germany. At that time nations did not exist as we think of them today. The Wurttemberg principality did not become part of Germany until later in the nineteenth century. I hope I'm not boring you with this."

"No, not at all. Tell me more. When was Michael born?"

"The US census in 1856 says he was born in 'about 1788.' The 1860 census says, 'about 1785.'"

"Do you have any idea why the family emigrated to America?"

"Legend has it that Michael and Hannah immigrated to America to prevent their sons from being drafted into constant European wars. Their first five children born in Germany were all sons. They were not without means but wouldn't have been able to pay the necessary fees to keep five sons out of the military service.

In perspective, Michael was a teenager during the French Revolution, Paris was only 300 miles away, like Des Moines to Chicago, as were the major Napoleonic battles of Austerlitz in 1805 and Waterloo 1815."

Sarah was fascinated by his historical knowledge. Her look encouraged Andrew to continue.

Wurttemberg's King Fredrick joined a few Germanic client states of the First French Empire under Napoleon's rule. In fact, Württemberg was an ally of France from 1802 to 1813. French Emperor Napoleon rewarded Württemberg with large territory grants. In return for this favor, King Frederick joined Napoleon in his campaigns against Prussia, Austria, and Russia.

"Wow, did your ancestor experience any of that firsthand?"

"According to his son Godfrey, Michael was conscripted into service by King Frederick and effectively ended up a soldier in Napoleon's army. Of the 600,000 Frenchmen, Germans, and Poles who made up Napoleon's Grand Army, only an estimated 25,000 men made it back home from the debacle in Russia. Michael was one of 16,000 King Frederick subjects who marched to Moscow, only a few hundred actually returned to the Kingdom of Württemberg.

That Michael made it back alive, married and had children was amazing. The battle of Waterloo took place after their first son was born. Given the European history Michael had experienced, moving to America must have, even with the unknowns, seemed a prudent risk."

"One can only imagine the stories he could tell," observed Sarah.

"Yeah, if we only knew the details," added Andrew.

CHAPTER 5

June 20, 1812 near the Neman River in present-day Poland

"Rumor is that other units are starting to pack for the long trip home," said Hans as Mikkel and he curried the handsome studs while wearing aprons protecting their uniform trousers.

"Yes, we should think about it. A week's worth of oats should suffice. Friendlies on our route back will supply more," answered Mikkel (Michael) Augustine.

"The Czar will come to his senses any day now and accept the emperor's terms. After his disastrous defeat at Austerlitz seven years ago when they outnumbered us, I'm sure he has no desire to face the largest army ever assembled."

Mikkel and Hans Beitert were properly dressed as soldiers in King Frederick's complement of 16,000 soldiers from the kingdom of Württemberg in the Grand Army of Napoleon. They proudly wore white braccae trousers, blue tunic, and a tall black shako hat with a white plume.

Friends since childhood, they joined the service in the summer of 1805 at the age of 19, a few months before the epic battle of Austerlitz. Volunteering avoided conscription and allowed them to care for horses instead of becoming cannon fodder for artillery. Napoleon's victory at Austerlitz had been brilliant. Though he was outnumbered, he defeated all of France's enemies except England. After their amazing victory, the Grand Army beamed with self-confidence. Mikkel and Hans had a written copy of the emperor's proclamation:

> *On the day of Austerlitz, you lived up to my expectations of your intrepidity. You have adorned the eagles with eternal glory. In less than four hours, an army of 100,000 men, led by the emperors of Russia and Austria, has been destroyed and dispersed… and you only have to say, "I was at the Battle of Austerlitz to hear the reply. There goes a brave man."*

The friends had moved up in the cavalry ranks of stable hands from grooms to ostlers. Württemberg's contingent in Napoleon's Grand Army of 600,000 Frenchmen, Germans, and Poles was small – but none were prouder. The seven years had been a great adventure, but grueling. Back home they would have status and stories to tell their children when a new life was started. As Napoleon promised, they were treated as heroes at home on a month's leave before assembling in Poland for the last display of military might near the Russian border.

"Did your families finalize plans for the marriage?" asked Hans.

"Yes, all is agreed, Hannah and I will be married a week after my return."

"Within a day the Czar will capitulate, a week to disband and three weeks journey home. You'll be a married man next month and starting a family – early congratulations," Hans teased.

Although never spoken, Hannah Houck and Mikkel Augustine knew before they became teenagers they would be married. No courtship as we may think of it – he held her hand once, daringly kissed her on the forehead during wedding negotiations – but they always knew.

Hans continued to tease Mikkel about becoming a married man as they finished currying two nearly identical Spanish Jennet horses. The Jennet horse was a common ride of European nobility. The black spotted white horses had a smooth, crisp gait and radiated pride in harmony with the owner, Count Ernst Busch.

Their friendly tease was interrupted by a shout of *"Attention"* from outside the stable. Count Busch entered and inspected his studs. "Have them both saddled and ready at dawn tomorrow. We'll make short work of the Mongols from the East."

The Count laid his hand on the stud near Mikkel. "I'll ride this one first. Be ready to move out at dawn and have the other one ready for replacement as we finish this quickly."

Napoleon's last bid for peace had been sent to St. Petersburg. An answer was not received, and the Grand Army was ordered to enter Russian Poland. Speculation abounded in the stables after the Count left.

"How foolish the Czar is not accepting the emperor's terms," observed Hans.

Would it be a week or a month before the Czar realized his mistake? Disappointment was overwhelmed by confidence that the delay returning home would be short as the Grand Army crushed the Czar's meager forces.

On June 24th they invaded Russia and moved relentlessly, stopping seldom as the Grand Army chased dwindling Czarist forces. Two wagons of horse oats dwindled to a few bushels as did their own supplies, but it would be over soon, thought Mikkel and Hans.

At the end of July, wagons were empty. The supplies lines had been outrun. They were living off the land as was seldom needed in Europe. Here on the seemingly endless flat steppes of Russia with all destroyed before them, it was near disaster. Mikkel and Hans had not eaten for two days. The horses were becoming restless.

"Wagons are coming!" a member of their regiment yelled in anticipation as the sun rose.

At a great distance, Mikkel could see dust rising. It was a column of a wagons. Dozens, then hundreds of soldiers surrounded the wagons upon approach. Someone pulled the tarp from the first wagon to find only gunpowder and cannon balls.

"Which wagon has food?" asked a sergeant.

"Only armaments on this convoy," a driver answered. Two days later another convoy arrived, same cargo.

In August, the advance slowed but continued. They moved forward; hungry, sick men deemed unable to travel were left behind. Rumors flooded the Württemberg stables that a similar Polish equine squad of ten soldiers had killed a sick horse for consumption. For an example, they were lined up in front of the Polish company and shot.

Mikkel had never known hunger as he now faced. Relentlessly his stomach ached; he could not sleep. In hopes of finding any animal normally edible or not, he wandered with rifle across a wheat field that had been burned by the Russians. At the edge of the field amongst sparse brush, he sat. He seriously contemplated circling the encampment and heading west, but to be caught was to die.

His thoughts wandered to Hannah and their walk in similar brush. He was looking at green growth on the stem of a bush, his mind not making the connection until he remembered her saying that lichen was edible. She had pulled some and had him taste it; it tasted terrible. Now he found the Russian lichen delicious.

That evening, he told Hans of his find. They next morning they ventured together scouring the countryside for lichen. It was sparse. Letting others know would soon deplete the supply. It would be their secret.

On the eastward march, multiple times the Grand Army prepared for a major battle only to have it end in a minor skirmish when Russian forces again retreated deeper into the country. The effort of deployment for battle both psychologically and physically drained the morale of soldiers who were hungry, and disease ridden. Because of hunger, units couldn't be held close. Soldiers spreading out in search of food invited desertion. On August 30 when they neared Gagarin, the ratio of the Grand Army to Russian forces had shrunk from 3:1 to 5:4.

The Russians were well anchored on the new Smolensk Highway—Napoleon's expected route of advance – in a pentagonal earthwork near the village of Shevardino.

Mikkel could see Count Busch, mounted on a non-battle trained mare, barking orders at an extra detachment of soldiers charged with guarding the cavalry's battle horses.

"What do you suppose he is ordering?" Hans asked.

"Look, they're picking up and heading toward the front," Mikkel observed.

The friends could see a boy near the Count. The boy was fleshy – unlike the Count or other soldiers.

The Count dismounted and exclaimed, "Good, both of my Jennets are saddled. This is my son. He will mount one. He just arrived for this historic battle. It will be recorded in history that two counts of Württemberg participated in history's greatest battle, the conquer of Russia."

The battle of Shevardino began on September 5. As Grand Army forces approached the earthen Russian barricades, Konovnitzyn's Russian cavalry attacked their flank. French Marshal Murat led Nansouty's First Cavalry Corps and Montbrun's Second Cavalry Corps, against the Russian cavalry. Simultaneously, Prince Józef Poniatowski's Polish infantry attacked the position from the south as did Württemberg's cavalry, led by Count Busch.

During the battle, Hans and Mikkel were equipped with Charleville muskets and placed in Napoleon's last reserve unit. Both had been trained in the standard issue rifle's use, but never carried one. The rifles were now in abundant supply abandoned by dead, wounded or starving soldiers. The final reserves were not called into action.

The great cavalry battle ended with Konovnitzyn's retreat when Viceroy Eugène de Beauharnais' Fourth Corps arrived. The battle ended with 5,000 French and 6,000 Russian casualties.

Hans and Mikkel had returned to the makeshift mobile stables when they saw the Count and son riding toward them. Both rode high in the saddle, and their Jennets strutted with pride from a victory. Once in the enclave in which the horses were kept, blood was visible running down Count Ernst's tunic; blood seeped from his ride in three places as well as his son Bastian's leg.

Confident they had some privacy, too proud to be seen injured, the Count collapsed from his mount. Mikkel broke his fall to the ground, and Hans was sent for a doctor.

The doctor removed the Count's tunic. In addition to blood seeping from the stomach wound, dark intestinal matter was visible. The doctor nodded his head at the Count and covered the wound. The Count knew.

After a priest give rites, the Count summoned Bastian, Mikkel and Hans. "You've been charged with caring for my studs, now I give you a greater task. You will care for the soon-to-be Count Bastian and see that he makes it back to Württemberg after this glorious victory is finalized. For your service, you will both receive a parcel of land."

It was two days of agony before the Count passed. The sword wound on Bastian's leg was showing infection. The doctor warned that if gangrene set in he would lose the leg.

Mikkel remembered on a walk in the forest Hannah had pointed out a plant of the nightshade family. She said it was the cause of her great aunt's conviction for witchcraft. She had administered a tea made from the plant to victims of a cholera outbreak. The men went crazy with hallucinations. The work of the devil obviously. She was burned.

The plant was nicknamed the devil's trumpet due to the shape of the blooms. In America, after use in the Jamestown colonies, it became known as the Jamestown weed or Jimsonweed.

Hannah said the plant could be used discreetly for wounds, swelling and snake and spider bites. Mikkel remembered seeing the weed as he sought lichen. He wrapped Bastian's leg in Jimsonweed leaves. Eventually the swelling subsided.

The French advance from the west after the fall of Shevardino threw the Russian formation into disarray. By September, the Grand Army had forced the Russians back to the outskirts of Moscow, where Napoleon won the battle of Borodino, suffering great losses but prying the road to Moscow open.

With winter approaching, the army was relieved that they would have winter quarters in Moscow with hopefully ample food supplies. It didn't work out that way. Food supplies had been moved or destroyed. Russian partisans sneaking in at night set the city on fire.

In an example of the brutality, a dozen wives of Russian soldiers paraded outside a hotel in only bloomers, luring French officers who had gone long without female companionship to the third floor of the hotel. The women escaped through a hidden staircase and underground tunnel. Fires were set in the hotel including the stairway blocking the officers' escape. Only one officer survived – breaking his shoulder after jumping from a third floor window.

Out of necessity, the city was abandoned by the Grand Army into the food-less countryside with the onset of brutal cold. All seemed to be on their own as the Grand Army slowly dissipated due to hunger, disease, and frigid temperatures. Count Bastian, Hans, and Mikkel shared what little lichen they had hidden under their tunics and slowly made their way west. At night they slept in spoon formation to utilize the others' body heat.

Desperate and willing to risk the penalty if caught, they sacrificed one of the Jennets that had been wounded for meat. Unable to stop eating, they gorged themselves and were unable to move for two days until their stomachs adjusted. On the third day, the Count rode the remaining steed and Hans walked as Mikkel eliminated evidence of their three day encampment.

Before catching up with the others, Mikkel heard a gunshot, then another. Mikkel cautiously approached and saw the Count fall from his mount. Two Russian partisans lay on the ground and a third was in the process of impaling Hans. Mikkel drove his knife into the partisan's back, but not before Hans was gone through by the man's sword.

"I'll be cold no more. See my parents," were the last words Hans spoke.

The Count was dead as two other Russians, one from the Count's pistol and one from Hans' sword. With regret but knowing the gunshot would draw anyone close and it would take days to chip through frozen ground, Mikkel left his friends unburied and mounted the Jennet. He rode well into the night. With frozen horse meat in his saddle bag, he rode for three days letting the Jennet forage on dead grass at night.

In western Poland and through Germanic country, Mikkel found residents were happy to share a meal in return for news from the Russian front. Mikkel said what he needed to, true or not, in order to continue his journey home.

Of the 600,000 Frenchmen, Germans, and Poles who made up Napoleon's Grand Army, only an estimated 25,000 men made it back home from the debacle. Mikkel was one of 16,000 King Frederick subjects who marched to Moscow. Only a few hundred actually returned to the Kingdom of Württemberg.

After joining his family, Mikkel took the Jennet to the Count's estate. He gave the younger brother and wife the seals worn around each Count's neck.

"Did you give them a proper burial?" asked the wife.

"Of course, they died valiantly," Mikkel answered with a half-truth.

The noble family surmised if it were not as Mikkel said he would not have notified them in such fashion.

They thanked him for coming. Mikkel thought better of advising them of the Count's promise of acreage. He had not, after all, brought Bastian home safely.

Within two weeks, Hannah and Mikkel were married. Their first son, Mikkel Jr., was born in 1814. Within nine years they had five sons. Albert – Andrew's third great grandfather – being the fourth.

Through the years, Mikkel talked little of his experience in Russia. "It was a bad time," was his usual response when asked. Renewed talks of war in 1826 brought back horrid memories. He was prosperous enough to pay the tokens necessary to keep two sons out of the army, but not five. Subjecting any of his sons to the ordeal he went through he would not do. It was time to make a voyage across the Atlantic to a place called America.

Chapter 6

Andrew answered Sarah's statement about what his ancestor must have seen. "You know, makes you wonder if Michael could describe his experiences now from above, how much would we find historians got wrong?"

"Doesn't it though? I need to get home," Sarah said, standing – not wanting to appear overly intrigued by Andrew – although she was fascinated by his family history. Why, she did not know.

"I'll walk you back. My car is there also," offered Andrew.

"At least it isn't raining tonight," observed Sarah.

"Yes, tell me about it. This long rainy period has delayed planting crops, makes farmers like me fidgety."

Between the ice cream shoppe and library parking lot they heard screeching tires. Sarah was ready to step off a curb into a street crossing when Andrew grabbed her arm and pulled her back. Two cars side-by-side vying for a lead accelerated past them. The startling exhaust noise bursting into the town's serene evening must have been heard at the police station. Two blocks distant they saw the cars enter opposite alleys and disappear.

"Wow, is drag racing on the street common here?" asked Sarah as his hand belatedly left her arm.

"Not that common."

"Why would dragsters race within a block of the police station? Don't they know it will raise the ire of the police?"

"I expect the thrill of doing it near the police station was the point," answered Andrew.

When they reached the parking lot, he stood until she opened her car door before entering his car. Not that he expected a kiss, but he found it strange they didn't even say "Good night." *Not her fault*, he thought.

In route to the farm, Andrew stopped at a convenience store for orange juice. He recognized the cars drag racing parked at the store. The only two young men in the store were standing by the beer display inspecting an ID.

"Who won the drag race?" Andrew asked.

"What are you talking about?" one answered with a question.

"You boys look young enough to have grandfathers; how old is yours?" Andrew asked the one who avoided his question.

"Seventy-one, why?"

"What would you boys think if you caught your grandfathers drag racing in the middle of town?"

"That's a stupid question; they're not that crazy!"

"Did you hear what you just said?" asked Andrew. "Not crazy, eh? It would seem to me that old men drag racing would be less crazy than two young whippersnappers like you two."

Unbeknownst to the three in discussion, Sarah had stopped at the convenience store for coffee creamer. She recognized Andrew's voice from the adjacent aisle and listened, peering through stacks of candy bars.

Andrew received looks as if the boys had encountered an irrational, weird creature.

Andrew continued, "I suppose your grandfathers have ten to fifteen years left on this planet. You boys, if you don't do anything too stupid, have at least sixty. As you have more to lose than your grandfathers do, it would seem rational that you should engage in less risky behavior than they. Think about it."

The boys had enough of the conversation, thought better of attempting to buy beer with the fake ID and skedaddled.

Andrew turned the aisle corner to see a smiling Sarah. "Well, besides farmer and history buff, you're also a philosopher, I hear."

"It doesn't make sense that proclivity for risky behavior and age are inverse."

"Do you think they will consider anything you said?"

"Probably not, but it couldn't hurt."

Andrew stood behind Sarah as they checked out. As she reached for a credit card in her purse, Andrew started to lean forward to get a view inside her purse before he caught himself. She fascinated him, he wanted to know more about her.

"That'll be $3.49," the clerk, having caught him looking in her purse, firmly said to Andrew.

With his eyes on Sarah at the door, he didn't hear the clerk. Halfway through the door she turned toward him. "Good night," he said.

"Good night to you," she replied and was gone.

"I said the orange juice will be $3.49," repeated the clerk, sternly this time.

It had been two weeks since Sarah had seen Andrew. He hadn't been in the library and another greeter was working the church door. She was tempted to contact him even though it was inappropriate, but she had no contact information for him. Suddenly, it struck her she could look him up in the library card list, but what excuse would she use to contact him? Perhaps it was just as well. Her relationships with men usually ended badly. Although she had to admit, she was a little peeved that he hadn't contacted her. Then again, he had no obligation. He was most likely on to someone else, perhaps the girl at the ice cream shoppe. She considered checking out the ice cream shoppe but thought better of it and ordered a pizza for pickup.

Corn planting had been delayed by inclement wet weather. Further delays would limit crop yields. Andrew worked fourteen hours a day, leaving no time for the library. Many hours in the tractor gave him much time to think. His failed nuptial plans were past tense, but Sarah entered his mind often. Busy as he was, two weeks passed quickly. Finally, planting was finished, and he had decided tomorrow he would ask Sarah out to dinner. This evening he would pick up a pizza and rest.

Sarah considered eating pizza at the restaurant but eating alone always felt strange. Would locals talk about the new 33-year-old librarian as a spinster whose only love was as a bibliophile and whose prodigy would never be more than a few added library card holders? Enough negative thoughts – after all, she needed to get home and work on the library budget.

Andrew parked and headed for the back door of the pizza parlor. He was wearing what he had for two days, soiled striped bib overalls and a seed corn advertisement cap. The overalls he only wore at crop time – unlike his father and grandfather who commonly wore them. It struck him he should have cleaned up before driving to town, but he was hungry and clean up would take time, hence he chose to be seen by few and entered the back door.

Sarah was picking up her pizza in front as Andrew waited at the back door for his. In his attire, if he had known she was at the front, he would have stayed away from the pizzeria. Had Sarah known he was at the back door; she would have ignored his proximity. Protocol dictated it was he who needed to make contact. And he had not.

Sarah was headed toward her car when a yellow Porsche pulled in the driveway. She was furious. Wearing an Armani suit with the collar and tie pulled open, he stretched himself up out of the low seated car. She recognized the tie as her outrageously priced Christmas present to him. He had only closed the door when she confronted him.

"What are you doing here? You know our deal. I'm sending emails of the report out in the morning."

"Hold on, hold on. I'm not here to bother or see you. I had a court appearance near and remembered how good the pizza was."

"Sure, you did – you, a descendant of slave owners!" she answered. Then she proceeded to open her box of pizza, flip it over and crush sausage, green pepper, and mushroom pizza on the shiny yellow hood of his car.

"You bitch!" he exclaimed loudly, grabbing her, and twisting her away from the car.

"Let go of me, I'll call the cops!" she screamed.

Clark's open right hand swung and made contact with Sarah's cheek. The blow turned her head and sent the sound of a single loud clap across the parking lot.

Andrew was rounding the corner of the building when he heard the words, "You bitch!" and saw a couple struggling. He dropped his pizza and headed for the couple as he would in defense of any abused woman. His steps quickened once he realized the woman was Sarah. Instinctively, as a former high school linebacker, at three strides from Clark, Andrew lowered his shoulder. The collision into Clark's mid-section ripped him from Sarah.

On the parking lot surface Andrew raised himself enough to land a solid blow to Clark's left jaw. He might have landed another if not for Sarah grabbing him hollering, "Enough, enough!"

Andrew got to his feet above Clark and watched him attempt to reclaim his breath that had been knocked from him. Turning to Sarah, Andrew asked, "Are you all right?"

"Yes but leave him alone. I can take care of him."

Andrew had to clinch his teeth to refrain himself from responding that it didn't appear she was successful at that.

Clark's hand was in his mouth, checking teeth. "I have a loose tooth, you throwback. I'll sue you for anything you may have."

Sarah restrained Andrew from taking a step toward him as a police car pulled beside them.

"What happened here?" asked the officer.

"This grease-stained Mongol attacked me, loosened a tooth and ruined a twenty-four hundred dollar suit."

A bloodied knee was obvious in the ripped Marino wool pantleg now soiled from Andrew's grease stained overalls.

"Andrew," the officer knew him, "what happened here?"

Before Andrew could answer, two from a crowd of a dozen who had encircled the combatants spoke. "He was abusing her." Another pointed to the left side of Sarah's face which was as red as a spanked baby's butt. "He slapped her hard, and I saw it," said another witness.

The sheriff arrived and pulled the police officer to the side. "She has complained to my office of him harassing her."

"May be, but I don't have any choice but to arrest both men for assault and battery and her for destroying private property."

While the officers were talking, Clark said to Sarah, "So this is a backwater boyfriend in this hoe duck town?

Sarah ignored the insult to Andrew and the town. "Don't worry, Clark. I'll call your mom and law firm and tell them all."

Andrew was aghast. After the abuse, would she stick up for him? He'd heard of women defending their abusers, but it was eye opening to see it firsthand. Women – he'd had enough of them.

The three were all deep in thought when the officers returned. Clark glared at Andrew and said, "Officers, there has been a misunderstanding here. I slipped and fell, and this man sought to help me."

Quickly, Sarah added, "We were just having a spat that couples sometimes do. No harm."

"Your cheek shows evidence you've been struck, I have no choice but to arrest someone for striking you."

"I was too hasty applying rouge this evening and probably got too much on one side."

"Okay, we'll let this go, but if it ever happens again someone will be arrested. I want you two to shake hands," the officer said exchanging glances at Clark and Andrew.

Clark reached out his hand, Andrew reluctantly accepted it, but found Clark's pressure more than usual. He returned the gesture with an overwhelming squeeze. Clark quickly withdrew his hand. Without another word to anyone, Andrew turned and headed for his car.

On the way to the farm, Andrew thought of the lyrics *"All women are fickle"* in a Rigoletto opera aria, the last opera he had seen,. As the melody bounced around in his head, he thought, *some things never change with time.*

Walking to church the next morning, Sarah could see Andrew greeting members of the congregation at the door, but he was gone when she entered. *Just as well,* she thought.

Before library closing Monday, Beverly, library board president, knocked and entered Sarah's office. "Tell me what happened at the pizza parlor Saturday evening."

"So, you heard about it?"

"Half of the town has. Are you okay?"

"That's nice," she answered sarcastically.

"Sounds like Andrew, the guy you've been seeing, was a hero from what I heard."

"Well, I'm not seeing him, and I could have managed it. And he stormed off mad when it was over and is avoiding me now."

"What caused that?"

"I don't know. I told my former I would contact his mother and law firm. Andrew grunted and gave me an unpleasant look."

Beverly carefully commented, "Well, if he got in a fight to protect you and you offered to assist the man who assaulted you after he went out on a limb for you, I can see why he might be hurt."

Sarah defended herself, "That wasn't it at all. Contacting his law firm and mother was a threat from me. And it worked; he immediately wanted to drop everything."

"Do you think Andrew saw it that way?"

After no comment from Sarah, Beverly said, "Well?"

"I guess it would look differently from his angle."

Sarah was ten minutes earlier than normal arriving at church Sunday. Her early appearance caught Andrew by surprise as he turned after greeting an older couple.

"Good morning," she cheerfully greeted him.

"Hello," he returned the greeting, then turned away from her and held the door open for another couple.

"I hope there was no misunderstanding about the parking lot episode," she reached out when momentarily alone with him.

"I think I understood, which is fine." He answered, turning, and welcoming another couple for more reason than one.

Sarah hoped to continue the conversation after church. As church let out, she turned from her pew and saw him already at the door, obviously wishing to avoid any after church mingling.

It was a warm early June day; she had enjoyed her walk to church and was game to explore more of the town by foot. Within a block she met a couple pushing a baby stroller. They greeted and Sarah bent down to look at the baby.

"She is so cute," Sarah offered, assuming the baby was a girl by the pink blanket.

"Thank you, she is our first. You're the new library director, aren't you?"

They spent a few minutes passing the time of day before moving on. Sarah had to wonder at 33 – she had maybe 10 childbearing years left. Would she ever have a child? What were the chances of a single woman adopting a baby in rural Iowa?

A few minutes later she ended up in front of the ice cream shoppe. "*Why not?*" she asked herself.

With two scoops of cherry nut in a dish, she turned, seeking a seat. Her eyes went to the back booth in which Andrew and she had sat a few weeks earlier. She caught her breath as he was sitting in the booth looking directly at her. Sarah ignored him looking at her. After being snubbed at church, she would return the favor.

The ice cream parlor was nearly full. An older couple was sitting at the counter with a purse occupying the stool next to them.

"Do you mind?" Sarah, while glancing at the purse, asked the woman, expecting the woman to move her purse for Sarah.

"Actually, I do," answered the woman. "There is an empty half booth against the back wall. Don't you think it is time for Andrew and you to settle your silly quarrel?"

Sarah was taken back by the suggestion. She was tempted to reply to the forwardness but found the woman's comment soothing to a degree she couldn't explain. Before she could think it through, she found herself headed for Andrew's booth.

"Do you mind?" she asked, gesturing at the empty booth seat facing the wall.

"Go ahead."

"I see you talked to Thelma and Ralph at the counter."

"Yes, I've seen them at church. Are they friends of yours?"

"They are friends of many. No one will see them for weeks and suddenly they will show up and help someone."

"They seemed to know about us, or I should say about the parking lot fiasco, but I guess many do. Do they live in town?"

"No one seems to know where they live. I'm glad you met them. Here's the funny thing; some in church think they're angels."

Through the window, Sarah could see Thelma and Ralph getting in a green car. *Ridiculous,* she thought, *angels would not need a car.* She would wait for Andrew to bring up another subject.

He didn't and Sarah broke the uneasy silence, "I want to explain what happened in the parking lot, so you understand.""I think I understand, not all relationships are... should we say... cordial? I'm sorry I interfered."

His statement struck her as funny. With a mouthful of ice cream, she chuckled. "Beverly was right," and answered his inquisitive look. "My volunteering to notify his law firm and mother was not to protect him but a threat to expose information which would make his life difficult.

Just as you punched him, my threat was as hurtful to him. No... actually, it was more effective. Notice that he quickly backed down. Nevertheless, I want to thank you for coming to my rescue. It was very chivalrous. Something that would seldom happen where I grew up."

"I noticed you described him and you as a couple to the officer."

"Couple? In the past, no more, no way. I said what I needed to keep you and I out of jail."

Seeking to change the subject, Andrew asked, "Where did you grow up?"

"I grew up in Chicagoland. My family, what was left of them, moved to a north suburb from the city fifteen years ago before the great exodus began.

"We come from completely different backgrounds. So, from whom did you learn of the wagon train rumor?"

"I heard my grandmother tell my mother when she was considering moving out of the city. She said something like, *it's okay to move. Our family has a history of moving in wagon trains.* That is the only time I ever heard it mentioned."

"Do you know more about your family history?"

"No, really not much. I want to hear more about yours. So how did your ancestors immigrate? What did they do when they arrived in America?"

CHAPTER 7

The family decision was made in February 1827 to leave Württemberg, the ancestral home of both Michael and Hannah. Back from the horrors of Russia for 14 years, Michael had no inherent desire to travel, but his family took precedent. Their marriage had produced five sons ranging in age from two to thirteen. His sons would not experience the terror or witness the inhumanity of war if Michael could help it.

"It doesn't seem right not planting a garden," Hannah lamented in late March.

"No use, we'll be leaving in a couple of weeks. And we needn't waste money on seed. We need to save all we can," answered Michael.

"What will it be like in America?" asked eleven-year old David.

"Will there be Indians everywhere?" thirteen-year old Michael, Jr. asked another question.

"I don't suppose it will be much different than here, but just less people," answered their dad.

All their possessions had been sold by the fifth of April except what the Augustine family had loaded in a cart. Pulled by two oxen, they headed north. The journey from the Stuttgart area, in what was later to become southern Germany, to the north Germanic state of Bremen near the North Sea was 400 miles. It took them 25 days.

After 1820, emigrants started leaving the Germanic states as people fled 19th century revolutionary years in Germany. Coming to America was more than simply a voyage; it was a whole set of adventures which could prove dangerous, even lethal.

The children saw the trip as an adventure – Hannah, not so much. After two days travel, she was further from home than she had ever been. It was like traveling to another world. In many respects, it was.

Upon arriving in Bremen, nine-year-old John, who was playing with three-year-old Albert (Andrew's third great grandfather) asked, "Are we in America yet?"

"Not quite," answered his father.

In Bremen, Michael made arrangements to travel by riverboat down the Weser River to Bremerhaven. It would be two days before space was available on a river boat. He spent a day seeking offers on the oxen and wagon and used part of the proceeds to buy two hand-pulled carts for their belongings.

While in Bremen, the family viewed the famous statue of Roland the Giant. The statue commemorated Roland who was killed by Muslim forces attacking the rear-guard of Charlemagne's army in 1404. They also spent time in a church praying for their safe passage.

Centuries of silt had rendered the Weser only passable by shallow flat-bottomed river boats. The riverboat journey to the sea was nearly 50 miles and took three days. At the final harbor Michael made arrangements for the passage. Hearing horror stories of families who booked steerage, he would only consider second class.

Steerage fees were the equivalent of $16.00 per person in American money at the time, children half-rate. Booking second class was $30.00. For Hannah, him and five children the second class fee was $135.00. It would have depleted all their savings. Arriving in America with no money was not an option.

Michael signed an agreement with a trading company to finance half the passage fee for a year's work near Philadelphia. Intermediary trading companies paid for the passage of immigrants, then effectively sold their client's labors to employers. Finding and particularly keeping workers was difficult with so much land and opportunity available in America. A horse stable owner in Pennsylvania had gone through eight stable hands in four months. The owner sought stability and someone with experience caring for horses. For the indentured servant, housing and food were provided, but no wages. Flight from the contractual arrangement would land one in debtors' prison.

Michael saw a year as an indentured servant as practical. It would give his family housing, food, and a chance to become accustomed to a new land. He paid half the voyage fee with gold marks and signed a contract for the remainder.

The final journey to the ocean-bound ship could only be taken during ebb tide, when water from the arm of the Weser flowed toward the North Sea. They were brought to the side of a large wooden sailing ship which had just returned and been unloaded with tobacco and flour from Baltimore.

Bremen authorities required complete passenger lists from the ship's owner for each voyage. Listed in the Augustine family were:

Michael	born 1786
Hannah (formerly Houck)	born 1791
Michael, Jr.	born 1814
David	born 1816
John	born 1818
Albert	born 1824
Godfrey	born 1825

As the ship departed, like others, the family stood in silence pondering the adventure that lay ahead as they watched their Fatherland slowly disappear. With a combination of emotions from fear to optimism, they faced several weeks at sea from Bremen to America, if all went well. They sailed through the English Channel, then out to the Atlantic Ocean and nearly halfway around the world.

The ship measured 124 x 20 x 15 feet and carried 700 passengers. It was crowded but less so than some ships. The ship was a 'bark' vessel, three-masted with foremast and mainmast square rigged and the third mast fore and aft rigged. There were very few laws governing safety, food provisions, or cleanliness; and storms were frequent and often fatal. Ship fires were common, as were other accidents and collisions.

The second class ship's quarters below the upper deck was made of rough sawn lumber fastened together forming compartments, each one holding four people. With children, trunks and baggage, the Augustine family had seven in a compartment. It was tight but better than the more crowded communal living steerage where all lived together in multilevel bunks.

Toilets on the deck consisted of buckets with privacy screens. Cooking grates were set up on the deck and turns had to be taken for their use. In the early 19th century sailing, ships took about six weeks to cross the Atlantic. With adverse weather it could take as long as fourteen weeks.

Ironically, legislation governing slave ships from Africa was often more humane than the legislation governing emigration ships. The same ships carrying 700 emigrants would only have been allowed by law to carry 500 slaves – although it was haphazardly enforced, and conditions were often much worse on slave ships.

However, Bremen was one of the better ports for departure. Bremen tried to improve the quality of life for emigrants and established a reputation as the most favorable place from which to emigrate. The Bremen Senate set up rules regarding the seaworthiness of the ships departing from her harbors, minimum space requirements and enough adequate provisions for three months at sea. They also required that a doctor be on board each voyage and mandated sanitary inspections.

Once upon the open seas, the entire family dealt with bouts of sea sickness. Even Michael had not imagined the degree to which the ship rolled in heavy waves. The children were first to overcome nearly constant ship rolling. Young Michael, Jr. and David found the trip to be an adventure often playing with other children on deck. The younger children and Hannah, more confined to the quarters, did not.

It was the late in the afternoon on the fortieth day at sea the captain announced that land was in sight. The deck filled with those wanting their first glimpse of America. They were disappointed as land could only be seen by eyeglass from the lookout cage high on the main mask.

The next morning David woke early and ventured to the latrine on deck. He came back and awakened the family exclaiming that land could clearly be seen. The deck was soon crowded with people looking forward, not backward as they had a few weeks earlier.

Immigrants from Europe were not a random sampling of Europeans. Some were destitute, yes, but many were seeking adventure or a new, better life and were willing to take a chance acquiring it. Scientists have identified 124 genes that can influence risk taking. Because of the gene pool, Americans are more prone to taking risks than Europeans. Such could be a reason Americans became more productive.

Individuals and families were not allowed to disembark without showing a receipt proving payment for the voyage. A representative of the indentured servitude procurement company that arranged for half of the Augustine family's fare was waiting. With the second half now paid and Michael's receipt for the first half of the payment, they were allowed to disembark.

Baltimore immigration passenger lists show Michael Augustine and family granted entry into the U.S. in 1827 and his date of birth 'abt 1791'. U.S. entry was much less paper detailed than emigration from Europe and the family members were not listed.

For those entering the Port of Baltimore and heading for Pennsylvania or other mid-Atlantic states, another voyage awaited them on the Chesapeake Bay. The next day was spent on water until they arrived near the port toward evening and anchored again. There, they were assayed any taxes or duties on items they brought into the country and quarantined until examined by a doctor.

A representative of the indentured servant company led three families to their commitment. For the Augustine family it was delivery to a man who had purchased their servitude in Columbia, west of Philadelphia.

From the upper part of Chesapeake Bay, they were taken by horse-drawn canal boat to Columbia, Pennsylvania.

"Are we finished riding on boats?" David asked as they departed the canal boat.

"Yes, we'll be on dry land now."

"Good," two sons replied, and Hannah agreed.

The company representative introduced the family to Herman Schmidt, owner of one of three horse stables in Columbia. Michael was pleased that both Herman and his wife spoke German as well as English. It would hasten the children learning a new language. Herman showed Michael and the boys what would be their quarters while Hannah was introduced to Herman's wife, Martha.

"You must be exhausted from the trip. It was excruciating for us twenty years ago," Martha commented in German.

"Six different boats, all questionably sea or river worthy, I couldn't have imagined worse our quarters, – the constant stench, the rolling seas," Hannah shook her head as if trying to dispel the ordeal.

"Did your stomach have problems adjusting to the rolling ship?"

"I never really got over it. More nausea than five pregnancies combined. Had I any idea of the ordeal, I would have balked at my husband's wishes," vented Hannah.

"I know it isn't much. We just finished last week, but I hope it will accommodate your family," Herman showed Michael and the boys their housing for a year. The makeshift home was a lean-to added on the backside of the stables with a cobble stone floor.

David ran to his mother, "Wow, come see it mom! It's much bigger than the ship's cabin and has two rooms."

It was not their home in Württemberg, but after the ship's cabin, Hannah agreed it would do. *Brighter times lay* ahead promised Michael.

The family soon fell into a routine. Michael was up at dawn, cared for horses and mended harnesses. The three oldest boys attended school in the morning and cleaned horse stalls in the afternoon and evening. Before supper, Michael would hitch a horse to a cartload of manure and spread it with a pitchfork on a farm field.

The youngest boys, Albert, and Godfrey, stayed with their mother. Hannah, always handy with a needle, soon was busy mending and altering clothes for people. While Michael and the older boys' work repaid the loan for their trip to America, Hannah's work added to their savings.

Within six months, the boys had become fluent in English and the parents had picked up enough to get by. After discussing it with Hannah, Michael announced to the boys with the most English he could muster. "It is important that we fit in our new land. So, from now on the conversations in this home will be in English. If your mother or I have trouble, you will help us."

At the end of a year, they had satisfied their contractual obligation, and the family was free to move on. Herman sought to keep them for wages, but Michael had other plans. He had tended horses for a large landowner living a day's ride west of town. From the man, Michael learned that farming land was available.

To Michael's delight, Herman gave him a good deal on a dual purpose horse. "If farming doesn't work out, remember you will always have a place here," offered Herman.

"You've been very fair with us, and I appreciate the offer," Michael replied.

On the second day after the servitude was complete, Michael rode west with their savings and met the landowner. He spent a day looking at various parcels. The price was higher than he expected, and he finally settled on 60 acres, 40 of which were wooded. It would take much work and he deemed the acreage small for a farm to support his family, but it would be a start.

The boys, having made friends in town, were reluctant to leave, but Michael artfully characterized the work to be done as adventures to look forward toward.

A neighbor was generous in his advice on cabin building, giving Michael and the boys their first adventure building a cabin from logs on the property. It was one room at first, but within three years it was four. A barn, chicken house and hog pens were also added. The forty acres of woods was now ten as the farmland grew to fifty.

Hannah gave birth to Martin in 1829 and Johanna in 1831. In 1833, Hannah was near childbirth again. The oldest, Michael, Jr. was 18, David 16, John 14, Albert 8, and Godfrey 7. It was obvious the farm could not support their growing family. Michael sought to buy parcels around them, but none could be had.

Michael left Michael, Jr. to look after the family and took David with him to explore new lands in the west. They were gone nearly two weeks. Confident that in Ohio a larger farm could be purchased at a lower price, he sold the Pennsylvania farm for three times what they had paid. In 1833, two months after Tobias was born, they packed and headed west.

It was time to move on.

Chapter 8

Both ice cream dishes were long since empty when Andrew finished sharing what little he knew of his ancestors' trip to America. Andrew only had a vague outline of what hardships his ancestors, like most, had faced. Sarah and Andrew sat pondering details that would not be known and could only be speculated upon.

"I cannot imagine what they must have gone through," Sarah thought aloud.

"Yeah, for instance, what do you suppose they ate for weeks on a ship? How did they sleep on the ship? Were there beds? I would guess all water was for drinking. Washing clothes or bathing wouldn't have happened," observed Andrew.

Sarah laughed when Andrew held his nose closed to emphasize the point. She put conditions in perspective, "And today people complain if there is an hour power outage."

"Well, I'm glad you stopped, and we had a chance to talk. I jumped to a conclusion I shouldn't have," Andrew said as he stood.

"You need not apologize; I can see how it must have looked to you."

Perhaps I'll see you at the library this week. The hectic part of the fieldwork season is over; I won't be as busy," Andrew added.

"Yes, I wish I knew more of my family's history to share as well. You have a good week," Sarah answered.

As Andrew got in his car, he wanted to kick himself. Why didn't he ask her out? He had misunderstood what happened in the pizzeria parking lot. He could have said asking her out was amends for misinterpreting what happened without revealing that he was attracted to her.

Sarah walked to her car unsure whether he really accepted her explanation about the pizzeria fiasco. She had hoped by clearing up the misunderstanding he would ask her out. Perhaps he was timid – she was tempted, but she would not take the first step. Joining him unexpectedly for ice cream was as far as she would go.

Andrew backed his car out to see Sarah starting to back out. Chivalry dictated that he let her leave the lot first. He stopped and waited for her. Near the lot exit to the street, she stopped and waited. He momentarily thought she was having trouble with the car. He could see she was not on the cell phone, just sitting in the car doing nothing.

An explanation suddenly hit him. She didn't want him following her. Whatever precipitated the unpleasant experience with her former boyfriend, she didn't trust men. Such a woman, thusly traumatized by a man, would harbor an innate fear that would make any relationship problematic. He gently pulled around her and left. He would move on in more ways than one.

Something about him made her nervous. She had always been self-conscious about her driving skills. If she turned a corner too sharp and struck the curb, what would he think, she was a klutz? She would wait on him and possibly avoid embarrassment.

It had been three weeks since Sarah had given explanation to Andrew about the fight with her former boyfriend. She had received nothing more than a nod and a 'Good morning' from him at the church door since. She was disappointed. Not that she had to have a man in her life, but she was 33 and not getting younger. Would she need to go outside this small town to find a suitable suitor? She had made special effort

A WAGON TRAIN LEGACY

to look as attractive as she knew how going to church. She even had bought a new sundress, shorter than she was accustomed to wearing; perhaps it was too short and gave the wrong impression. Obviously, more needed to be in place than common interests and beliefs to draw a couple together. Perhaps underneath his mannerly, interesting façade, he was plain weird. Reluctant as she was, it was time to try an online dating service.

Beverly was in her office going over the annual library budget. Nothing stood out; it was simply rudimentary, and both signed off on the budget.

Beverly had held off asking the question and did so delicately. "I haven't heard of Andrew and you doing anything?"

"No, I thought we had much in common, who knows?"

"I don't want to be forward, but I have a nephew who'd love to meet you. He plays trombone in the city band. The band plays every Thursday in the gazebo in the center of the town square. Would you accompany me and allow me to introduce you after the concert?"

Sarah looked at Beverly differently than she had and said, "I've been wanting to attend a concert, why not?"

"Great, the concerts start at 7:00. Many people park around the square to listen, but I suggest we arrive by 6:30 to claim a bench before they are filled."

The town square with a band gazebo at its center had eight sidewalks geometrically spoking out to a sidewalk encircling the city block. Each spoke had green wooden benches on either side. The entire block was canopied with tall trees. On a summer day it was a great shady place to meet a friend or share town gossip.

It was good Beverly and Sarah had not arrived later. They took one of the last benches to be seen. While they waited for the concert to begin, Beverly started boring Sarah with the history of what she said was the oldest city band in the state. Sarah's eyes surveyed the benches around the park. A few library patrons she recognized. She recognized a girl sitting alone on a bench but not from the library. It was Melanie, the ice cream dipper.

Looking further to the side she saw Andrew enter the maze of sidewalks and benches. He seemed to be looking for someone. Melanie waved at him— after a short conversation he sat.

Beverly noticed Sarah's observation of what appeared to be a couple. "Amazing, isn't it, how guys seem to go for younger girls. I suppose it is in their DNA."

The concert was better than Sarah expected. The selection ran from Rossini's *William Tell Overture* to Simon & Garfunkel's *Homeward Bound*. Particularly interesting, which the younger people didn't understand the music connection, was a man dressed as the Lone Ranger milling around.

Sarah took notice that Andrew and Melanie sat very properly on the bench, no hand holding or touching. Silly, she knew, but it gave her hope. She also noticed that Allen, whom she was to be introduced, looked young.

After the concert, the band dispersed in the crowd, Beverly introduced Allen. He seemed nervous, immaturely so. She surmised he could not be much over twenty. Although Andrew might be attracted to women much younger, Sarah was not attracted to young men. She was aloof as possible without appearing less than courteous. Leaving the park, she saw no sign of Melanie or Andrew.

Twice Allen called Sarah, asking if she would meet him for a drink. When she said she did not drink, she thought he would give up. A week later he called her and asked her out to dinner. She thanked him but said she would be out of town. Having told a lie and pondering how doing so might impact her relationship with Beverly, Sarah left town for a movie theater twenty miles distant.

"Give me a heads up when Sarah is close," Ralph said to Thelma as they waited in a parking lot.

"She's getting close, and Andrew is headed to town only a mile away. Working out just as we planned," answered Thelma.

When they saw Sarah's headlights, Ralph left the parking lot and swerved his green car in front of Sarah, forcing her to leave the road.

It was a warm night. Andrew had planned on early bed but remembered the refrigerator was void of milk. A late night run to the grocery store substituted for watching another rerun of *Gunsmoke*. He was a block from the grocery store when he saw a car with a wheel over the curb at an intersection. The driver was haplessly spinning the wheel attempting to free the car. Andrew thought the car looked familiar and realized why when he walked to the driver side and saw Sarah.

"Oh, it's you." She said startled.

"Yes, it's me. Looks like you are in a predicament."

"A driver with a passenger in a green car – whom I suspect is drunk – came veering to my side of the road. I swerved trying to avoid him and not only didn't he stop but like disappeared."

His look of skepticism embarrassed her. With nothing to lose, she exclaimed, "Yes, think it, say it – I'm a bad driver."

"Could have happened to anyone. Quit spinning your wheel. I'll nudge you with my truck bumper and you'll be out."

Sarah's car was soon free, and Andrew stepped up to her window. "Nothing is damaged, you're okay to drive."

"You can go first."

"Don't worry, I won't follow you home."

"What are you talking about? I just don't want you to see my driving."

"Huh?"

"I know it is crazy, but I'm a bad driver. That's why I let you leave the ice cream parking lot first a few weeks ago."

Andrew could not help himself and burst into laughter causing him to lean forward with both hands on her car door. "I thought you had a phobia about a man following you home."

"Now that is just as crazy as my paranoia about driving."

"Let's go get some ice cream," Andrew stated more than asked.

"What about Melanie?"

"What about Melanie?" he countered.

"Aren't you, you know, you and she?"

"Now that is crazy also. I saw you watching us at the park concert. She offered me a seat when there was none, that's it; she's too young and immature for me. Come on, let's get some cherry nut."

Suddenly, Sarah was struck with a dilemma, ice cream again? Would they never do any more than ice cream together? Her mother had always emphasized that a girl must never appear too interested in a guy. Did noticing her watching Melanie and him cause him to believe she had a crush on him?

"No, I think I'll pass tonight. Too much ice cream... well, for health reasons I must watch my figure."

"Your figure looks mighty fine to me," he countered.

Sarah turned from him and looked out the windshield hoping to hide the blush she felt on her cheeks. "Well, thank you for helping me out, see you around."

Andrew wondered if what he had said was wrong. He intended his comment about her figure to be a compliment, not a come-on. Women these days were so oversensitive to flattery. But her declining his invitation and pulling away challenged him. He decided that it would take more than one no from her to dispel his interest.

Immediately, she regretted leaving him abruptly after he had helped her out. *Why play silly games with him?* She liked him. In a small town with few prospects, she had just rejected a man who was cute, smart, and shared many common interests with her.

Clark, Sarah's former fiancé, had taken Sarah's advice and asked Debbie out, the cute paralegal in his office. They had become an item, together most every weekend, but Clark still felt offended by Sarah's dumping him. Debbie was a prolific oil-on-canvas artist and supplemented her law office income by selling paintings at art shows. It was the third weekend in a row Clark had accompanied her to an art show. This art show was called 'Art on the Square' in Oskaloosa. Clark had no intention of looking up Sarah while in town.

"Sarah's leaving too early, they won't meet on the way to the art show," said Thelma to Ralph, seeing Sarah stepping outside her apartment.

"I'll hold her up with a phone call," said Ralph as they watched from a parking lot.

"Won't work – her cell is in her purse," responded Thelma.

"Are you sure about that?" answered Ralph.

Sarah had hardly closed the door when she heard her cell ringing inside. She was sure she had placed it in her purse, but the ring tone left no doubt that it was hers.

By the time Sarah unlocked the door, answered the phone to find it was a wrong number, put it in her purse and stepped outside, Andrew was five minutes closer.

"Just right," said Thelma.

Andrew parked his truck at the closest available spot two blocks from the square. At a pedestrian street crossing, he waited for traffic and saw Sarah walking to the crossing from the other side of the block.

"Hi, are you going to the art show?" he asked.

"Yes, and you?"

"Yes, I attend every year."

"I guess it shouldn't surprise me that you are an art enthusiast in addition to a pig farmer."

"Was that a compliment or was it intended to hurt?" he said while chuckling. She joined him in laughter at their exchange.

"Well, whether be it fate, serendipity or planning from above that put us on similar paths at the same time, would you allow me to escort you to the art show?"

He raised his elbow slightly inviting her to lay her hand in it. After she timidly laid her hand inside his elbow, he asked, "I think we make a great couple, don't you?"

"I thought we were just going to an art show."

"Can't blame a guy for trying," he answered causing them to both to smirk while looking straight forward hoping their expressions were not seen by the other. He had never been this bold nor had she ever expected it of him.

After her dismissal of him at her car predicament, Andrew vowed to himself to try another track. To Sarah, his new aggressiveness validated her standoffishness strategy.

Sarah and Andrew studied a display of acrylic landscapes longer than they had the dozens of other displays by which they had walked. The same painting caught the eye of both.

"What do you want for it?" Andrew asked the artist.

"For that one, I need $300," replied the artist.

Sarah could not help envisioning how it would look on her living room wall. But the price was beyond what she would spend. She was frugal with her money, lived on her salary and would not touch her investments.

"I'll take it," Andrew said, shocking Sarah.

The artist took Andrew's money on the condition that the painting remain until the show was over and the judges had made their selections.

In the next aisle, Sarah and Andrew walked by a booth in which they had no interest. The art took modern art to another level, a weird level. Beside abstract, each painting had a hint of what appeared to be bright red blood oozing invoking a macabre aura to the entire booth. Andrew quickly moved on but before Sarah passed she caught a view of a familiar face. It was Debbie, Clark's paralegal. She turned to see Clark standing on the other side of the booth staring daggers at her.

With Andrew at the next booth, Sarah stopped long enough to give Clark a *leave me alone* look. Clark returned it with a tight forced smile and overly crisp wave. Sarah sharpened her expression and moved on before Andrew came back.

She joined Andrew. He asked. "Did you like that ghoulish display?"

"Absolutely not, and I'm glad you didn't," she replied.

At the next two art displays, Andrew thought little of the paintings and found himself pondering Sarah's comment. If she were glad they shared the same taste in art, what could it mean about her feelings for him? If she saw no future for them, why would she care about their art tastes? He came to the conclusion he was over analyzing.

Andrew saw someone carrying the painting he had purchased heading toward the band gazebo in the center of the square. His first thought was that someone had stolen it until they climbed the stairs of the gazebo.

"Attention everyone," a speaker said on the gazebo's sound system. "The judges have picked this acrylic of a woman in a garden as the grand prize winner of the show."

"Perhaps I should add art critic to your list," said Sarah.

Before Andrew left the square with the painting, four people had offered him a profit on the painting. While carrying the painting to the car, he asked, "How about something different for dinner. Perhaps Asian?"

She looked at him bewildered, "Are you asking me to dinner?"

"Yes."

Clark was discreetly watching the couple leave the park. "Nice painting, he bought, eh?" a stranger asked.

"Do you happen to know who he is?" Clark asked ignoring the question.

"Yes, that's Andrew Augustine. He farms ten or so miles east of here."

At the Asian restaurant, Sarah, and Andrew both ordered chicken—him orange, her General Zoe's.

Sarah wanted to hear more about his family's history. How much more did he know? "So, if your ancestor scouted land in Ohio, how did you get to Iowa?"

"It is a long story."

"I've no immediate plans, and no one is waiting on our table."

"I know that they moved to Ohio, then Indiana and eventually, according to records, bought land in Iowa for $1.25 an acre," he answered. "They were the first pioneer settlers in an Iowa county east of here. Family legend has it that Michael killed an Indian in an encounter, but I don't know the details."

CHAPTER 9

Summer, 1833

The Ohio farm the Augustine family moved onto was 120 acres, twice the size of their Pennsylvania farm. It had a log cabin, barn and two outbuildings already built but in need of repair. The family who had owned the property moved to Indiana.

Albert, now age nine and old enough to work, joined by three older brothers, gave Michael a hardy crew. Roofs were replaced, brush eliminated from the pasture and more land plowed for crops. The run-down farm was soon as well-kept and prosperous as any in the area.

By 1835, with the family's abundant labor supply, Michael Jr. and David took jobs outside the farm.

"Dad, here is half my pay from last week," Michael, Jr. offered his dad.

"No, from now on you boys keep all you earn off the farm. It is time for you to think about starting your own life," responded Michael, Sr.

Junior was working for a blacksmith ten hours a day and had become quite good at the trade. The blacksmith's shoulder problem worsened, causing him to spend more time at home. He sent his 17-year-old daughter, Silvia, to deliver daily noontime dinner to Junior at the shop. Junior couldn't decide whether he liked her fried prairie chicken or cherry pie better. One day after the blacksmith's daughter left with dinner for the shop, Junior stepped from behind a tree and knocked on his door.

"Where is Silvia?"

"She's at the shop."

"Why are you here then?"

"I must ask you something."

"Well, speak up."

Junior's gaze scanned the house and his weight shifted from leg to leg. Having an idea what was coming the father asked, "Is this about my daughter?"

"Sir, I wish to ask for your daughter's hand in marriage."

Three weeks later, Michael, Jr. and Silvia were married.

One year later, David was married.

Hannah gave birth to her ninth child, her second daughter, Nancy, in 1836. The loss of two sons by marriage had not diminished the available family labor force as John, Albert, and Godfrey were all growing into strong young men.

It was fall when the man whose Ohio farm they had purchased rode onto the property.

"My, it is hard to believe all the improvements you have made," he observed.

"Yes, I have a big family and it is good to show boys how to work," Michael answered and continued. "That is the primary responsibility of a parent, to prepare young people to live on their own. We won't be here forever, you know."

"You've got that right. It's what my wife keeps telling me," the man answered.

Michael knew there was more to his reply than he verbalized but waited for him to expand upon it.

"We've got a great place in the South Bend area of Indiana, 320 acres of prime farmland. It is all I hoped for, but my wife misses her family around here. I thought she'd get over it, but she hasn't. She has grandchildren here, you know. A week ago, she said she was moving back here whether I came or not."

"So, what are you going to do?" Michael asked.

"I was thinking, you've got a growing family. Look what you've done here. A challenge for your boys would be good. And I've only a boy and girl at home. The half section is too much for me. Having twice as much land would be good for you, and I probably should scale back."

"What are you proposing?"

"That we swap farms. You'll have more and better land and we are closer to our grandchildren."

Hannah and Michael pondered the proposal for two days. As reluctant as she was to pack up and move again, she knew it would be good for her younger sons. Within a year she would have help in the kitchen from 5-year-old daughter, Johannah, and her two oldest sons were making their own life. She also recognized the itch in her husband to explore new lands.

A local lawyer helped them swap deeds and while the ground remained frozen for easy traveling they moved on west. This time with two fewer sons, and an infant daughter. Five head of cattle including a milk cow, two riding horses and two wagon loads of possessions, one pulled by oxen and another by draft horses were included in their moving caravan.

Spring had set in when they reached the South Bend area. The 320 acre farm they found was not as they expected. The log cabin was small, and the land was mostly brush and poorly drained, almost a swamp area. However, the biggest disappointment was the prevalence of swamp fever. The disease, now called Malaria, had wreaked havoc in the area, killing many. Within fifteen days of dealing with hordes of early mosquitoes, Michael developed a fever. Soon Albert, Johannah, and Hannah were stricken with tiredness and headaches. They all recovered but were told natural immunity would last only a year and to expect reinfection next year.

Michael was tempted to return to Ohio and confront the man about his misrepresentation of the farm and omission of swamp fever in the area, but he knew he had no recourse and confronting the man would waste his time. His focus had always been looking forward. To dwell on the past throughout his life would get him nowhere. They had to leave the area before someone died of swamp fever.

The future lay further west, Michael was convinced. A neighbor offered to buy the farm for $3 an acre. Michael agreed as long as possession wouldn't be given until the first of the year. As Godfrey, age 12, was the only family member who had not contacted swamp fever, he had no natural immunity to the next round of infection and was in the most danger. Although young, he would learn fast. Michael and Godfrey saddled up, bid the family farewell, and headed west to seek new land.

They carried a few food provisions, a leather water bladder, axe, shovel, crosscut saw and steel wedge to split wood. Game would be the primary source of food. Michael carried a Pennsylvania Rifle with a 38-inch octagon barrel and 45 caliber bore that had been converted from flintlock to percussion.

Often they stopped and scouted areas as they crossed Illinois seeking farmland, but most was flatland and Michael was leery of settling in another poorly drained area prone to swamp fever. He also had a desire to settle far enough west that the move would be permanent.

They approached a river wider than they had ever imagined. It was called the Mississippi. Zebulon Pike had split off the Lewis and Clark Louisiana Purchase Expedition to follow the Mississippi. In 1805, Pike landed at the bluffs on the west side of the river and recommended that a fort be constructed there. It never was, but the settlement was incorporated as Burlington in 1833. What later became Iowa was part of the Wisconsin Territory.

Although Godfrey was too young to remember the journey from Europe, he had heard many frightening stories of boat travel. It took much persuasion to convince him that the ferry was safe to travel across the river.

Godfrey refused to take his eyes from the raft as they ferried across the mighty river. A pioneer settlement was being built on the west side. River barges docked, unloading lumber, and temporary shacks were being constructed haphazardly with no plan for future streets or organized layout The whole scene created an aura of each for himself in what was a lawless enclave.

For two days they slept outside the settlement. During the day Michael gleaned what information he could from those passing through. Information varied; rumors spread of a gold strike a hundred miles west. Others said it was a planted rumor by a peddler with an excess supply of shovels.

Michael was trying to sort out all the advice and rumors he had heard when a stranger wearing buckskins from head to toe and riding a mule rode into Godfrey and their campsite.

"Mind if I stay by your fire tonight?" he asked. Hearing no reply, he added, "Don't like to hang around those highfalutins over yonder," nodding toward the emerging town.

"Dismount and take a rest, where are you from?"

"Been as far thataway," he pointed west, "to the other big river, a good two week's ride."

The more they talked, the more Michael began to trust him, he showed no inclination to lead them astray.

"If I were hankering a good farm, which I ain't, I'd find land betweensth these big rivers. Best I'd stay on this side of what here they call the Skunk River and mosey northeast a couple of days. There's them Sac and Fox Indians around; they don't like to fight, but sure enough – steal you blind."

Before the man left, he said, "If I was a mind to settle up there, I'd get a few packets of sugar to give the hooligans. It'll go a long way."

Godfrey was fascinated by the ruffian, particularly his colorful language. Michael cautioned the boy to never repeat words that he had heard in front of his mother.

Michael had enough information. After picking up a few supplies in the settlement, they followed the Skunk River for two days and camped where Dutch Creek joined it. A mile up Dutch Creek, a hill overlooked farmland above the floodplain and close enough to the creek for water. It would be here they would settle.

Useful trees were close to the top of the hill where they would build a cabin. They had the luxury of being able to cherry pick the straightest, tallest old growth trees for the cabin without much need for chinking. Utilizing the techniques shown him by the Pennsylvania pioneer, trees were cut, and logs were laid. They would build one room now and add more once the family arrived.

Two layers of logs had been laid when four Indians appeared. Whether Sac or Fox, Michael did not know. They rode ponies around the construction twice before the leader waved his hands in language Michael could not understand. Michael reached in a bag of supplies and handed the leader a pouch of sugar. The Indian tasted it, waved his hand around, then pointed a finger at him. Michael interpreted it as recognition that the space would be his.

In another day, they had the cabin walls four logs high with each log saddle notched for fit. That night they placed their supplies inside the unfinished enclosure and tied the horses to a rope line within sight. During the day, the horses could graze, but at night they would keep them close.

It was nearly dawn when Michael heard a horse neigh. He peered over the four foot log wall. An Indian had a rope around one of their horses and was starting to walk away. Michael grabbed his percussion rifle and hollered, "Hinken!," the German word for halt. German or English, the buck could not understand. When Michael took a few steps toward the Indian, the Indian grabbed an arrow from his scabbard and loaded his bow. Michael pointed his rifle at him.

The stalemate was lengthy. Eventually, Michael lowered his gun, waved the Indian toward him and took a step in his direction. The Indian let loose the arrow. It missed Michael and grazed Godfrey's arm who had taken a position near him. Turning back from his injured son, Michael saw the Indian pull another arrow. He raised his rifle and shot him.

Within five minutes the Indian was dead. Luckily, Godfrey's injury was not much more than a tree limb scrape he had received the day before. With daylight now upon them, Michael tossed the Indian over his horse and buried him in dense timber a quarter mile from the cabin. He camouflaged the grave with dead leaves as well has he could.

Extra prayers preceded breakfast that morning as Michael sought forgiveness. Although he had no choice, an amount of guilt flooded him. He would not chance staying where they were.

They rode ten miles up Dutch Creek, crossed it and found an area Michael deemed more adequate than what they had left. This time, after identifying a cabin site, they didn't start building for a week. Game was plentiful as were berries in addition to corn meal they had brought mixed with water. It was as if God had the spot waiting for them. They camped at the site with the horses close, rifle prepared and assessed the safety of the site.

Again, dad and son had two logs placed on the cabin wall when five ponied Indians rode up. Michael gave them two packets of sugar and waved his hand around the perimeter then pointed at himself. The Indian leader seemed to acknowledge it. Michael then pointed to both horses, then at himself. The Indian again acknowledged and they left.

With the cabin walls over six feet, they used the purlin and rafter technique for the roof which involves two gable walls which support the roof. Finished with a door and no windows, the one room cabin would be a start – rooms would be added later. Water was plentiful at the nearby creek and a well could be dug later. Michael rode half a mile in four directions from the cabin setting markers in the ground.

Satisfied that he had found what he sought, Michael and Godfrey headed back to Burlington. At the federal land office, he described best he could the location and markers he had placed. With the payment of $1.25 per acre, the section, one mile square, 640 acres, was marked on paper as his.

It was late summer when they returned to the family in Indiana. Two weeks later, the entire family was headed west for new land. They became the first pioneer settlers in what was to become Washington County, Iowa.

The first winter in Iowa was tough, provisions from the wagons were supplemented with game. Firewood was ample to keep warm. The boys were put to work building fences to contain the horses and six head of cattle. Before the winter was over, another room was added to the cabin. Curious, Indians visited a few times without any problems.

It was said they were strong, rugged people. Michael and one of his sons could split a thousand wood rails a day. Their herd of cattle grew. They added to their land holdings until they had a thousand acres in the Dutch Creek area with several sets of good buildings. Martha, the tenth and last of their children, was born on the Iowa farmstead.

At this time Burlington, Iowa on the Mississippi River was the largest city in the territory, the territorial capital, and the only place to get supplies. Often they would drive livestock the 70 some miles to Burlington and trade for supplies. Some of the men stayed and worked in Burlington part of the year. Other men in the family worked as lumberjacks in Wisconsin when they needed cash.

Three of Michael and Hannah's children – John, Albert, and Tobias – went to California. John made some money and came back to Iowa. Albert returned but had acquired "gold fever" and traveled many times captaining wagon trains to California and Oregon. Eventually, he opened a general store in a mining town.

Michael and Hannah Augustine
Hannah passed in 1854 at age 63
Michael passed in 1864 at age 78

Chapter 10

"So, you don't know all the details about the family's journey from Pennsylvania to Iowa, but why did your third great grandfather, Albert, move back to Iowa from California?" Sarah asked Andrew.

"He went broke with the first general store he owned in a California mining town when the gold ran out. After bringing another wagon train west, he opened a second general store. He sold that one before the gold was depleted. With twelve thousand dollars from the store sale, he purchased a farm in the Springfield, Missouri area. But his abolitionist Methodist beliefs were not popular in the area, and he left before someone was hurt. Taking a loss on the farm, he returned to Iowa with his wife, Dorothy, and three children."

"How many children did Dorothy and Andrew have?"

"Thirteen total, five died in infancy or childhood."

"Wow, eight adults put in the world. How many children did Albert's parents Hannah and Michael have?"

"Ten, they had 70 grandchildren." Can you imagine having 69 first cousins? And I cannot imagine the number of great grandchildren."

"Oh, my goodness, it would be neat to have one cousin, I don't have any first cousins. Mother was an only child and Dad's brother died young," lamented Sarah.

"Have you any second or third cousins?"

"Not that I know of,"

Andrew could tell it bothered her to be alone family-wise. He didn't know how to console her.

Sarah changed the subject and summarized the legacy of pioneers, "It's unbelievable what pioneers went through. Children grew up fast out of necessity. And, as history shows, it didn't hurt them. Look at what they did as adults, built cities, industry, prosperity, and a country in which most of the world wants to come. Many of the most prolific achievers in history were given adult tasks early in life. Davy Crockett at twelve years of age had to walk hundreds of miles home alone after helping herd cattle."

"Yeah, and look at how children have it today," added Andrew.

"Many of my teacher friends say the majority of parents are either helicopter parents, hovering over their children to the point of hindering initiative, or absent parents either physically so or absent in directing their children. I've noticed schools in Des Moines with cars lined up blocks to pick up children when most live within a few blocks in safe neighborhoods. On the other hand, many children live with their grandmother, don't know who their father is and hardly ever see their mother.

In the Chicago suburb of Northbrook, where I grew up and went to school, state agencies are taking seriously someone's comment from the area, *it takes a village*. They are taking it to a new level believing the state has a preemptive right to overrule parent's decisions in which they don't agree."

"Have you heard of the movement called, *'Free range children'*?" Andrew asked.

"Yes, you can take anything too far, but the idea is to teach kids initiative, responsibility, and consequences as an alternative to coddling. If I have children someday, I'm going to take my responsibility seriously, and prepare them for life."

"It is not just children who are coddled," added Andrew. "Look at adults. My ancestors fended for themselves, built cabins from scratch, cooked meals without gas or packaged foods. Tomorrow morning I'll mow my yard; that's not clearing land of brush with an ax, but most of my friends in town hire a lawn service to mow their grass.

It's in vogue to be at the health club Saturday morning instead of pushing a lawn mower. Pushing a mower puts you in a group that cannot afford a lawn service, rather than offering a sense of pride for having done it for yourself."

"Aren't you so right," Sarah continued with the same thoughts. "How many women clean their own home today, although it shouldn't be just a woman's job?" Andrew felt the comment was directed toward him. In a way, he hoped it was.

She continued, "Let's take this a step further. A few weeks ago, I went to one of those dystopian movies, you know – the bomb, asteroid or some catastrophe strikes the earth – and we must revert to living like our ancestors. How many people today would have the skills, stamina, or ingenuity to survive? With hunger rampant and few moral values, like the movie portrayed, would humankind devote more energy on theft and murder for survival than making do and helping each other?"

Sarah saw Andrew with a smile on his face. "Something I say funny?"

"No, not at all. Talking about depressing scenarios should dishearten me but being with someone who thinks and sees the world as I do is very uplifting."

He laid a hand over hers on the table and said, "I see people waiting for a table, we should leave."

Andrew walked her to the car. He was tempted to kiss her but held off. He didn't want her to think his only attraction to her was physical. "Good night, I'll see you Sunday. Oh, and you can leave the parking lot first. I promise to neither follow you nor judge your driving skills."

She playfully waved him off as she opened the car door. It was a wave off of his tease, not him. She found herself somewhat disappointed he hadn't tried to kiss her. She would have welcomed it.

The next morning Andrew rehashed the Asian restaurant conversation as he mowed lawn. Sarah gave her apartment the first thorough cleaning since she had moved in. Her focus was on the diametrically opposite personalities and beliefs of her former fiancé and present boyfriend. She caught herself in mid-thought; Andrew was not her boyfriend, yet anyway. She pushed her mind away from thinking about them as a couple, but soon stared at the blank wall in her apartment and thought how great the painting Andrew purchased would look there.

A week after the art show Andrew was headed to town for tractor parts when he noticed a white truck parked on his bottomland field that a creek ran through. With closer inspection he noticed a man walking along the creek. He pulled behind the truck and noticed an official 'State of Iowa' license on the truck. More ominous was a DNR (Iowa Department of Natural Resources) emblem on the truck door.

The agent was inspecting the flow of the stream called Middle Creek when Andrew approached him. "Hi, lovely day for a walk," Andrew asked realizing it sounded awkward.

"Yes, you wouldn't happen to be the owner, would you?"

"As a matter of fact, yes, can I help you?"

"No, not really. I'll soon have what I came for."

"What would that be?"

"Just doing a compliance inspection."

It was as much the tone of what the agent said as the words that sent tension up Andrew's spine. "You don't have permission to be on this property."

The agent's condescending look was as a professor might look if a student audaciously pointed out it was the instructors job to provide more answers than questions. "Don't be ridiculous, I could have a court order tomorrow."

Andrew pulled his cell phone and called the sheriff, "I have a trespasser on my property."

The agent folded his notepad and started walking to his truck. Over his shoulder, he said, "You'll regret not cooperating with a public official."

Clark was working on a legal brief when his phone rang. "I believe, I've found enough to give him trouble. A creek that runs across his property appears to have changed course according to our aerial maps. If he had anything to do with it, that is a big no-no. It was nice to get out in the field for a change. I'll go to make the case, but you owe me one now," said the DNR administrator in charge of field agents, who had been a college friend of Clark.

After picking up tractor parts, Andrew was at the library researching Iowa administrative laws, specifically DNR prohibition of any stream alteration. Sarah had seen him enter and found him at a table with administrative code books open.

She glanced at the books, "A little more boring that history, looks like to me."

"Yes, I know but I caught a DNR agent on the property this morning which usually means trouble."

"What kind of trouble could they accuse you? You didn't dump animal waste near a stream, did you?" She asked.

"Heavens no, I play by the rules as ridiculous as many are, because tangling with them would be expensive, even if you prevail," he answered.

"Probably just some bureaucrat putting in their hours. But if you need help, I know someone who is a good friend of an agent supervisor in the department." The statement had barely escaped her mouth when she realized the futility and possible risk of what she said.

"Let me see what happens. From all I've read, I've done nothing to worry about. Hopefully, I never hear from them. But it would be good to have an inside track just in case."

Sarah had hoped he hadn't caught her remark, but he had. Now she regretted it more. Why had she been so anxious to help him before she thought?

Andrew usually sat in the back pew at church after he had greeted the worshipers at the door. The prior Sunday following the service, Sarah was surprised to find him sitting directly behind her. They passed the time of day before he suggested they visit the ice cream shoppe. It was very impromptu, certainly not a date.

This Sunday the crowd was larger than normal. Sarah sat two thirds of the way toward the back on the left hand side. It was her usual spot. She was comfortable there. She often wondered why, when there were certainly no assigned seats, most everyone sat in the same location every Sunday. Were people afraid of change? She promised herself that she would sit elsewhere the following Sunday.

She was reading the bulletin when Andrew stood in the aisle by her pew. "Could you squeeze someone else in here?" he asked.

"Sure," she replied, scooting over expecting a late comer to sit beside her. Without saying more Andrew sat beside her. An older lady, who recently lost her husband and always sat in front of her, turned with a smile carrying an *I told you* look. Sarah was sheepish returning the smile as she had recently commented that they both sat in the predominantly single women section. The lady's reply was that Sarah would not be single long.

Sarah caught a few others around her discreetly checking out their new church neighbors. *People would think they were a couple*, thought Sarah. The thought chilled her, but it was what she wanted.

Belatedly, without turning to him she said, "Sure, there's always room here."

Pastor Ken usually made rounds greeting people as the choir sang the first song. Making his rounds, he stood in the aisle and shook Andrew's hand, then put his hand on Sarah's shoulder. "Good morning to both of you."

Soon the assistant pastor, Stan, stopped and greeted them. The coy smile on his face was recognition that their sitting together was not happenstance. Sarah was pleased.

Amanda led the choir in the next song, a traditional favorite, *Just as I Am*. Did Amanda glance in her direction sensing Sarah was out of tune? No Amanda couldn't hear her from that distance, but Andrew could. Sarah turned the volume of her regular voice down a notch and carefully tried to stay on tune. For her it took effort, she was not a candidate for the choir, and she didn't wish to embarrass herself. Into the second verse, she mouthed silent words and attempted to hear Andrew. His voice was soft, for good reason, she thought. Every other word from him was off key. It struck her as funny. She lowered her head trying to disguise and stifle her laughter.

"Is something wrong?" Andrew whispered.

"No, not at all," she answered.

Pastor Ken's sermon was on patience, "Blessings will come to those who are hopeful and steadfast in their quest for what is meant to be," his words stuck in Sarah's mind.

When church broke up, Andrew asked what she was doing the coming Wednesday evening. He asked her to dinner at an Italian restaurant in a nearby town.

"Are you asking me out on a real date?" she asked the obvious.

"Yes, I am," he replied. Then added, "Even though you couldn't help snickering at my singing."

As usual, Wednesday's mail came by noon at Andrew's farm home. Often he went through it as he ate lunch, this day the usual four ads for services he did not want or need, two bills and an unexpected yellow card. The card was notice that he had a registered letter at the post office. Registered letters were never good news.

Andrew had planned to stop at the post office before the five o'clock close, sign for the registered letter, then kill some time in town before picking up Sarah at six. But curiosity got the better of him, the more he thought about what it could be, the more worried he became. It could be from the IRS – his politics invited audits – God forbid. Maybe it was a recall on his truck, and he was worrying for nothing. He would get ready for his date when he got back. He cut short his farm chores and headed for the post office at 3:00.

The postal clerk he had seen around town but did not know her name. With the post card given her, she left and came back with an official looking letter. Was she particularly somber or was it his imagination? He signed. The first thing his eyes caught was the return address. DNR, Des Moines, IA. He had forgot about catching the agent on his property. In his truck, he opened it and read.

> It has come to the agency's attention that you have violated an
> agency rule by diverting the flow of a state controlled steam.
> The fine for such activity is $25,000. The fine will be limited to
> such with your immediate payment and rerouting the stream
> to its original state. If you wish to appeal this ruling, notify the
> agency within 10 working days.

An IRS letter could not have been more frightening. Any problem with the IRS would have been due to a simple error. He had done nothing to divert the stream, his lawyer would straighten it out, but at what cost?

Date, date, with Sarah, he kept telling himself. He would deal with the DNR mistake tomorrow. Now was the time to shower and get ready for his first official date with Sarah.

Sarah looked radiant as she stepped out of the apartment, and he opened the truck door for her. She was wearing the sun dress she wore the first time he saw her, white with roses painted upon. She wore fancy sandals with a matching painted leather flower on top. He would not mention having seen the dress. Doing so would disclose his immediate interest in her and perhaps make her feel bad she had not bought a new dress for their first real date.

Andrew did his best to set aside recurring apprehension about the DNR letter. But between engaging subjects of conversation at the dinner table, Sarah could sense something on his mind.

"Anything going on special at the farm? You seem distracted at times."

"Wow, you can read me. I don't know whether that is good or bad. Yes, I got an upsetting letter today."

She didn't want to pry and said nothing.

He answered her thought, "Remember I told you a DNR agent was on the farm, I got a letter today, a big fine and demand that I correct something I didn't do."

"If you didn't do anything wrong, I'm sure you'll get it straightened out. Tell me more about your family history, what more do you know about the wagon train?"

"No, it's your turn. Tell me what you know about your family's history in Chicago."

"I don't really know that much, but my grandmother told me that her grandmother had a vegetable and fruit produce farm and moved there after the great fire in 1871. Where the wagon train connection came from I don't know."

CHAPTER 11

Nevada City, California

At a saloon-eatery, Sarah's ancestor, Tobias, chopped beef carcasses into steaks for hungry miners wishing to celebrate their newfound riches with more than whiskey. After two years of this and now at age 20, he left the saloon-eatery job and started a butcher shop in the California mining town. Over the years the shop grew, employees were added, he was married and became a father of two girls and a son.

With no ice, meat had to be eaten fresh, salted, dried, or canned. Tobias's shop specialized in fresh meat, but they would salt any that wasn't sold fresh before it spoiled.

The man who walked into Tobias's shop was well dressed, like few he had seen. He wore a frock over a checkered vest. His tie was as white as his shirt. He wore a silk top hat, which tilted to the right on his head giving him a confident, distinguished appearance. He was obviously a newcomer or passerby, because even the richest miners didn't have access to the latest fashion.

"Are you the proprietor here?" he asked.

"Yes, sir, may I help you?" Tobias answered, thinking a large order might be in the making.

"I'm exploring the west and always wanted to see firsthand a boom mining town I've heard so much about. Must say... it's a haphazardly built, decadent looking place. But your shop is a delight in this pigsty. Mind if I look around?"

"Sure, go ahead. Where are you from?"

"Chicago, I say."

The next morning the man came back. "Is this town where you see yourself in 5 to 10 years?"

"Eventually, no."

"I am the owner of a state of the art meat packing plant in Chicago. We process more in a day than you'll see here in twenty years. I see you may have an aptitude for the packing industry. I need good plant managers. Follow me to Chicago, soon to be the packing capital of the world. I'll show you the latest, pay you a good wage and moving expenses, provide housing and a chance for advancement. But most importantly get you out of this wayward village of sin."

Tobias's wife and he discussed the job offer. California they did not desire to leave, but getting out of the mining camp, they were ready. The ratio of men to women in the camp was 50 to 1. With the exclusion of women working at three sporting houses, it was higher. They had young daughters who they would not let out at night --escorted or not. The danger would only increase as they got older. The law that existed could be bought off with a few nuggets, and there was plenty gold floating around.

The saloon-eatery owner in the past had offered to buy the butcher shop. They took him up on his offer and packed their belongings in three trunks. The debonair Chicagoan showed up with five train tickets to Chicago. He said two adults were on him but the half-price fare for the children he would deduct from future wages. Tobias cringed at what he saw as backtracking on a promise, but it was too late to turn back.

The transcontinental railroad had been completed one year earlier in 1869. The 1900 mile route from California to the Missouri river at the Nebraska-Iowa border took four days traveling through the new state of Nevada, the future state of Wyoming and across Nebraska. The arduous wagon trip had taken Tobias's family five months when he was young. A stagecoach trip would take 25 days. Although they traveled by coach fare, the train trip was comparatively luxurious. In Council Bluffs, Iowa, they switched to the eastern U.S. rail network in route to Chicago.

A driver met the family at Chicago's Union train station and loaded their three trunks on a wagon. They headed south to a company bungalow built for packing plant managers. It was a small two bedroom wood framed house which had more comforts than their mining camp home, but two people could not walk side by side between their bungalow and the adjacent one. The backyard was smaller than the house floor plan.

Tobias's wife was happy. The children would have a real school and be in a safe neighborhood as long as they didn't venture north of 22nd Street which was becoming known as the Levee district.

The district became home of the Everleigh Club and a range of lower end establishments of gambling, drinking, racketeering and prostitution. Although all were illegal, payoffs to Republican aldermen of the time kept the police away.

With the opening of Union Stock Yards in 1865, the packing industry boomed. Three million cattle and hogs passed through the exchange in 1870. Working conditions were horrendous at the packing plants. Workers, including immigrant children, worked twelve hours a day and lived in one-room company shanties. Although Tobias had seen despicable conditions in western mining towns, the near slavery conditions of the workers abhorred him. He was often reprimanded by higher management for cutting injured workers some slack.

The long drought of 1871 persisted into the fall. The city had received only one inch of rain from July to October. On October 8th, a strong southwest wind lasted two days. The most popular tale is that Mrs. O'Leary's cow knocked over a lantern in a barn. A more likely explanation is the weekly meeting of a group of drunken gambling men in the barn knocked a lantern over.

The consequences were severe. Winds caused a great conflagration of predominantly wood structures and took out a water pumping station early. The two day fire killed 300 people, destroyed 17,000 structures, and left 100,000 residents homeless.

The Tobias family was lucky. Flames moved slower in their direction, giving them time to escape, but lost was their home and all they could not carry. With a shortage of housing throughout the city, they moved into company housing for low wage migrant workers. Their three room bungalow had been a move up from the mining town house, but this move was two steps down.

The conditions were intolerable. Tobias rented a horse from a stable and rode west. He was gone for two days. Back in the packing plant he was reprimanded for missing work and warned that it could not happen again. He didn't respond to the threat, just turned, and walked out of the plant.

With savings from the sale of the California butcher shop, he was able to buy a 60-acre farm south of the village of Aurora, forty miles from Chicago. The farm was too small to sustain a family growing regular crops, and too small for livestock raising. He had noticed how quickly fresh vegetables were snatched from carts in the city. Sixty acres and enough hard work would generate ample produce to make a living. His produce farm (truck farm as they later came to be called) was successful and grew over the years. The farm was passed on for two generations.

As a young girl, Sarah's mother, who lived in the city, often overheard her grandfather talking about his experience running a produce farm. Because he loved to talk about old times, she was never sure how much of her grandfather's recollections were real and how much was bloviating.

"Yes, things were getting out of hand in the early 20s. My farm, now 240 acres, was producing well, but it was a nightmare getting produce into the city and getting it sold. Our trucks would get hijacked periodically, sometimes they would be found empty of produce, sometimes never found. The trucks delivered to grocery stores, and we'd also sell directly from the truck. Thieves would take what they wanted. The police would turn their head.

The Democrats who had ousted the corrupt Republican politicians in the city were becoming just as crooked. Many Chicago policemen earned more money from payoffs than from the city. We had to payoff aldermen and policemen to park a truck and sell produce off it.

It wasn't right. Our farm was more productive than ever. But our losses in the city were so great we began to lose money."

"How did you survive?" asked a nephew.

"One day two men showed up at the farm. In double breasted pinstriped suits, they were not dressed like someone you'd expect to see on a farm. They said they understood we'd been having considerable losses. At first, I thought they were from the police department wanting more payoffs but soon figured out they weren't. Policemen were seldom out of uniform as the uniform gave an aura of authority. With 45s bulging under their jackets, these men didn't need a uniform to convey power.

"We can help you," one said to me.

"What would you want in return? I asked.

"Twenty-five cents for every trip of a truck into the city."

"It was far less than I was paying politicians and the police. And, frankly, I was apprehensive about telling these guys no. "What's the terms?" I asked."

"We'll stop back next year. You keep a tally on how many trips have been made into the city and pay us. But be warned slighting us will not make the boss happy."

"Who is the boss?" I asked.

"They turned and left without answering. How they did it I don't know but we never lost another truck after that. Petty thefts of vegetables from trucks also were reduced greatly. It was the best money I ever spent."

"Did you ever find out whose operation it was?" the nephew asked.

"Yes, it was Scarface's, which is Capone's. The word got out that my trucks were not to be trifled with. I eventually stopped paying off politicians and policemen."

"How often did you pay them?"

It varied, sometimes every few months, other times nearly a year before the same guys would show up. I never cheated them. It was the best money I ever spent. I had a neighbor who raised turkeys. They showed up at his place and bought every turkey he had one year before Thanksgiving and distributed them free to people in the city during the depression.

Call it the mob if you wish, but they had many more friends than the police. I know they were sometimes ruthless. But did they kill as many people as get killed every year in the city by gangs today?"

Demographically over time, Chicago like many large cities reverted to the past, before the industrial revolution. Cities were predominantly inhabited by the wealthy, cultural leaders and working class poor with high populations of immigrants. Small towns and rural areas were enclaves of the middle class. With the industrial revolution, unionization and the agricultural revolution which cut the need for farm labor,

A Wagon Train Legacy

the middle class grew and thrived in cities. The population of large cities exploded and became centers of cultural activity.

The tide reversed itself in the post industrial age with the onset of rising crime, high taxes, and declining school quality. Large cities became less desirable for those who could not live in protected areas or afford to pay rising taxes.

Large cities continued to be a magnet for young people fresh from college. It was the place to be. Popular culture gave young people in small towns and rural areas a much better understanding of urban life than the reverse. Most often, even after the popular situation comedy 'Green Acres,' rural people were portrayed as backward, beholding to archaic values and unimaginative. But as young people married and thought about having children, the cities lost their luster.

A recent study showed that 39% of Chicago public school teachers send their children to private schools, compared to the national average of 12%. Most families leave for the suburbs when their children reach school age unless they can afford private school. Immigrants and the poor have no choice but to remain.

At nearly school age, Sarah had a pet golden retriever. The dog got away from her mother on a walk. Her dad put up posters in the neighborhood offering a fifty dollar reward. The next day two policemen came to the door. Sarah was joyed when she heard they had the dog.

"Where is it?" asked her dad.

"She's in the car. First how about the reward?" an officer said.

"But you're policemen on the city payroll. Isn't that part of your responsibility?"

"So, let me understand you, you refuse to pay the reward." Sarah, who was in the kitchen, heard them respond to her dad.

Her mother brought her dad to the kitchen. "Do you really want to chance what they might do? She asked her dad.

"You're right, I don't want heroin found in my car."

He paid the reward, and they got the dog back. After an hour of discussion in which Sarah heard, remembered but at the time understood little, the words taxes, crime and corruption, a decision was reached. Sarah's parents saw the trend developing and moved the family to a northern suburb.

Sarah received a good public school education and majored in library science in college. While she was in college her father died of a sudden heart attack. After college Sarah worked at a local library. Her mother developed cancer. As an only child, she took care of her ailing mother for years until she died. Working and caring for her mother left little time to socialize or date. Sarah remained reluctant to talk about her years in Chicagoland, her parents' plight made the time too painful.

In a suburban library, Sarah knew a woman who often brought her children aged 6 and 13. She would sometimes leave them in the children's section and venture off to a section on the arts. The mother said her children needed to learn to make do without their mother always present.

One day she heard whispers in the library about a patron. When asked what it was about, Sarah was told to check the Tribune. She found an article about a court hearing in which the DCFS (Department of Child and Family Services) was attempting to deny the mother and father custody of a boy and girl. It seemed a neighbor had notified the DCFS about the mother allowing her 13-year-old daughter to walk her 6-year-old son to a park two blocks from their home. After hearing arguments from the family's lawyer, the DCFS administrative judge allowed the family to keep the children under the condition that they not be allowed to leave the yard unaccompanied.

It was a safe neighborhood. Sarah knew the mother was keen on keeping her children safe while teaching them self-reliance. What was the area becoming? It is the parents' job to teach their children to live without them. Children would be without parents someday as Sarah had found out. A mindset that the village had more responsibility in child rearing than parents was permeating the area. Where would it end?

Sarah often wore a necklace with a Christian cross on it at the library. It had been her mother's. She was called in the library director's office and told that the oversized cross was found offensive by some new inhabitants of the community. She was instructed to no longer wear it to work. Sarah decided that if her future children were to be raised as she saw fit, and if she were to hold her values, she would need to move. After her mother passed, Sarah sold the Northbrook family home, invested the money, and took a job in Des Moines.

CHAPTER 12

"I'm sorry, I just don't know much about my family history," Sarah told Andrew at the Italian restaurant between dinner and dessert. She actually didn't know as much as Andrew did about his, but she knew more than she was comfortable talking about. The early deaths of her parents brought back unhappy memories. Talking about the past was fine unless it breached a barrier erected by unpleasantness. She preferred to focus on the future not the past.

"Too bad you don't know more about how and when your ancestors were on a wagon train. Wouldn't it be interesting if our ancestors traveled the same path, the same year or – highly unlikely I know – were on the same train?" Andrew asked.

"It may be fun to speculate on that, but where will it get us? I'm more focused on the new children's programs we are implementing at the library."

Andrew thought this was a good time to ask the question which might give him a hint whether they had a future.

"Do you find it difficult adjusting to small town life? As a young girl, did you ever envision yourself exiting big city life to a mid-sized city, then to a small town? Quite a transition you've gone through."

"No, not at all. Crazy isn't it? I suppose the next step in the sequence would be to a farm."

The words had hardly reached Andrew's ears before Sarah realized the implication of what she had said. How would he interpret her off-the-wall comment? How could she take it back? Could she?

The break in conversation was poignant for Sarah. Their conversation had always been easy and fluid. Immediately, Andrew didn't read anything into her comment at the dinner table, but later he did. She broke the lull in conversation by again answering his original question and dropping the tailing farm comment. "I think I'm adjusting fine. I don't miss anything about the cities."

Like a gentleman, Andrew walked her to the door at her apartment. She punched the code, twisted the door handle, and turned toward him.

"Well, good night. It was a great meal and I always enjoy our conversations." She had about said she enjoyed being with him but that was too forward.

"I enjoy being with you," There he said it first and continued. "I'd like to kiss you, but I don't want to seem forward on our first date."

"I appreciate that, perhaps our next date," she answered before she realized it sounded presumptive.

"Good night, again," he answered turning toward his car.

Clark picked up the phone on his law office desk. "Hi, it's Sarah."

"Oh, nice seeing you at the town art fair," he answered contradicting the look he'd given her there.

"Yes, I was glad to see you and Debbie are together at the art show. I think you are a good pair."

"Well, thank you. She – what can I say – is much better suited for me than you ever were. But I suspect that is not the reason you called."

"You promised you'd mail me the painting you have of my mother's." Her mother had painted in watercolors. Sarah had some of her paintings, but never liked her mother's attempt at abstract. Clark had it.

"Yeah, yeah, I forgot, I'll send it."

"Perhaps you can keep it if you'd do me a favor. Do you still defend clients who have problems with the DNR?"

"Yes, why?"

"A man I know received notice and a fine from them. Can you look into it and see if it is serious?"

"Oh, you're talking about that farmer boyfriend of yours. I have to say he was cleaned up pretty well at the art show. I can't believe you're going with a farmer."

The insult peeved Sarah. Although a different kind of farmer, she was a descendant of farmers. And how could he insult Andrew without knowing him?

"Just forget the whole thing. Keep the painting. I no longer want it.," Sarah answered and hung up. She decided never again would she make the same mistake.

As soon as Clark finished the brief he was working on, he called Jason, the legal director of the DNR, a common courtroom adversary.

"What kind of loopholes to get around administrative law are you working on now?" Jason sarcastically asked.

"Well, isn't that a nice greeting?"

"What do you want?" Jason was not one for baloney.

"Last month you offered me contractual work for your department. I've been thinking that since I know the other side, I could be helpful. You know what they say, your best debate performances are representing the viewpoint in which you disagree."

"What is it, your law firm short on work?"

"No, not at all; let's just say I have special interest in a case."

"Where?"

"Mahaska County."

"Yes, an appeal of the ruling and fine has been filed and is on my desk as we speak. Okay, I'll send you the petition and our case file. I assume the fee I offered earlier still applies."

"I'll look forward to receiving it," answered Clark. Whatever he could do to harm the man who punched and embarrassed him would be sweet payback. Beyond that, he felt Andrew had prevented him from reconnecting with Sarah --a farmer replacing him, the world had turned upside down.

Jason was all smiles. He had reviewed the Augustine case file and found it very weak. It was the weakest case that had been submitted by the field agent administrator. With a legal challenge to the ruling in the works, he had decided to withdraw the charges. But with a normally adversarial lawyer volunteering to assume their banner, why not? It might be good to see him hammered. He attached all their case information to the email and struck send.

Clark reviewed the information and immediately recognized the case's weakness. He called his friend, the field agent manager.

"I'm looking at this Mahaska County case file. What can you tell me?"

"You are defending the man? I thought you wanted to pester him?" He was surprised.

"Pester, an interesting word choice, but yes I do. Actually, I've an agreement to represent the agency this time."

"There was just no evidence to be found that he encouraged or had anything to do with the stream change, although he peeved me with his attitude. You asked me to put together what I could, but the judge will toss it."

"Probably so, but in the meantime it will cost him legal fees and worry."

"What do you have against the guy?"

"I'd rather not say," Clark answered.

"Well, the good news is the judge. She is inclined to rule in our direction and favors the agency, but she can't rule in our favor all the time or red flags arise. This will be a good one for us to sacrifice. Losing this one will make it easier to win others."

Saturday evening, Andrew invited Sarah to the pizza parlor. It was the place where Andrew had asked his fiancée for his ring back and Sarah had gotten into a disagreement with Clark.

"I hope this place doesn't bring back bad memories," he thought aloud.

"No not at all. In fact, if anything it is a good memory that he and I parted ways. How about you?"

"Ditto. Shall we talk about something other than recent history?"

"Sure, how about the forward or backward question?"

"What is that?"

"Reach in your pocket and pull out a bill without looking."

He gave her an inquisitive look, then pulled a picture of Lincoln from his pocket.

She reached out and took the five from him. "Okay you pulled out a five, it is a question of five hundred years forward or backward. If you pulled out a Washington picture it would be a hundred years. Now tell me, if you were given a choice to be transported 500 years in the past or 500 years in the future, which would it be and why? Unless you give me a thoughtful answer, I will keep the five."

"Boy aren't you a gamester. Let me think on it."

Their pizza was delivered.

"Now that is a very deep question," Andrew said as he took the spatula, placed a piece on a plate and handed it to her, then served himself.

He filled his mouth with a bite of pizza, giving him time to think of an answer he could support.

"My curiosity tells me to go 500 years into the future to learn what life will be like. Will the culture be recognizable? Do we assume recent trends of the last 50 years will continue and extrapolate them? If so, people will live in a dystopian state with the powerful using technology to control everyone. Or have those trends accelerated? Or has some unexpected event or intervention from above caused an awakening? Unfortunately, the default position is to assume trend lines continue."

Continuing to analyze the choices as he spoke, he added, "Having said all that, going forward would scare me. Could I even relate in that future era? No, I'd feel more comfortable in 1523 than 2523. At least I would know what is there."

"Interesting answer. Can't say I disagree with your sentiments," Sarah observed. She returned his five.

"Is such a deep question one you ask all your boyfriends?"

This time Sarah hesitated answering, not that the answer was embarrassing; it was that his question presumed they were boyfriend-girlfriend, a term seldom heard in the present culture.

"I'll be frank if you will. My experience with boys or men is limited. Seven years of caring for my invalid mother didn't allow time for socializing. Clark, who you met – or I should say wacked – was the only man I ever had more than two dates with."

Without blinking, Sarah's eyes piercing his in an attempt to view deeply into his soul. The stare told Andrew it was time for him to answer his own question.

"I was only engaged once, for a month. The women I've dated, once I get past the luster, just… well, never felt right."

Having thought more about the big question, he changed the subject. "Whether I would go forward or backward would depend upon whether the time travel was permanent or temporary. If it were permanent, I definitely chose backward. If the travel was temporary I'd go forward. Once back either warn people of where we were headed or have confidence in the future. Now I want to hear your answer."

Sarah took a deep breath and gave her well thought-out answer, "In the sixteenth century little freedom existed, but a trend was started toward more liberty. With the apex of freedom sometime in the last fifty years, the trend now, as you pointed out, is toward more state control, and economically a more striated society.

The middle class is squeezed. How ironic that the proponents of this change call themselves progressives when their policies regress us to the past. Although money is still important in occupying the privileged class, proper views are as important if you want a coveted job.

If the decay in moral values continues, where will we end up? Whether you are a believer in a greater power or not, the laws laid down to Moses are a set of good and necessary rules to maintain an orderly society.

I have confidence in good prevailing. It is either A or B. If the secular materialists are right, our species has been successful over all others. As our species has evolved for success, we will continue to evolve, solve our problems, and sustain ourselves.

On the other hand, which I believe, if we are put here for a reason, our Creator will not stand by and let us destroy ourselves. I guess I didn't answer the forward or backward question."

"No, you didn't, but you answered a greater one," observed Andrew.

As on the first date, Andrew walked her to the door. This time after the code was entered, Sarah opened the door and walked in without turning. "Come on in and see my humble abode before you leave."

The qualification of her invitation was obvious to Andrew, but he had not planned to stay. She was not that kind of a lady.

She took him on a tour of her mother's watercolors. They were good, but small. "I like your decorating taste, but have you thought about putting something on the big bare wall over there?"

"I've been thinking about it."

"Thank you for inviting me in and showing me around, but I probably should leave now."

"Thank you for dinner and great company," she said walking him to the door.

He turned back toward her at the door. She was close. He kissed her. The kiss was not bland, neither was it erotic. It was comfortable as if they had something in common, which they did in their view of life.

In the truck on the way home, he pondered. They had explored the question of backward or forward at dinner. The kiss – it was as if he had experienced it – as if it wasn't their first kiss, but was it from a backward or forward experience?

Andrew was headed for the hearing with an administrative judge in Des Moines. In the passenger seat of his truck was his lawyer, Clements. Clements was a friend and handled tax, deed and will matters for him. Perhaps he didn't have experience in dealing with the DNR, but Andrew trusted him.

"How many hours do you have on this at present?" Andrew asked him.

"Prep work has taken around 25, not including today, of course."

Andrew did a quick calculation 25 times his fee of $200 an hour. He'd sunk five grand into this problem before today. If they weren't successful getting the order nullified, he'd have the $25,000 fine plus another $15,000 in cost moving the stream to where the DNR wanted it. Even if his legal fees totaled 10 grand, it would be a good investment to save 40 grand, but he would limit his investment in overturning the order to 10 grand.

Knowing Andrew was worrying, Clements said, "I wouldn't fret about today. I consulted an attorney who deals with these people. He says they don't have squat. In fact, he doesn't understand why they are wasting time and taxpayer's money on it."

Andrew had never been in a courtroom. Once he had been called for jury duty but got off because it was harvesting season. He didn't know what to expect. He didn't expect Sarah's former fiancé to be sitting at a table with the agent who was on his farm.

Clements carefully laid out notes and outlines in preparation for his argument while Clark presented the DNR's case to the judge. Andrew had difficulty hiding what was fuming inside him. But even with the distraction of his anger, he could tell Clark was not confident, without energy and only going through the motions.

Once Clark was finished, Clements stood ready to submit his defense, but the judge waved him down and asked Clark, "What evidence do you have that this farmer purposely altered the stream?"

"He plowed the ground, thus loosening the soil, facilitating its erosion."

"For your information, Counsel, that's what farmers do. Hearing no evidence of intent, tampering or complicity in the stream's change, I'm dismissing the charges. And please do not waste this court's time with such frivolous charges in the future."

Andrew was pleasantly stunned at the quick ruling and looked for Clark in order to give him a belligerent smirk, but he was already headed out the door. Clark was also happy; although he had lost, he received retribution for the parking lot embarrassment by costing Andrew thousands in legal fees.

At Clements office in the afternoon after the charges were dropped, Andrew called Sarah. "I won; the judge threw out the charges. I want to celebrate. How about I pick you up at six and we get a steak at the Stonehenge restaurant?"

"Sure, I want to hear all about it," she answered.

Andrew's elation at being finished dealing with the DNR overshadowed Sarah's former fiancé representing the agency. It was as if he'd landed a second blow to Clark, this one figuratively.

Early for his 6 o'clock date, Andrew turned around a mile from his home. He went in the house, picked up and loaded an acrylic painting of a woman in a flower garden he'd purchased at an art show and headed back for town.

CHAPTER 13

Andrew parked in Sarah's apartment lot, carried the acrylic painting to her door and rang her buzzer. She was still fussing with her hair when she heard the buzzer.

"You're early," she said.

He looked at his watch, "I can go sit in the truck for five minutes."

"Don't be silly, come in and I'll finish getting ready."

"You already look pretty good to me," he said with an ornery smile.

"Flattery will get you… well, it'll get you a dinner partner."

He reached around the door and picked up the acrylic he had placed there. "Why did you bring that here?" she asked.

"You've got a barren wall in your living room, and you said you like the painting."

"I couldn't, that cost you a lot of money."

"Well, I know where it's at; get me a hammer and something to hang this on."

She brought a Tupperware container intended to store food. It held two screwdrivers, a few mismatched nails, glue, fingernail polish and one of those do-it-all-poorly gismos people threw in Christmas grab bags years ago.

"Is this it?"

"Yes, do you think I'm a carpenter?"

She could hear him hammering a nail with the gismo thing while she checked her hair. She fluffed up her shoulder length crimson hair on her right side, looked at herself in the mirror and felt better, although he would not have noticed. The picture was hung when she entered the living room.

"What do you think?"

"I think it looks wonderful."

"I think I deserve something for that," his ornery smile had returned.

She gave him a quick peck on the lips. "There, I'm ready to eat. Winning that court hearing certainly has put you in a frisky mood."

He hadn't wanted to ruin the evening by telling her who represented the DNR. But when she asked him to give him the details of the hearing, avoiding mentioning Clark would have been deception by omission.

The steaks were delivered to the table as she pondered news of Clark's part in the hearing. Andrew was starting to regret telling her when she said, "I can't believe he would do such a thing. I only knew him to represent clients fighting the DNR."

"Well, it all worked out. I won. I'm willing to leave it at that."

"I'm not sure I am. In openness, I must tell you something. After learning you had trouble with the DNR, I called him, knowing he had legal expertise in the area. I thought he could provide useful information to us, I mean you. But he was such an ass, I hung up on him. He took my breaking up with him hard. I suspect he wanted to get you. It is my fault. I'm so sorry."

Sarah put her knife down and reached over and held his hand. "Can you forgive me?"

"Nothing to forgive, like I said, he lost. If he went after me, he got slapped again."

"Thank you. I always want to be honest and forthcoming with you," Sarah said, surprised he brushed her call to Clark off so easily, but glad.

"Reconsidering, I'll have to think of a way for you to make it up to me."

She pulled her hand from his and playfully slapped his hand, "You're incorrigible."

Clark, still smug from causing Andrew legal fees, followed Debbie into her condominium. He was carrying his mini overnight bag containing men's products purchased in the cosmetic section at the front of an upper end department store. It was the third Saturday night in a row that he intended to spend the night.

Debbie fixed him a scotch on the rocks before he asked for it. "You're such a sweetie, unlike the uptight excuse for a woman I almost married." Her thrust as they toasted glasses made a louder clink than he expected. It caused him to laugh. She didn't.

"Why do you bring her up every time we are together?"

"You aren't going to get all fussy and bothered about her again, are you?"

"Nothing uptight about me, you're the one who can't seem to let her go," Debbie retaliated.

"Okay, okay, I won't mention her again tonight, I promise."

"What time are you going to pick me up for the law firm's summer picnic party tomorrow night?"

"Maybe it would be better if we went separately," Clark thoughtfully answered.

"Why would we do that?"

"You know, working in the same office, someone might get the wrong idea."

"What would the wrong idea be?"

"I'm hoping to move up in the firm and you are a legal assistant, might not look good, you and I."

"Last year you saw no problem taking a librarian to the party."

"I thought we were not going to bring her up again. But now that you did, her status wasn't a concern as no one knew she was only a librarian and my mother had plans for her. People know your status."

"So, a librarian is okay to be seen with but not a legal assistant?" Debbie's words now had an edge to them.

"Don't get so wrapped up in crazy comparisons," he cautioned her.

Debbie grabbed his leather overnight bag and tossed it toward the door. "Your bag is at the door waiting on you."

"Fine, many women seek the companionship of a man in my position without the turmoil. Have a good evening." The door shut with a bang.

It was 9:00 Sunday morning when Clark sought a parking place in front of his mother's modernistic home in the Des Moines Sherman Hills neighborhood. The house was painted metallic silver, which added to its square sharp corners gave it the appearance of a sterile stainless steel shoe box. The box replaced the middle house of what had been three old Victorian style homes in a row. Only a political favor from a member of the planning and zoning commission allowed her to raze the old home and build the modernistic one. Clark drove around the block twice seeking a place to park. Disgusted, finding none, he parked in front of a fire hydrant.

"You're earlier than normal," his mother, Andrea, observed as he entered her kitchen.

On Sunday, she was alone. Her cleaning lady-cook, who had immigrated by wading the Rio Grande two years previous and was paid in cash, had the day off. Andrea's husband and she had amicably parted ways a few years earlier. Both wished to expand their sexual horizons.

"I'd have been here earlier but the churchies have the streets clogged."

"Yes, that's not all that church around the corner is doing. They're demanding that certain books be taken out of the children's section of city libraries. Their wish is to keep children boxed into an archaic belief system, but we have the upper hand. I see you parked in front of a fire hydrant."

"So what, I'll get no ticket. That's an advantage of driving a Porsche. They know I can spend enough to beat any ticket."

"You mean with my money. You arrived sooner than normal. Have enough of Debbie early today?" inquired Andrea.

"I've had enough of her period. I'm dumping her."

"Well, I can't say I'm disappointed. She's just not right for you. You need someone of similar background and prospects. I'm going to start working on finding you a proper partner. Neither Sarah nor Debbie came from a proper background. And much training would have been needed to bring Sarah around to a forward looking perspective. They were both cute and nice, but not, I dare say, at our level."

"By the way, did you see Sarah when you submitted your children's book recommendations to that small town library board?"

"Of course, I saw her. I'll be going back there to lobby further when the board makes the book purchasing decisions. Let me tell you she is completely off the rails; she revealed a much more important reason for you to leave her alone than her background. I can't believe you never detected such backwardness and closed-mindedness in her. Perhaps it is my fault for not mothering properly."

Clark knew better than disagree with his mother who was usually right and changed the subject. "What did you do last night?"

"Oh, your father came over for dinner that Fernanda prepared before she left. It's so wonderful we still get together and encourage each other in our life's explorations."

"Will father be teaching the same sociology classes at Iowa State University as last semester?"

"Yes, but he said this Fall his schedule will be cut back to two classes from three allowing him to focus on writing more research papers."

"How did he get that pulled off?"

"There is a new appreciation for professors, and the administration took notice of him when he led the effort to terminate Dr. Gonzales, that astronomy professor who wrote the popular astronomy book acknowledging the possibility of intelligent design."

"Yeah, I heard about that."

"That reminds me, he asked what you found out from the Background USA test you planned to submit."

"Oh, I changed my mind and didn't submit it. How would any ancestry discovery help us?"

"You are right. Just as well we leave the past alone. If family rumor is correct and we did have an ancestor take a wagon train as far west as Wyoming, most anything done by pioneers was not good. The way Indigenous Americans were treated, rape of the land with mining, obsession with firearms, women treated as objects, and wild unsupervised living – it is all not to be associated with today."

Clark, knowing a family background he could never reveal, hoped his mother's betrayal of the wild west hadn't caused his face to blush.

"Your face is flushed, are you okay, honey?

"Yeh, maybe too much sun yesterday." Flipping the subject, he added, "What are you doing the rest of the day?"

"I'll make an appearance at a charity for the homeless and pitch the idea of a mobile book trailer. Got to keep myself ingratiated with the right people. Will you join me?"

"I'd love to, but I have a brief to work on," he lied.

At the church door, Andrew saw Sarah walking at a distance. He was immediately reminded of the goodnight kiss the night before. He wanted to hug her as she approached but thought better of it. "How was your night?"

"Fine, but I should have eaten less steak and taken more home. Hopefully, you have not reconsidered forgiving me for contacting Clark about the DNR."

"No, not at all. I know you were trying to help." Their conversation was interrupted as more people arrived. Sarah stepped back, not entering the church. She would enter with him. They exchanged a few smiles as she visited with people while waiting.

With no one in sight and time for the services, Andrew approached her, "Where would you like to sit?"

"Let's try somewhere different. New leaf, that's what we're doing, aren't we?"

"Yes we are," he led her to the second row from the back, middle aisle.

As church dispersed, Assistant Pastor Stan approached Sarah. "An interdenominational consortium of young peoples' Sunday School teachers would like to an opportunity to visit with you and the library board about young peoples' books."

"I would welcome the opportunity. The board is meeting Tuesday evening and we look forward to the input from the community," Sarah answered. "All taxpayers should have input into what we do."

It was 7:00 Tuesday evening when Beverly, the president of the town library board, called the quarterly board meeting to order.

"We have much on our agenda this evening including approval of next year's budget; but at the request of our out-of-town visitors, first we will discuss approval of books to be added to our children's section."

Sarah was not surprised to see Andrea at the meeting. As director of Des Moines Public Libraries, she was a member of the state library association's committee for book recommendation. Sarah was surprised to see that Andrea appeared to have brought a woman with her who distributed a list of state recommended books to the forty people in attendance. She had hoped Andrea would not be back after her initial recommendations were made.

Beverly announced, "Our library director has studied the merits of a list of state recommended children's books, which I see has been distributed among you. She will make her recommendations. You have the floor, Sarah."

The library board secretary distributed Sarah's list for approval, while Sarah scrolled a PowerPoint list on screen briefly reviewing each of fifteen books she was recommending.

"I move approving the purchase of the list as submitted by our director," a board member moved. There was a quick second.

"All those who approve, say 'Aye,'" Beverly stated.

The women with Andrea stood and booed. "I object," Andrea loudly protested. "The list is not inclusive of all the recommended books."

"State your objection," answered Beverly.

"Madame Chairperson," a town resident jumped up and stated before Andrea could answer, "You are this town's library board, this is a local decision, not the state's, or nation's decision. Why should non-residents, non-taxpayers be allowed to influence this board's decision?"

Beverly replied, "I hear your objection, but we will not be accused of forbidding input on our decision. We respect free speech here unlike other places. Andrea, please state your objections."

"Your temporary director has omitted five books from our recommendation. The books *Lawn Boy, All Boys Aren't Blue, The Bluest Eye, Beyond Magenta,* and *Gender Queer* were all recommended to immerse children into the culture in which they will live. Would you ban books that immerse children in modern technology and force them to live in pre-digital times? I think not."

"Sarah, would you care to support your recommendations?" Beverly said.

"A huge gap exists between books that push unwanted change into a culture and books that reflect the culture that actually exists. Advocation of the cultural change those mentioned books promote, I do not believe represent the desires of this community.

Banning is an inappropriate word to describe my recommendation. Parents of our children are free to purchase these books for their children if they see fit. Does your use of the word banning," Sarah looked at Andrea, "also apply to numerous books that your state committee has rejected?"

"That analogy is preposterous," Andrea retaliated. "We are experts."

"I call for the question," a board member moved.

The vote was six in favor of the board director's recommendation, one opposed.

"The motion carried. Next on our agenda…"

Andrea sarcastically said as her group left the room, "If you want your children to remain in the twentieth century, perhaps you should harness them."

Andrew, who had been sitting in the back of the room, stood when the out-of-town women left and began clapping. He was joined by Assistant Pastor Stan, and a group of Sunday School teachers. Soon the whole room joined. When quiet returned, Beverly said, "The next item on our agenda is the budget."

"Madame Chairperson," a board member interrupted her. "I move we revoke the six-month probation period of our new director and immediately make her position permanent at full pay."

The motion passed unanimously.

Andrew was waiting for Sarah in the hallway after the meeting adjourned. "I guess I severed all prospects of going back to Des Moines for a library job."

"Were you thinking about doing so?"

"No," she answered as their eyes met.

"Ice cream time?"

"Why not? I'll buy with the big raise I'm soon to get."

CHAPTER 14

When Andrew returned the engagement ring of his former fiancée, the jeweler had treated him well, and his loss of money was minimal. Buying a second engagement ring from the same jeweler could cause gossip and paint him as a habitual unsuccessful proposer. This time he went to another jeweler.

"Do you know her ring size?"

"No."

"We can always size it later. Did you have a style in mind?"

The only style Andrew had in mind was something completely unlike the one he had returned. Partially because it would be tacky giving a similar ring but mostly because Sarah was unlike his former fiancée.

Andrew had only known Sarah six months. Some would think it was too little time to get to know someone. He was 35, her 33, both mature and past the fly by-the-seat of your pants mentality. They'd both been around the rodeo and had dismounted a bad ride before it was too late.

Upon advisement of a friend, Andrew had created a spreadsheet of traits he deemed important in a mate. Twenty-six items he listed ranging from spiritual beliefs, music tastes, physical attraction, health, six personality traits, political inclinations, intelligence, honesty, trustworthiness – among others. With the spreadsheet, he rated his former fiancée, and from memory other women with whom he had more than two dates. Sarah's score was double any previous woman he had known; in fact, it was near perfect.

He knew many people would consider such cold analysis contrary to the belief in a love arrow delivered by an angel. However, it gave him discipline and tempered any short-term infatuation.

The moment would have to be right before he presented her with a ring and the question. But his decision was made. He would plan and do what it took to make her his wife whether the opportune time was two weeks or four months.

Saturday, at Sarah's insistence, she and Andrew were again at the Stonehenge Restaurant and Nightclub. She insisted on buying dinner this time with her raise as he had when prevailing against the DNR.

"I'm considering making a major change in where I live," she announced.

Andrew was taken back. He thought she was happy. A great job, tremendous support in the community and he'd hoped that he was a reason to keep her in town. "Why, I thought you liked it here?"

"Oh, I don't mean leaving town. I think it is time to buy a house, never did in Des Moines because I wasn't sure how long I'd stay. And Clark… well let's not get into that. Renting apartments was never about necessity for lack of money; I have investments which I made when I sold our family home in Northbrook that have done quite well."

Even engaged to Clark, she had not discussed her investments with him. Money and he did not have a good relationship as he easily parted with it. His expensive suits, car, and attendance at fundraisers he could not afford. Sarah would not see her family's money thoughtlessly cast away. She knew at some point before their marriage it was a discussion they would need to have, perhaps that was part of the reason she ended the engagement.

Sarah didn't have any idea about Andrew's financial situation, although she knew he owned farms. But she knew he didn't frivolously spend money. He had priorities other than impressing people with his finances. Although their relationship was nothing more than dating for a few months, she trusted him. From experience she had learned that trust was paramount in building a successful relationship.

They were seated in a booth that overlooked the bar, stage, and dance floor. Before they finished eating, a country band started. Their music tastes were similar, both found country music okay along with oldies, but preferred classical. As they shared tiramisu for dessert, the dance floor filled with two-steppers.

"Do you dance?" Sarah asked.

"About as well as I sing," Andrew answered causing them both to laugh. He was not about to ask her to dance.

"Well, hi Sara and Andrew," they heard before they saw Beverly and her husband Jim, approaching their booth. The library board president wore jeans and boots as did Jim.

"I want you to know, Andrew, my tenure as board president is secure forever after hiring your date as library director. Everyone loved the way she handled that know-it-all from Des Moines."

Andrew wondered whether it would be proper to thank her for a compliment of something his date did, when Beverly asked, "Come on Andrew, let's dance."

"Oh no, you don't really want to. I'd scare everyone from the floor."

"You can't be that bad," she reached for his elbow and pulled.

"Go ahead, Andrew," coaxed Sarah trying to hide a smirk.

The intense look on Andrew's dance floor face brought chuckles to Jim and Sarah as he tried desperately to stay in step with Beverly.

"At least he hasn't fallen down," Sarah observed.

"We're next," Jim reached for Sarah's hand.

"I'm just as bad as he is," she warned him.

"Come on, you can't be as bad as him."

Before the third song started, Beverly and Jim dumped their temporary partners near each other and took off dancing together in a carefree, upbeat style. Sarah and Andrew found themselves standing alone, somewhat envious of Beverly and Jim and not knowing what to do.

"What do you say? It can't get any worse," Andrew said as he reached for her hand.

At the end of the second song together, they were still bad dancers but no longer bad enough to catch sympathetic sideways glances. The third song was slow, Andrew's hand encircled her waist. She rested her head on his shoulder. Both realized that they had burst through a barrier in which neither had been comfortable.

"This is fun. Perhaps we should take dance lessons," Andrew said.

Sarah ignored his suggestion.

Watching from near the door, Thelma said to Ralph, "Your suggestion that Beverly ask Andrew to dance worked out well."

"Yes, money well spent," he replied.

In Andrew's truck after church the next day, they headed for the farm. "How does it feel riding in the shotgun seat?" he asked.

"Do you really have one behind the seat?"

"Yep, want to shoot it when we get to the farm?"

"Someday," she replied realizing that her answer was a presumption that she would be at the farm again.

"I thought we were going to have lunch before you showed me around the farm," Sarah asked.

"I've a little surprise for you."

"Am I to assume you are cooking lunch?"

"Yes, we are going to have porkburgers on the grill and homemade ice cream. I've a few things to do first, however."

"Must I ask?"

"We are going to make the ice cream together after I show you how to milk a cow. The porkburgers, we have to pick out a volunteer pig first; that's what the shotgun is for."

"What!" she exclaimed, then looked across the seat and saw him trying to stifle laughter.

Sarah playfully swatted him on the shoulder. "I may have grown up in the city, but I wasn't born yesterday. And you want to remember I have ancestors who ran a produce farm, so it is in my blood."

It was three quarters of a mile from the last house Sarah saw before he pulled in the driveway of his place. She knew but hadn't really thought about someone living as secluded as his farmstead was.

"I'll show you around the farm and the house after we get the porkburgers started."

In the modern kitchen, he turned the sink faucet on. "See – we have running water."

She ignored him and he got the clue, no more teasing about farm misconceptions. It was the first time she had porkburgers. "Are these from your own pigs?"

"Yes, I have some locally butchered a few times a year and share it with the employees."

After a tour of various buildings full of hogs, some cattle feedlots, and a building full of farm equipment, he said it was time to make ice cream. "This will be joint enterprise," he told her while carrying a wooden staved bucket and a bag of ice to the garage driveway. Next came a stainless steel two gallon container of an ice cream mix from the refrigerator, then an old rusty cast iron contraption with a handle.

"I've never seen this done, but where is the cord?" Sarah asked.

He pulled up a chair on each side of the heirloom ice cream machine. "This one doesn't take electricity," he answered as he started turning the wood handled crank.

"Where did you get the ice cream mix?"

"I make my own."

"Really, a family recipe?"

"No, every time it is different. Following a recipe is plagiarism."

"Okay, what's in it?"

"The flavor will be a surprise, but it contains cream, eggs, sugar, and malted milk mix. Now it's your turn." He spun the bucket around, so the handle was in front of her.

Sarah got the message and started cranking. "This doesn't turn easily. How long does it take?"

"Around 45 minutes. I told you this is a joint affair."

"Do your parents come home often?"

"No, maybe once a year, the longer they've been in Texas the less they come home," he answered as he took over cranking.

He had promised himself he would not ask her what she thought of the farm. The crank was turning harder when she said, "I'm surprised at the farm, not that I thought you had pigs running around outside, or T-shirts and underwear on a clothesline. It is all kind of like an up-to-date factory."

She saw the car lights coming down the road and watched the car pull into the hog building complex a few hundred yards from the house.. He answered her unspoken question, "That's Jason, he's on duty tonight."

"No cars have driven by. Don't you ever get lonely out here?"

"If I get lonely, I can go to town. If you get burdened by too many people, too close, where do you go?"

"I lock myself in a closet."

"That sounds like fun," He took his hand from the crank and cupped his hands around his mouth as if they were a megaphone, then shouted at the top of his lungs, "The world is crazy." Followed by "Flowers are pretty." Then looked at Sarah and said, "Try it."

"What?

"Yell anything you want as loud as you can."

Timid and giggling she yelled, "Merry Christmas."

"Come on you can do better than that and it's August."

"Birds aren't real!" She yelled louder.

"Have you ever done that before, been able to unabashedly yell anything to the world without worrying about what someone thought?"

Softly, in contrast to her yell, she said, "No, guess not."

Andrew left her long enough to shut off the outside lights.

"It's kind of scary sitting out here in the dark," Sarah observed."

"Depends on your perspective, I guess, not as scary as being outdoors at night where you came from."

"Well, you have a point there," she agreed as she noticed him looking up at the sky.

Her eyes followed his upward. "Oh, my goodness, look at all the stars here. There're everywhere. There are so many."

"Same as everywhere, it's just that you can see them here."

Sarah was transfixed gazing at the sky. "Something about it radiates oneness. Does that make any sense?" Sarah asked.

"I know it is crazy, but I feel closer to God out here with an unimpeded view of what He created. I wonder if He can hear us clearer out here." Andrew then yelled, "I like Sarah."

"That's enough," she said. "Isn't the ice cream about ready?"

They remained outdoors sitting in the driveway under twinkling stars and a rising crescent moon eating blueberry pecan ice cream. Andrew noticed her shiver after a bowl of ice cream. He moved his chair close to her and put his arm around her.

"Do you think there is anyone out there?" she looked up, asking herself as much as him.

"I presume you mean other life forms. A big question for centuries. We'd be somewhat self-centered if we assumed here on earth was the only life God created."

"If there are others, why, with our technology, have we not made contact? The SETI (Search for Extraterrestrial Intelligence) effort began listening for non-random radio waves from outer space in 1985. That's 37 years ago, and we've heard nothing. No life capable of making radio waves within a distance 37 light years from us."

"Perhaps they don't want to be heard," Andrew responded.

Sarah continued, "If you believe that a few photos were taken of UFOs in the '50s and '60s when one out of a thousand people carried a camera, it makes sense with everyone carrying a camera today we should be flooded with UFO pictures. If they were here, we should have more evidence today."

"Again, that is if they wish to be seen."

"You, I take it, believe in life elsewhere," observed Sarah.

"And you are a skeptic. Have you noticed the similarity in the depictions of aliens people have claimed to have seen? Some green, smallish, most with big heads and eyes, but their head is between shoulders. They have two legs and stand upright. If they are real and emerged accidentally as secular humanists believe we did, but in a faraway solar system, why is their structure similar to ours? If we have no relationship, perhaps they'd have seven legs, eyes on their legs, or a structure we wouldn't readily recognize as a lifeform."

"Are you saying that if they exist, they were created by the same God?"

"Yes, just variations of the same blueprint." Andrew continued, "Of course, there is another explanation. They are us. Sometime in the future we've discovered time travel. Curious historians of the future travel back in time on research projects. That theory would explain why they are very reluctant to make contact as doing so could or would change history."

Sarah posed a question, "Remember on our first date when I asked the question of choosing between going back or forward in time? We both chose backward. Are you suggesting people from our future may make the same decision?

"Yes, I am," he answered. And I must ask, weeks ago did you ask me that question as some kind of test?"

It was close to midnight when Andrew took Sarah home and walked her to the door. Their embrace and kiss lasted until Sarah pointed out the plastic container of ice cream she held would soon melt.

With one last kiss, Andrew turned and left.

In addition to the ice cream warming, across the street Clark could feel heat rising in his core as he watched the couple with binoculars. He had planned to return her mother's abstract painting as an excuse to see Sarah. Two hours he waited in the car, but this was not the time. The good news was that the farmer didn't spend the night.

On the trip home, Andrew was more sure where he wished his relationship with Sarah to go. Now he needed to carefully plan the steps to get there.

Unaware of Clark's proximity, Sarah thoughts regressed to discussions she had with Clark, his obsession with clothes and optics and compared those with Andrew and their discussion of God and aliens. It was night and day. A choice between the stars and the right necktie.

Clark tried to tell himself he was frustrated because of his wasted trip from Des Moines, although he knew losing the affections of Sarah to another was the root of his irritation. His Porsche hit 54 mph in a 35 before he was out of town. Only red lights and a siren took his mind off his loss.

"Thank you for the warning, Officer," was Clark's preemptive attempt at avoiding a ticket as he handed the officer his driving license.

"I don't write warnings for speeds 19 mph over the limit. Let me see your insurance card?"

"Of course," he handed proof to the officer and added, "I'm a lawyer from out of town and was unfamiliar with the limit."

"It is posted."

"I bet going to court, wasting half a day on a speeding ticket, isn't high on your priority list, right?"

"Here is your ticket, have a nice evening."

Normally Clark would have pleaded guilty and paid the fine by mail avoiding the drive but contesting the fine would give him an excuse to return. And make amends with Sarah.

CHAPTER 15

Melinda entered Clark's firm shortly after she passed the bar. Ten years younger than Clark, she was attractive – although her loose fitting slacks and jacket hid her figure well. Her hair was shorter than average and not coiffured, indicative of a woman who made her own way unbound by traditional gender expectations. With a little research, Clark found her father was a director in the motor vehicle agency and her mother was a social worker. Although her college grades were on the low side and her bar score was just high enough to pass and below the standards of his firm, she went to a prestigious university. Melinda would pass his mother's standards.

Clark made a point to head to the lunch area when she was there, also the media room. She had no ring on her finger. He introduced himself and made small talk with her whenever the opportunity arose.

"Mind if I sit with you?" he asked one day at lunch, sitting down before she could answer.

"Go ahead."

"How do you like the firm so far?"

"I'm happy to date," her answer was short. Clark couldn't help reading another meaning in her statement.

"Let me know if you have any questions, or how I may help you – you know… questions you might not want to ask a partner. I'm not a partner yet, but I soon expect to be."

"Thank you, I'll keep that in mind," she answered. "I better get back to work now."

The second time he had lunch with her, he asked, "There's a great bar around the corner, how about I buy you a drink after work and we can talk shop or anything?"

"Thanks for the offer, but I won't be able to."

A week later, thinking she might not drink, he asked her to join him at an overpriced chain coffee shop.

"Thanks, but no."

"Do you have a boyfriend?"

When she avoided eye contact and didn't answer, he tried another track. "It's not a date, just offering my friendship in the firm."

She turned and gave him eye contact, "I have a girlfriend... no, no... I'll be honest. I don't have a girlfriend, but if I had that kind of a friend it would be a girl."

All made sense to Clark now, hired below the firm's standards, dress, standoffishness. He wanted to kick himself for his naivety. "Oh, please don't take offense at me. I have upmost respect for your decision and wish you the best."

"I'll have you know it is not my decision, I was born this way and I'm proud of it."

"Please, bad wording on my part. I didn't mean that, of course you were. My family gives generously to pride causes."

She left him sitting at the table.

Clark realized that it was a fine line between a woman who didn't overplay her womanhood which his mother would approve and one inclined toward the same gender.

Frustrated striking out with unavailable Melinda, Clark took a shortcut through an alley for a bar where depression sometimes took him. Strike out – heck no – he'd been swinging at a nosediving sand-bag, not a baseball. He was too hard on himself.

As he walked past a dumpster, a hand reached for his shoulder. "Step behind here and don't make a sound."

Clark was ready to flee for the street when he felt the tip of some-thing sharp poke through his expensive suit and scratched his back above his kidney. He let the man walk him behind the dumpster.

"Just hand me the briefcase and your billfold."

"Just legal papers in the briefcase and maybe only twenty dollars in my billfold," Clark pleaded.

Feeling the knife again on his back, Clark dropped the briefcase and reached in his pocket for his billfold. "That's better," the robber eased the pressure on the knife.

"Buster, I'd back away from him," Clark heard in a feminine voice.

The would-be thief's hand left Clark's shoulder and the knife his backside. Clark turned to see a short blonde pointing some kind of pistol at an unshaven man wearing a torn weathered trench coat. An open purse hung over the woman's shoulder. She wore a jacket that didn't cover her nurse's uniform.

"Just drop the knife where you are standing and hustle on out of the alley, Mister."

He hesitated, causing her to flex her pistol-holding hand in a threat-ening gesture closer to him. "And drop that disgusting coat also," she added.

The knife clanged as it fell to the alley pavement followed by his coat. With his hands raised he walked away from Clark and the nurse. Clark noticed the man wore designer jeans underneath the filthy coat.

"I guess I owe you," Clark said to the nurse.

"Why would you walk through this alley wearing such an expensive suit? Like putting a target on your back," she offered as she slid her 9mm Sig Sauer into her purse.

Clark ignored her question and asked, "How about I thank you with a drink where I'm headed? My name is Clark."

She momentarily stared at his outstretched hand and then reached for it. "I'm Janice."

After taking stools at the bar, he said, "I take it you are a nurse."

"Yes, and I surmise you are a wealthy businessman or an important lawyer."

"Half right. Do you enjoy caring for people beside rescuing helpless lawyers?"

"I guess."

"Do you always carry that… you know… with you?"

"You mean my piece? Don't be afraid to call it a gun; doing so will not cause it to bite you."

"It's just, I'm not used to seeing one."

"Good thing for you I was carrying, right?"

"Your accent tells me you are not from around here," he changed the subject.

"Originally, Philly. And I like traveling exploring the country. In a couple of months, I'll be moving west."

"Must be nice to have that kind of freedom."

"I have freedom, and I help people. What more could a person ask for? And you?"

"Expectations, you know from family… kind of like a harness," Clark surprised himself exposing an innermost feeling that he seldom admitted to himself.

"Harnesses come off you know," Janice offered.

He ignored the comment, ordered another round, and asked, "Want to share a couple appetizers?"

"Sure, that's a nice suit you are wearing."

"Thank you, I'm about to make partner in an important law firm."

"Will that make you happy?"

"It will be a secure job and pays well."

"That's not an answer," she said.

"How far do you live from here?" he asked on their third drink.

"On the far east edge of town. I should go because I must be back for the early shift, I've double shifts for a couple of days. I hope my old car holds up."

"My condo is only two blocks away, why don't you stay with me and save the trip?"

"Oh, I couldn't do that," she replied as if it was the proper response.

"Maybe we could have the next drink at my place."

"Why not?" she asked and reached for her jacket surprising him.

It was 7:00 in the morning, Clark had dozed back off when Janice headed for the shower. Clark's phone rang, it was his mother. He didn't answer. The thought of his mother caused 'What the hell was he doing?' to vibrate through the ache in his head. Was it too much drink or his mother pulling a string?

Dressed in yesterday's uniform, the nurse stopped to kiss him on the way out. "Look forward to soon seeing you around again before I leave in a couple months."

"Sure," he replied, making a note to avoid the alley and bar. Reality and his mother's call reminded him except for one night she was off limits for him.

Her look changed. It was as if she had read his thoughts. "Good luck making partner. I wish you the best."

He watched Janice head for the door never looking back over her shoulder. After she was gone, he felt envy and a loss he could not describe. She was who she wanted to be, said what she wanted, and her feelings she wore on her arm. Her status, carefree attitude, and honesty would disqualify her for his mother's approval. Otherwise, no... he forced thoughts of, *if only he could be like her* from his head.

Andrew saw it was Sarah calling. It was a welcome distraction from a discussion about a potential swine disease with his manager.

"Andrew, could I ask a favor?" Sarah knew the answer but asked anyway.

"Sure, what is it?"

"I've an appointment with a realtor to tour a house. Structurally, I'm somewhat lacking in knowledge. Would you join me and give me your opinion?"

He picked her up and found the realtor waiting at the house. It was a two story, three bedroom, two bath frame house with a brick streetside face.

The house appeared sound to Andrew before they toured the basement. Water stains on one wall raised concern about the foundation. The realtor said the owner would pay for an inspection and stand the cost of any repair.

Andrew gladly pointed out that water problems could reoccur even after repair. Sarah took his advice and scratched the house from possibilities. On his drive home, he felt little guilt exaggerating the potential for leak recurrence. Sarah purchasing a house was not part of his plan.

Clark sat with the firm's lawyers in the oversized conference room for the Monday morning pep talk by a partner. Debbie and the paralegals sat toward the back. Clark avoided looking at her. Melinda took a seat beside him. They greeted each other, but Clark would have preferred someone else sit near him, but not because she was unavailable. She was new and the optics would be more fitting with his rising stature if he sat adjacent to more senior attorneys.

A Wagon Train Legacy

The partner's motivational speech was about perseverance. "You should never take a 'no' if what you are doing feels right. Never let a judge discourage you with a couple of bad rulings, just work harder. *Blah, blah, blah,*" he went on after Clark had tuned him out.

Although Clark had tuned out the Monday morning *rah, rah, rant* by a partner, after a second Glenfiddich at home the word perseverance bounced in his head. His mother was anxious for him to get married. She had her standards, yes. Within the social parameters set for him, Sarah was a compromise – acceptable to his mother and attractive to him. She was the one with whom he would compare other women. Although Janice's comment *'I have freedom and I help people. What more could a person ask'* bounced around in his head. He would force himself to delete Janice's words. She was like in another dimension off-limits to him.

Probably good that Sarah had a short thing with a farmer, she would appreciate his stature more now. Why would he give up when now likely was the time to get her back? So, she had some errant views, why under-estimate his own skills bringing her around to the proper way of viewing things?

He would avoid the weekend when the settle-it-with-your-fist farmer might be around. He would surprise her Wednesday evening. Settling the speeding ticket would give him an excuse to be in town. Contest the ticket, then pay the ticket, he would. It would all worked out, like the time he got a C in Algebra, his mother worked it out with the teacher as he would this. He would prevail.

Clark had two stops to make before he headed to Oskaloosa. At an overpriced candy boutique, owned by the senior law partner's wife, he bought a box of chocolate covered cherries. Anything cherry Sarah liked. Online research convinced him that white roses were associated with new beginnings and weddings, he would make a statement rather than blasé red. He ordered two dozen. He would not be chinchy in his effort to reclaim Sarah.

His credit card was declined. His second card took. He would need to remember to ask his mother for money. She was comfortable helping him until he made partner at the firm.

Gradually, Sarah and Andrew had been finding a reason to see each other on most evenings of the week. Wednesday and Saturday were their regular dinner dates. Sarah was still at the library when Andrew called.

"Would you mind terribly if I was an hour late? The veterinarian is due at five, and he may delay me until seven."

"No," she looked around making sure she was alone, then continued, "However, it will mean one less kiss at the door."

"You are mean," he said, "really mean," replying in a tone that meant anything but what he said. He had planned to toss out feelers about their future that evening. Perhaps he still would. He kept the engagement ring locked in the glove compartment of his truck, so it was handy when the time was right.

Clark held the box of candy under the arm of the hand holding the roses. His free hand rang Sarah's buzzer, then he switched the candy box to his free hand. It was 6:00. Sarah was sure Andrew had arrived early and pulled the door open without looking and said, "Glad you are early," before she caught herself.

"That's the greeting I was looking for," Clark answered.

"What are you doing here?"

"Do you want me to get on my knees?" he held the white roses in front of him.

"No, I just want you to leave."

"I will, I promise but let me say a thing or two, please."

Sarah didn't answer, she just stepped away from the door. Clark followed her in. With his hands full, he pushed the door with his elbow but didn't get it closed.

"Here take the flowers. White is the color of new beginnings. And here, I know these are your favorite candies."

"Say your piece quickly because I have a date tonight. He'll be here soon. You'll not want to deal with him a second time."

"Sarah, you and I were good together. I understand that I took you for granted. I've learned my lesson, and I expect you've come to realize this is not the place for you with that farmer."

"There you go again, jumping to conclusions for me. I happen to like Andrew a lot – no, maybe more than like. Get out now or I'll call the sheriff."

Andrew finished with the vet sooner than he expected. At a quarter past six he pulled in the apartment parking lot and saw a yellow Porsche. There couldn't be more than a couple in the state, it had to be Clark. He was early. Whatever was going on between Sarah and Clark he thought it best to let Sarah manage it and waited nervously in the truck. But as the minutes went by, he became more agitated. Once he noticed her door ajar he headed for it.

As he approached the door, he heard Sarah say, "I happen to like Andrew a lot—no, maybe more than like," which caused him to hesitate.

Then came Clark's response to her asking him to leave, "Hell no, I won't leave! You accepted my proposal once. If it was right then, it remains so. Here is your ring, give me your finger. I'm putting it back on you."

"What do you think I am, your chattel?" Sarah hollered at him as Clark stepped toward her.

Sarah was ready to scream when she saw Andrew step through the door. Her eyes left Clark and moved to Andrew. Clark saw her eye movement and turned to face Andrew.

"I think the lady asked you to leave," Andrew spoke slow and deliberately. There was no doubt in his meaning.

"What, are you going to do assault me again? I'll sue your ass and you'll be in jail this time."

Andrew ignored him and spoke into his phone. The call was not to 911, "Yeh, sheriff, we've got a problem here. Can you send someone quickly?"

"I'm a couple blocks away."

Clark moved within a foot of Andrew and taunted him, "You hillbilly, heck— what's your IQ, 80? I'll bet Sarah isn't as good for you as she was for me."

Although Andrew was sprinkled with spit from Clark's shout, he wasn't as angry as he would have expected. Sarah's comment about possibly more than liking him had a mellowing effect.

"What's going on here?" the sheriff asked as he entered.

Sarah spoke boldly, "I'll tell you what, Sheriff… the genes this man inherited from his slave-owning Springfield, Missouri family – the thieving, murdering, hung by-the-neck ancestors are coming out in him. He is threatening me, refusing to leave my home, and trying to provoke my boyfriend."

"Is this the guy who harassed you months ago?" asked the Sheriff.

"Yes, it is in his blood."

The sheriff told a deputy who had joined them, "Handcuff him and lock him up. We'll decide what to do with him in the morning. If I'm late for dinner again, the wife will be unhappy."

"You can't treat me like a criminal. Do you know who I am?"

The deputy recognized Clark and his attitude from the magistrate's office earlier that day as Clark nastily contested then paid a fine, "King Tut, for all we care. You're going to jail."

Clark didn't go easily, tugging at the handcuffs as he was escorted to the deputy's car. "I can't leave my Porsche here; someone will vandalize it."

"Now that'd be a shame, wouldn't it?" replied the deputy.

With Clark and the police cars gone, Andrew asked, "Still in the mood for dinner?"

"Yes, let's put this behind us." Picking up the flowers and candy, she added, "First a stop at the dumpster."

On the way out, a neighbor lady stood at her door. "Is all okay?" she asked.

"All is well, and here… for those cleaning supplies you loaned me," Sarah said, handing her the candy and flowers.

"Oh my, years it has been since my late husband gave me flowers."

During dinner, Andrew asked, "Did I hear you say you more than liked me?"

"Possibly," she responded.

"Just so you know, I more than like you."

"Well now, that is interesting. What are we going to do about it?"

"We should have that conversation soon," Andrew said, not wanting a memorable night to fall on the same night as another confrontation with Clark.

"Did I hear you say Clark had ancestors who owned slaves in Springfield, Missouri? My ancestors also lived in the area for a time, but they were Methodist abolitionists."

Sarah explained her having a copy of Clark's Background USA report and how she obtained it.

"Wouldn't it be interesting if the families knew of each other in Springfield?"

Chapter 16

Ten Miles Northeast of Springfield, Missouri

It was the last day of 1860; the temperature had topped at 40 degrees – six degrees cooler than normal. The Adams family planned a New Year's Eve celebration and had invited five neighbor families and a land realtor and wife from Springfield.

Thomas Adams walked in the kitchen. It was warm, filled with pleasant aromas of food preparation. He would not enter for curiosity or passing the day with the kitchen help.

"What can I do, Massa?

"Have you all the wood you need for cooking?"

"Yes."

"Go find Mingo, send him to me," he answered and quickly departed.

Mingo was a lead in the fields during growing season. In off season, he oversaw maintenance of the plantation buildings. "Yes, Massa, I'm here."

"No need for more wood in the kitchen, get the fireplace in the drawing room stoked with more wood. We have company coming."

"Massa, we short on wood, have more next week."

"I say bring more wood here. You can get by with less in your shacks. Sleep closer together. Perhaps it'd be a good way to grow my chattel."

After leaving his brother to face a small crowd and a hastily hung rope from a century old oak tree in Wyoming, Thomas – Clark's third great grandfather – had gathered their cache of gambling winnings and horse stealing and headed for Missouri. He never made it to California. A different direction from where most people were going seemed prudent in case someone sought to find him. The cache bought him a 1,000-acre farm along with twenty-four slaves. He enlarged and fixed up the house which made him an attractive catch. Within a year, he married a local girl and now had a seven year old boy and a five year old daughter. Now a respectable member of the community, he seldom thought of his hanged brother James.

Rumors about the fate of the Union dominated conversation at the New Year's Eve party. The Winfred family was late arriving. Alfred Winfred explained their tardiness.

"I went to Springfield this afternoon and the rumor we've all heard is true. On December 20, South Carolina gave notice they intended to leave the Union, but to date no other state has followed."

"Looks like South Carolina will be a loner since no other state has joined them," offered an attendee.

Another wondered, "Will that crazy, skinny Northerner let the state go, or will they send federal troops?"

As the room erupted into all kinds of speculation about what would happen, Thomas asked the Springfield land realtor into another room.

"With all this uncertainty, I think it prudent that your client accept my offer on the parcel next to me before land prices plummet."

"I believe it is much too early to speculate on that," he answered.

"My offer still stands, but I cannot guarantee I will not reassess it should things deteriorate."

"We should rejoin the others before the conversation shifts to us," offered the realtor.

Six hundred acres adjacent to Thomas's property had been on the market for a year. It was fine farmland with a good set of buildings. On numerous discussions, Thomas's banker had stood firm requiring a 20% down payment to secure a loan for the remainder. Thomas only had 10% in liquid funds for the down payment. He could acquire another 10% but it would require selling one third of his slaves. Sixteen remaining slaves would not be enough to work both properties since no slaves came with the property for sale. Other owners cautioned him about breaking up slave families as it caused discontent, adversely affecting their work. His offer was 30% less than the parcel's asking price.

"What did you find out from the realtor?" Thomas's wife, Martha, asked after the company departed.

"No budging on price yet, but they will soon with trouble brewing in the country," Thomas answered.

"Maybe, maybe not, I think it is time you swallowed your pride and talked to Dad."

Martha's dad had been very skeptical about allowing her to marry Thomas. Although he had money, he had no verifiable background. Her brothers simply detested Thomas. Both Thomas and Martha were ambitious – Thomas to gain respectability, Martha to show her brothers she made the right decision marrying him.

Martha's father was a man of means. He helped his other daughter and husband often. He would help Martha and Thomas for the asking. But Thomas knew there would be a price for any assistance from her family. His father-in-law was a religious man, very much opposed to gambling and saloon drinking, although he often took from the bottle at home.

Gambling and saloon frolicking were in Thomas's blood. Twice he had won enough at a table to make the down payment on the property only to soon lose it before the night was over. Once the loss was a sleight-of-hand withdrawal from his pocket as he celebrated his winnings with a redheaded bloomer-wearing diversion. Regrettably, he discreetly took the loss. To protest the loss with the sheriff would bring family scrutiny.

It was a new year and as Thomas headed toward Springfield he vowed to himself that once he had won enough money to secure the new parcel he would leave the table and not become sidetracked.

The second general store in a California mining town opened by Albert Augustine after his fifth wagon train trip was more successful than the first. This time he would not wait until the gold ran out and render his holdings worthless.

His first attempt at merchandising was in Nevada City, California. It was a tough life; Dorothy, his wife, was the only woman in the mining encampment of hundreds. They accumulated $7,000 in property before the mine played out and they lost all, forcing him to return to wagon training. With what little remained, they left via water route to Iowa. They found the water route no less arduous than the land route traveling by ship around Cape Horn in South America, up the Atlantic, through the St Lawrence Seaway and river routes to Iowa.

Before opening his second general store, he took wagon trains to California in 1853, 1855 and 1856. His last wagon train was the largest at 90 wagons. With the sale of his second store for $12,000, they headed for southern Missouri where the winters were less severe than Iowa. It was time to settle down.

Thomas had been at the table from noon until 6 pm. He kept his senses and drank not this day; however, the other players were as shrewd as he. He won no money, fortunately neither did he lose any, and it was time to depart. He knew arriving home after nine caused Martha to ask too many questions.

"How was your day?" he asked Martha as she approached him.

"Fine, exceptionally fine, and I can smell no liquor on you. A good man you are I told my father."

"You saw him today?" Thomas wondered.

"Yes, I met him and told him of our dilemma with the bank. He said he'd helped us little compared to my brothers and sister. His plan was to look for you in town, then go to the bank and provide half of the down deposit to the bank. On the way home, he stopped and said he couldn't find you but made the bank deposit. Where were you?"

"I was looking at another property across town," he lied.

"Were you at that place?"

"You can't smell liquor on me, can you?" he avoided the question.

"No, I can't; anyway, dad said he will be here in the morning to talk to you."

Thomas planned to leave for the bank and realtor before his father-in-law came, but as Mingo was hitching the buggy, his father-in-law arrived early.

"Thomas, we should have a discussion about part of the down payment I arranged."

"That was very thoughtful, Sir. I should get to town soon and finalize the real estate deal," Thomas answered.

"I think you should be aware that I didn't provide cash for half the down payment, rather I provided collateral with the condition I could pull the collateral anytime. If I choose to do that, you would have to cover it immediately to prevent foreclosure."

"But why…"

His father-in-law interrupted him, "I looked for you yesterday and saw you at a table in that sinful place. You shall not embarrass my daughter or besmirch your reputation further by ever darkening those doors again."

Thomas was at a loss for words. He had been trapped, "Well, I better get along, I understand and will comply."

"Good, Martha is fixing our breakfast, then you should leave."

Terms of the financial arrangement were not spoken of at breakfast. Breakfast talk centered around news that Mississippi had voted to leave the Union January ninth and Florida followed the next day.

It was late morning when Thomas left to purchase the parcel. He fumed on the buggy ride to Springfield. How did he go from a man of means from the Wyoming territory to a slave of his father-in-law? His hanged brother would spin down deep if he knew his work had ended in his brother's enslavement.

Thomas would not be trapped by his father-in-law. Plans spun in his head. His father-in-law was over sixty now, overweight, and not of good health. The man enjoyed hunting in Arkansas. To show his appreciation, Thomas could volunteer to take the old man hunting. Accidents happen. He would work out the details over the next couple of weeks.

"I've come to meet the seller's demands on the parcel," Thomas told the realtor.

"Should have come yesterday. I sold it this morning."

"What, how could you without giving me notice?"

"How was I to know you'd ever be able to close the deal?"

Thomas's disappointment soon dissipated. He was no longer indebted to his father-in-law. Today he drank whiskey as he played poker. Whiskey agreed with him, and he won money. He was tempted to stay the night but did not. Home late, Martha excused the whiskey on his breath as consolation for his frustration at not getting the property. She had learned that having him home after drinking was preferable to him staying in town and engaging in God-only-knew-what sins of which she did not wish to know. She would make him glad he came home.

It was April, after the siege of Fort Sumter began, when Thomas ventured to meet his new neighbors. Ignoring them would not allow him to acquire what should have been his; he would find a reason to discourage their stay.

"Hi, I'm your neighbor Thomas Adams, sorry I haven't been over to welcome you earlier, Mr. Augustine, I understand?"

"Yes, Albert. Well, glad to meet you. Our family has been terribly busy getting the crops in."

"I can see that, corn mostly, it looks like?"

"Yes."

"Tobacco, cotton or hemp for rope will yield you more per acre."

"I understand, but I don't have the labor for those crops."

"Slaves can be acquired; the best and cheapest source is over in the Oklahoma territory from the Indian tribes."

"I didn't know Indians had black slaves," noted Albert.

"Oh, yes, and they will deal much better than the auctions in Springfield."

Native Americans who moved to the Oklahoma territory did own Black slaves but buying them was an ordeal. Many who ventured into the Indian territory never returned, becoming victims of bandits or Indians. Albert would find that Thomas's advice was not the most helpful.

"We will not own slaves," Albert stated.

"Are you one of those abolitionists?"

"We simply believe one man should not own another."

"Well, it is a free country. Do as you wish, good luck to you."

Dorothy and Albert were abolitionists but not crusaders. They knew some sympathies in Southern Missouri would lie with plantation owners as they held a good deal of economic power. Actually, more slaves were held north of them in the area called "Little Dixie" where the Missouri River crossed the state. They were surprised two fold, both in the amount of support for slave owners and the stark division developing in the area. Neutrality was like being in no man's land. But they were convinced that the turmoil in the country would simmer down. Since the bombardment of Fort Sumter, armed conflict had been very minor and sporadic.

Missouri's governor, Claiborne Jackson, favored secession. He appointed a state constitutional convention to decide the issue. The convention met off and on for two years. The convention held "conditional Unionist" beliefs, meaning they neither favored secession nor supported the United States warring against the Confederacy. Missouri was claimed by both the Union and the Confederacy and had rival state governments sending representatives to both the Union and Confederate congresses. Eventually the Union established control and forced the Missouri Confederate government into exile.

By the 1850s, most slaves were given Sunday off from the normal dawn to dusk workday. Sunday's activities included church and tending to a small garden plot, but generally they were not allowed to leave the plantation.

Cuffee had turned eighteen and loved to fish. On Sunday after the garden was weeded, he grabbed a pole made from an Osage Orange branch and headed for a creek that divided the Adams plantation and Augustine farm. Daniel, Dorothy, and Albert's 10-year-old son, also liked to fish. It became routine for them to end up on opposite sides of the creek and talk. They each learned about lives they did not know.

Albert went to Springfield for supplies a few days after the July 21st battle of Manassas, called the first battle of Bull Run by the North. The town was still in celebration, feeling prevailed that the North would capitulate, and the war would soon be over.

Albert had half his supplies loaded when the store proprietor approached him. "I'm sorry to do this, but your purchases must be in cash from now on."

It was common for farmers to pay local merchants when their harvests came in unless their credit was deemed unworthy.

"Why? I made a down payment at the start of the season," Albert asked, his experience in running a general store in California told him something was awry.

"I've been pressured, I must stay in business you know. A group – they call themselves *Bushwhackers* – they will withdraw business from me if I sell to you."

"Why? I haven't done anything. I may be opposed to slavery, but it's live and let live for me."

"I believe it is in response to the looting and burning Jayhawks coming over from Kansas are doing."

"Who is leading these *Bushwhacker's?*"

"Thomas Adams."

"I shall go talk to him."

On a day most farmers were working, Albert found Thomas sitting on his front porch. "I must speak to you," Albert said.

"Have a seat," he motioned to Albert, then hollered at an aproned woman slave, "Sary, fetch us two glasses of lemonade."

Albert got to the point of his visit before the lemonade arrived, "I understand a group you lead has demanded that credit not be extended to me."

"Unfortunately, many things are happening in this country that are not right. Sometimes events are out of our control."

"But I have not agitated. Yes, I oppose slavery, but whom have I bothered or where have I caused trouble?"

"Yes, you are right. I'll lobby for the group to take your name from the list."

"Thank you," Albert answered, but drinking lemonade with Thomas did not set well with him.

Thomas had no intention of portraying the Augustine family as anything other than northern agitators. At a meeting of the Bushwhackers, he reported, "One of my boys has been getting crazy ideas put into his head from a son of Albert. To maintain order, I've had to ban him from being anywhere near the creek. It seems the family has ties to the Jayhawks."

The revelation caused quite a stir in the group. Jayhawks were molesting plantations near Kansas. The only part of Thomas's report that was true was he had banned Cuffee from fishing in the creek on Sunday.

"We need to get them out of here before there is trouble," remarked a group member to acclamation of others.

The first crop of corn on Albert's farm was ripening in the field in mid-September. The yield would be quite good, more than he hoped. Harvesting would start in a week. He had drawn down his savings paying for supplies as needed, but the crop would replenish his nest egg.

It was past midnight when Daniel awakened Albert. "Something is burning!" he exclaimed. Albert peered out the window to the barn and outbuildings— no fire, but he too could smell smoke. Once outdoors he looked in the other direction to see fire devouring his corn crop.

At daylight he surveyed the damage. Eighty percent of his crop was gone. At the far edge of the field, he found evidence the fire had started at three separate places. Three oil cans were upset. Whoever did it wanted him to know.

As much as Dorothy desired this home to be their last, she agreed with Albert. They had no choice.

"I wish to put the farm on the market," Albert told the realtor who sold him the farm.

"With the war, prices have gone down," the realtor cautioned him.

"How much?"

"At least 30% less than what you paid."

"Put it on the market, We're moving out in two weeks as soon as what little corn we have left is harvested."

The day before the family was ready to pull out, Daniel asked his dad to follow him to the creek. "Son, there will be a creek for fishing in Iowa where we are going."

"It's not that, Dad, please."

Once at the creek Albert said, "Okay, I'm here what do you want to show me?"

Daniel waved his hand and Cuffee stepped from behind a tree. "Could I travel north with you?"

"I'm sorry, wish we could but we can't ask for any more trouble."

"I won't be a burden, I promise. I'm leaving here whether I travel with you or not. I want to fish again."

"I'll need to think about it," answered Albert.

"I must leave now, or I'll be missed," Cuffee replied.

"Okay, you cannot stay in our camp, it is too dangerous, but if you follow us and stay a mile behind, well what can I do?"

The next morning the Augustine family left with two loaded wagons. As usual, in the morning, Cuffee was sent to the creek for water. This time he never returned. Twice in route the wagons were checked for runaways. None were found. An hour after dark it became routine for someone to venture a quarter mile west of the camp with a plate of food for Cuffee. On a cold evening they delivered a blanket.

Thomas was furious with the loss of a promising slave. He was convinced that the neighbor family was involved. However, chasing them north would take time. Enforcers in Little Dixie would search their wagons passing through.

One week after the family left, Thomas Adams (Clark's third great grandfather) purchased the farm. This time without any of the caveats his father-in-law had attempted to impose. He spent the night in Springfield celebrating. Martha was not happy when he returned late the next morning.

Albert Augustine purchased a farm in Iowa, a farm which Andrew, his third great grandson, farmed.

CHAPTER 17

Sarah answered Andrew's speculation about Springfield, "You told me your ancestors were abolitionists, since Clark's ancestors owned slaves I hardly think they ran in the same circle."

"Perhaps they came in contact and were protagonists. From what I can gather, Albert and his family were run out of the area for their views about slavery."

"I really don't want to think about it," Sarah tried to change the subject.

"If you had an ancestor in the area, wouldn't you like to know? You said you have his Background USA information. What is the name of his ancestor who lived there?"

"I believe his name was Thomas—Thomas Adams— the brother of the murderer they hanged in Wyoming," Sarah reluctantly answered.

"All property records can be accessed online now. I discovered a few years ago Albert owned a section, 640 acres, northeast of Springfield for only one year. For curiosity, I'm going to research what property Thomas Adams may have owned, and it might give an indication of whether they crossed paths."

Sarah turned her head away. Andrew could tell something was bothering her. When she turned back toward him, she gripped his hand with both of hers. "This whole mess with Clark is something I'd really like to put behind me. I want to move on. I believe we have more in common than dislike for Clark or his extended family. Perhaps we have a future. Let's not base it, even partially, on dislike of my former boyfriend."

"You are right," Andrew answered. "I'm sorry I got carried away, just the history buff part of me. I'll drop it and not investigate property in Missouri. What good would it do us if we found out the worst?"

"Thank you; I have a favor to ask. Could you get me an appointment with your lawyer in the morning?"

"Sure, I can call him now. May I ask why?"

"I want to get a restraining order against Clark."

Andrew glanced at his watch. It was 8:30, not too late. He pulled his cell and dialed Clements. After a few words he handed the phone to Sarah.

When Sarah handed the phone back, he asked, "Well?"

"I have an appointment with him at 10 Monday morning."

This time Andrew covered her hands with his. "I'm glad you mentioned our future. I want to discuss that, but only when Clark is out of town and out of our minds."

He pulled his hands from hers and started to get up. She had hoped for dessert, but was he wanting to leave early? She received the answer when he moved to her side of the booth and scooted her over.

"Does this mean you kind of like me too?" she teased.

"How could I not like a 695?" he answered before he caught himself.

"What did you mean by that?"

"I said, how could I not like a nice lady like you."

"No, you said 695. What does that mean?"

"Just a figure of speech."

Her look graphically indicated she didn't believe his explanation before she said, "Explain."

He was stumped, many possible answers flew through his head, but they were all lies. Whatever they had was based upon honesty. He opted to keep it that way.

"You know I was engaged. She was not right for me. It took me too long to figure that out. A couple earlier girlfriends neither were good choices. I decided I needed to structure my pursuit of the right woman and focus on what was important. So, I put together this spreadsheet. And frankly you scored 695. That's what I meant; it was positive. It was an inadvertent compliment."

By her look, he immediately realized the use of the word *scored* was a mistake.

Sarah had been holding the dessert menu. She slid it under her plate in silence while looking straight ahead. Finally, she said, "So am I to be judged like the speed of a fast ball or marbling in a piece of meat? Is my marbling score sufficient for you?"

"No, no, you're not interpreting it right."

"I think you should take me home."

In order to avoid a scene, Andrew said no more until they got in the car. "Please, you are taking it all wrong."

"I must think about that," she said as she got out of his car. "I can find my way to the door."

On the drive home Andrew contemplated flogging himself. Mentioning the number was a slip-up, but he never dreamed she would take it so negatively. Sleep didn't come easy.

Neither did sleep come easy for Sarah. *Two boyfriends, they both treated her like a commodity. Would a score of ten less, a 685, mean dumping her? Men, were they all like that? She could do without them.*

Sunday morning, Andrew extended his greeter service outside the church until after services had started. No Sarah. It took much discipline to refrain from going to her apartment and begging for forgiveness. After church he kept busy with chores at home finally convincing himself that if his slip-up caused this kind of discord perhaps a 695 rating was too high.

Clark was furious. It was Monday morning. Since Saturday evening, he'd been held 36 hours in the Mahaska County lockup without charges being filed. He was allowed a call Sunday morning. Calling anyone in his firm would be embarrassing. He called another attorney he knew and left two messages, none of which were returned. He could be held 72 hours without charges but anything over 48 opened the door for harassment charges.

The hours had gone by slowly in the jail with nothing to do but contemplate his situation. *How did he come to be locked up in a county jail? It wasn't an adolescent slip-up caused by risk prone behavior. He was thirty-five years old. He was following a script laid out for him the best he could. Was it a script he was destined to follow? Crazy question, he had no choice.*

Two o'clock Monday afternoon Clark saw a familiar face holding a blue bound document walking toward his cell followed by a deputy. He recognized the man as Clements, Andrew's attorney, at the DNR hearing.

"This is a restraining order issued by Judge Blomgren forbidding your presence from within one thousand feet of Sarah Conner's residence, workplace, or her person. Have a nice day," without further words Clements turned and left.

"When are you going to let me out of here?" Clark asked the deputy.

"Now," he replied opening the door.

"You know I'll half break this county when I get done suing."

"Sure, you will," taunted the deputy.

"As Clark gathered what had been stored from his pockets, he asked, "How do I get my car when it is parked at her apartment?"

"It's not there. We had it towed to a lot out of town. The address is on this business card."

"How do I get there?"

"Ever hear of Uber?"

Clark left the county jail in a huff. He tried to call Uber; his cell was dead. He was lucky enough to borrow someone's charger at a coffee shop. Then he waited what seemed like hours but was actually thirty minutes for the ride.

"That'll be $260 for your car," the lot attendant said.

"You've got to be kidding me?"

"It's past noon, so two days plus the tow charge."

"I'll give you a check."

"We don't take checks, only debit, charge card, or cash. If it's cash I'll deduct a little," he offered with a wry smile.

Clark looked at his credit cards, one was at limit, another was likely within a couple hundred of the limit and the third was held jointly with his mother. He had no choice; he would come up with a story for Andrea.

Andrew had waited long enough for amends to be made with Sarah and headed toward town. He would someway patch up the disagreement – no, it was just a misunderstanding – with Sarah. Spreadsheet aside, she was right for him, he could feel it. Pride was a burden to set aside in matters of the heart.

He buzzed her door three times before he noticed her car was gone. He thought of checking the library, or ice cream shop, but no – he would wait for her. Any conversation needed to be private. An hour later he still waited in his car, as he did two hours later.

Sarah thought much about the idea of assessing potential mate compatibility with a cold spreadsheet analysis. Although the concept initially turned her off, she thought of the pluses and minuses of past dates. Clark – she would dismiss that disaster. She found herself mentally appraising what was important to her. Next thing she knew she sat at her kitchen table with pen making a list: affection, closeness, honesty, similar beliefs, trust, ease of conversation, similar goals in life, and interesting personality. Suddenly it struck her, she was doing what Andrew had done. And if she scored him on paper as she had subconsciously already done in her mind, he would rate above anyone she had known or likely hoped to know.

There were no lights on in the farmhouse. His truck was not in the driveway, but it could be in the garage. She checked the swine office lot, no truck there. After getting no reply at the house door, she sat in the driveway. *Was he at the ice cream shoppe chatting with Melanie? Should she have checked there before driving to his farm?* No, she needed to calm herself. She breathed deeply, turned the audio to her favorite Sirius station and relaxed. Two nights with little sleep caught up with her and she was soon sleeping in the driveway of a man she hoped to have not run off.

It was now close to midnight. *Where was she? Had she gone back to Des Moines? For what?* Clark was out of the picture, Andrew was sure. It struck him that wherever she was if she came home at this hour, he would look like a stalker in her parking lot. He had little choice, he headed home.

Suddenly, she was awakened by noise and a light. The garage door was opening in front of her. A truck, his truck, was pulling beside her. Her clock showed it was midnight. What would he think? Backing out and driving home crossed her mind, but before she decided he was standing beside her car door. Immediately, her embarrassment was overcome with joy to see him. Her finger hovered over the window toggle momentarily as they assessed each other through the glass.

"Hi," he said with the glass halfway down.

"Hi," she answered.

"I've been at your apartment waiting for you."

"Yeah, well I guess you know where I've been." There was tension in their mutual laugh which she broke by asking, "So, I'm a 695 out of a possible what?"

"Seven hundred, almost perfect."

"And what caused you to deduct five?"

"When I hung the painting in your apartment I saw a dirty dish in the sink."

"I guess I'll need to be more careful about that," she answered before her mouth was covered with his kiss.

They were soon sitting at his kitchen table with a mug of coffee. Although it was now past one in the morning, she was completely awake. "I better get back to town," she said.

"Too dangerous, with many deer out this time of the year. Stay here."

"It might be more dangerous here."

"I'll behave, I promise."

They were soon curled up together on his bed, properly clothed. "What if I snore?" Sarah asked.

"I'll only deduct one point."

Andrea was in her office at the main library in Des Moines when her secretary buzzed. "A certified delivery has arrived for you."

The interruption was disturbing as Andrea had asked not to be bothered while amending library pronoun protocol. Priority was given to being on the cutting edge by adjusting meanings to the they/them/ their pronouns. Nevertheless, she signed for the 9 by 12 envelope and tossed it on the side of her desk. Later, her eyes drifted to the sender name on the certified letter – Sarah Conners.

She couldn't imagine for what employment slights the former employee might be seeking restitution. In the envelope she found two documents – one was a restraining order preventing her son from proximity to Sarah Connors. The other was a Background USA ancestry DNA analysis obtained from Clark Adams.

The enclosed letter warned any breach of the court order by Clark would trigger the attached documents being sent to the state and Des Moines library boards, Clark's law firm and the Des Moines Register.

She spent the rest of the afternoon reading the documents. She remembered trying to reach Clark the previous weekend and failing. She had assumed he'd picked up a floozy to satisfy a young man's urges and didn't want to be disturbed. Curiosity caused her to open the online credit card site she shared with Clark. The most recent charge was a vehicle towing and storage charge in Mahaska County.

Clark thought it odd receiving a text from his mother. She seldom texted. It simply said, *Be here for dinner at seven.* His dad's car parked in front of the house surprised him. Only on an important occasion did the three have dinner together.

Both parents were solemnly waiting for him in the dining room, seated at the oversized ornate mahogany table which Andrea inherited along with her trust fund. At Clark's usual table place, two documents lay on his dinner plate. He recognized them. They both waited patiently for him to respond.

"It's not what it seems."

"Oh really, I investigated and found you were locked up over the weekend for floundering over a girl who was beneath you to start with."

"Mom…"

"Don't *mom* me! Combine the restraining order with this abominable ancestry report – do you wish to destroy us all? Why would you give her the report? Is she blackmailing you?"

"It's a long story."

Gerald, Clark's dad, spoke up, "You are overreacting to that ancestry report. Our culture has long absolved children from the transgressions of parents. In this case, parents multiple times removed from you, Andrea."

Andrea cringed from his less than subtle reminder that it was her genes they were discussing.

"Nonsense, in our circles some will say the views we hold are not genuine but guilt compensation for the actions of Neanderthals in our past. While others will say racism, sexism, homophobia, and elitism are in our genes. You can kiss a law partnership goodbye if you violate this order, son. And my future advocating for enlightened learning will be quelched."

"By your analysis, I guess our divorce is fortunate for me, absolving me of guilt," sarcastically commented Gerald. She responded with a piercing stare at her ex.

"Mom, I hate to say it, but in many respects perhaps elitism is in our genes," boldly stated Clark.

"That does it. You can't afford the luxury condominium in which you live. I have plenty of room here. You will move back home with me where I can keep an eye on you. Is that understood?"

Clark hung his head and whimpered, "Yes."

The boy's response was validation of what Gerald always knew – Clark might carry his genes, but he was Andrea's son, not his.

Chapter 18

Sleep did not come easily for Clark. He had a week remaining on his condominium lease contract. His mother had pulled her co-signature and would no longer provide half the rent. No way he could afford it on his own without drastically altering his lifestyle. Soon he would be in the room he inhabited before college – twin bed with a Star Trek comforter and the boyish baseball and Harry Potter posters. His mother hadn't redecorated the room since he left – how depressing. Where had the last twelve years gone? Only in a circle. It made his head spin.

Half asleep, his thoughts drifted to forbidden territory. Janice and her carefree life. The opposite of his. As a nurse she cared for people, as a lawyer he stoked controversy. Further drifting focused on her inherent beauty and a weird connection of their opposite personalities – no, he corrected himself, opposite situations. Had fate put them together for an evening? As he finally drifted off to sleep he found himself struggling to avoid drowning in a river and desperately grabbing for a rope thrown to him by whom? A vision of Janice struck him before sleep overcame him.

Wide awake and drenched in sweat from the nightmare, he speculated what in his psyche had produced the trauma. Did it come from deep inside his subconscious, a twist of Janice's alley rescue of him, or was the nightmare's source from elsewhere?

His choices were to live as a schoolboy under the thumb of his mother or force the issue with the senior partner for a raise. But was another choice available?

In the morning after a shower, Clark reached for the Armani jacket he had tossed in a hamper. He held it and shook it. The knife tear in the back from the alley encounter was hardly visible. It was a connection to Janice. Was she his savior? He would wear it. He was nervous, but deep breathing gave him the courage he sought as he walked into the firm's office.

"Is Jason available now?" he asked the receptionist who all knew was professionally discreet but intimately close to the senior partner.

"I'll need to check. What is this about?" she asked.

"About my tenure here."

"He said to come in."

"What can I do for you?" Jason asked.

"I need some clarification about my future here. Am I on track to be offered a partnership soon?"

"That's possible in the future, we value your service to the firm."

"I know no one can predict the future. Bluntly, am I on the fast track? Can I expect an offer within a year?"

"Again, we value your service here, and your credentials are impeccable, but we must take performance into consideration."

"Please drop the bullshit and be blunt with me."

The sharpness of the request shocked the partner into being forthright, "Two of the newer attorneys are outperforming you. At present, they have the inside track. However, with more effort on your part that could change."

"Thank you for your clarity," Clark said, as he turned and stepped toward the door.

"By the way, you have a tear in your jacket. You should get it repaired or replace it," the partner said.

At the door, Clark turned, "It happens to have special meaning to me."

In the media room Clark found a box. Within ten minutes, personal items from his cubicle were in it and he was headed for the door.

The receptionist asked, "Going somewhere?"

"What would cause you to think that?"

She immediately relayed what she had seen to Jason. "That worked out fine. Dismissing him would have caused problems for the firm, given his family's stature."

Back in his condominium, Clark called a friend who had expressed interest in his yellow Porsche. "You made an offer for my Porsche last month, still interested?"

"Sure, as long as it is in the same shape."

"It is, I'll stop over later."

Clark spent the rest of the day sorting through what was important to him in the condominium. He didn't find much. After signing over the car deed and receiving a check from his friend, his friend dropped him off at the condominium. "Have you bought another car?"

"Not yet, I will in the morning."

Once he deposited the friend's check and opened a checking account without his mother's name on it, Clark purchased an eight year old Toyota Highlander for a third of what he'd received for his Porsche.

At first, Janice didn't recognize the blue-jeaned man sitting on a flower bed retainer as she left the hospital. "I was afraid I'd never see you again," she said.

"Well, I'm here as a free man. Looking for a friend who cares without relying upon others for protection and is unafraid of the future."

"That's great, but I've quit my job here and was planning on heading west tomorrow if my car will make it."

It was the most uncalculated out-of-the-box thing Clark had ever done, but it felt right, "Want company? I'm also headed west, and my car has a three month warranty."

They spent the night at his condominium and made only short-term plans. The next day, she sold her old car for what she said would be plenty for gas money. In one more day, both their stuff worth keeping was in the back of the Highlander.

Clark called his mother. Before any greeting, she said, "I want you to move home this weekend, no sense delaying. I've a mover booked for tomorrow to pick up your things."

"Mom, what is left in the condo you can discard or keep to your taste. But I'll be gone."

"What are you saying?" she asked to a dial tone.

In a few minutes, she had Gerald on the phone, "What has gotten into your son? I suggest you straighten him out before he destroys his life."

Again, she was answered with a dial tone.

It had become a habit for Sarah and Andrew to have coffee after dinner. They were at her kitchen table trying different coffee flavor additives. Her favorite was French vanilla, his hazelnut. Their discussion was centered on environmental issues and the hyped environmental porn in which the country was inundated.

"I'll start worrying about the environment when elites advocate for clean nuclear power and stop burning private jet fuel for every whim," stated Andrew.

Sarah took the subject to another track, "What do you see as the ideal number of children for a couple to have?"

"You mean as it relates to the environment or what?" he evaded.

"Just generally."

"I suppose couples need to average over two in order to sustain the population."

His answer did not satisfy her curiosity. "How many children would you like to have someday?"

"I don't know," he stumbled. "It would be nice to have a boy and girl, but all would depend on my mate and forces I cannot see. How many children would you like to have?" He threw the question back at her.

"I agree with you. I want a boy and girl. If having more than two was necessary for that result then so be it."

"What about all the other genders?" he teased.

"I want a serious conversation," she answered. "I believe a similar desire for children is paramount for a successful relationship."

"I guess we're in agreement about children then," he followed. "In what kind of a relationship would you see that happening?"

"A marriage, of course."

He was dumbstruck. *Why hadn't he carried the ring in his pocket for an opportunity like this?* After some time, he asked, "Where do you see yourself in a few years?"

"What do you mean?"

"Do you see yourself moving to a library directorship in a larger town?"

"No, I like it here, that is if things head where I hope they will. I don't suppose you'd leave the farm, would you?"

Her comment about *where things may head* was not lost on him, but he ignored it and answered her question, "It would be difficult running the farm from elsewhere."

"Well, I need to get some sleep. See you tomorrow evening, right?"

After kissing her good night at the door, he said, "We've a lot to think about, haven't we?"

"Yes, we have."

He considered returning to her door with the ring from the truck glove box but didn't. From tomorrow on he would carry it in his pocket until an opportunity arose to put it on her finger.

On the drive to the farm, he mentally played out scenarios of ways to propose. Should the proposal atmosphere be lavish, perhaps a catered meal to the farmhouse? Perhaps on that quiet loess rise in the north 80 he liked for peaceful retreats overlooking fields of corn. Would a spectacle be more memorable, after church him waiting for her in the vestibule with much of the congregation present? At the ice cream shoppe where they first were together, with the ring on top two dips of cherry nut ice cream encircling a maraschino cherry? – no, too tacky.

As the truck entered a river bottom area on his way home, Andrew focused on compartmentalizing his decisions, first decide whether the proposal would entail an audience or be private, then whether lavish or simple.

The whitetail buck was entering his sixth mating season. He had survived all including the hunting seasons which followed. Perhaps it was his father's genes which engendered him with caution exceeding others of his species. His sense of smell was acute, a hint of human odor sent him to flight. His skills would be increasingly tested as the twelve point antlers he carried made him a prize trophy. Now was the season that primordial instinct grasped him in God's way of propagating the species.

The proximity of his desires overcame his caution as one leap took him from a grader ditch to a concrete slab. Lights encompassed him causing him to jump again in an attempt to avoid the glare.

Andrew thoughts were interrupted by the danger he had warned Sarah about. The deer seemed frozen straight ahead as if he were trapped and unable to move. The light reflection in the deer's eyes

Andrew would not forget. The brilliant eyes rose from hood level to his height in the cab as the deer leaped. No time to jerk the steering wheel sideways, only time for this right foot to fruitlessly connect with the brake.

It seemed to happen in slow motion for Andrew. With the jump, the deer's center of gravity was above the hood of the truck. The deer's legs made the first contact with the truck's bumper. *Did Andrew hear a snap as legs were broken?* First contact with the deer's legs turned the deer 45 degrees such that the deer's back slammed into the windshield. Andrew ducked his head as windshield glass burst inward. Glass penetrated everything inside the vehicle including Andrew. The steering wheel broke the deer shoulders momentum from crushing Andrew's downturned face.

In a daze, fighting unconsciousness, Andrew's foot fell from the brake. Idling slowly, the truck – carrying an extra passenger – moved off the road and was stopped by a roadside culvert. All was dark for Andrew. Was he half unconscious, in a coma, or in route to the hereafter? He did not know. He felt a warm blanket covering him. The blanket was in rhythmic motion every few seconds, and a warm liquid was spreading in his lap. Had he lost control of himself or was it his blood?

Gradually, traumatized Andrew began to piece together what had happened. The blanket was fur. The movement was labored breathing of the animal. His shoulder ached immensely and was immovable. His other hand was trapped beneath the deer's weight. As he pondered his fate and waited for what God would bestow upon him, the labored breathing of the deer stopped. The meaning struck Andrew hard; he would not join the deer and succumb. For the despondent it might be an easy way out, but he had so much ahead of him – no it was not his time. God had not come for him yet.

It was a woman in the fifth car driving the road that night who noticed a truck in the ditch pitched up against a culvert. She backed up, moved her car lights to the truck, and saw deer antlers protruding from the windshield of the truck. At first, she thought a hunter was carrying his trophy on the hood. Then it struck her where the rest of the deer's body was.

Within 40 minutes a deputy, the sheriff, a highway patrolman and an emergency rescue team from the fire department were at the scene. A paramedic was able to reach through a side window and find a pulse on the driver. A strategy was necessary to disengage the deer from the vehicle without further injuring the driver. Removing the door or hood would not work as the deer had the driver pinned.

Three grapple hooks were placed in the buck's body and a cable was attached to an emergency vehicle. The buck was pulled from Andrew's truck. They found Andrew conscious but groggy, "The deer is dead," he told a paramedic checking his vitals.

"Yeah, good news is you're not," the medic answered.

Andrew's lap was saturated with a mix of deer and human blood. His shoulder was obviously dislocated, glass abrasions covered his body, and they suspected he had a concussion. An emergency team was waiting at the county hospital as the ambulance arrived followed by the sheriff. The sheriff waited for a preliminary prognosis from the emergency doctor before contacting anyone. The sheriff's contact list was small.

A fireman who was on the scene knew Andrew's swine unit manager and gave the Sheriff a telephone number. The manager had Andrew's parents' Texas contact information. He awakened them with the news. Knowing that a relationship of sorts existed with the library director, the sheriff found her number from a restraining order in which he was notified.

It was two a.m. when Sarah's phone rang in the kitchen on a charger. At night, she habitually turned the ringer down to avoid being disturbed by spam. On the way home from the hospital, the sheriff was in a quandary whether to wake her. Normally he would not notify a non-family member in person, but if Andrew woke from medication who would be with him?

The second time the buzzer chirped, Sarah was unsure what it was. At the third buzz, she pulled a robe on. *Andrew, it had to be him, what would he... him now... would be so unlike him.* She felt herself anxious with excitement for an answer to her conjectures as she opened the door.

"Madam," the sheriff tipped his hat. "Sorry to disturb you, but I thought you should know that a friend of yours has been taken to the hospital as the result of an accident."

"Who?" she asked fearing the answer.

"Andrew Augustine."

"Is he okay?"

"Don't know, but it is serious. He is in surgery."

Within ten minutes, Sarah, still wearing her pajama top covered with a jacket, was at the hospital emergency waiting room. The room was empty until a man arrived. "Are you Sarah?" the man asked.

"Yes, and you?"

"I'm David, Andrew's swine manager. You look as nice as he described you."

"He talked of me?"

"Yes, he went on and on about future plans with you. Whoops, I'm sorry, I'm speaking out of turn here."

"I see, but let's not use past tense here."

"Of course not, didn't mean it that way."

"What else did he say?"

Any answer was cut short by a doctor's arrival. "Are you here concerning Andrew?" he asked.

"We both are," David answered. "His parents will catch the first flight out of Dallas in the morning."

Although the doctor was curious about their relationship to his patient he updated them. "Andrew will require surgery on his shoulder.

We've pulled half the windshield from lacerations on his skin, but most of all I'm concerned about a concussion. He is being sent to get an MRI."

"Is he conscious?" asked Sarah.

"No, we have him on medication and sedatives. We don't want him moving until we determine if there is brain or spinal damage."

Sarah opted to stay at the hospital. At morning, she called Beverly, gave her the apartment entry code, and asked her to bring a change of clothes and her makeup bag. David had left the hospital at daylight. On his way back to the hospital in the early afternoon, he received a call from the sheriff requesting he pick up personal items found in the truck. He picked up a small box of items from the glove compartment and console storage and gave them to Sarah.

She scooted the box under her chair near the hospital bed as David said, "His parents called and said they picked up a rental car at the airport and will be here in an hour."

Beverly arrived with Sarah's clothes and makeup kit from the bathroom all stuffed into a white garbage bag. "Sorry about the bag, it is all I could find."

Sarah hastily freshened up to meet his parents, returned with the bag, added the box of Andrew's things to the bag and placed it in the hospital room cabinet.

CHAPTER 19

A day into their trip west across Nebraska on Interstate 80 to who-knows-where, it struck Clark that he'd never been happier in his life. It was as if the zookeeper had opened the gates; he was no longer constricted by the expectations of others. Laughter had come more easily and often with Janice than he'd ever known.

After spending the night in Cheyenne, Janice suggested they explore Wyoming and head north on I-25. The interstate skirted the north side of Casper from the east, then turned north. Clark could see Janice was giving Casper a thorough looking over until they drove by a hospital.

"Turn around," Janice suddenly insisted as if hit with a premonition. "I want to see that hospital again."

Clark exited and turned on an access road into the parking lot without asking why.

"I feel this is where I belong. Pull in here, I'm going to apply for a nursing job."

"Now?" he asked, stunned at her sudden declaration.

"Why not? This town needs lawyers, too. Let's give the town a try."

"I'd have to pass the bar in Wyoming."

"Can't be that difficult for a smart guy like you," Janice said as she got out of the car and headed for the hospital entrance.

Her comment *'smart guy like you'* vibrated in his head. No one had ever said anything like that to him. It was always, *'You deserve it,'* or *'We expect it.'* While waiting on Janice, he Binged 'Wyoming bar exam.' He found that 72% pass the bar exam the first time in Wyoming, placing the bar's difficulty in the middle of the country. Why would it be trouble for an experienced lawyer and smart guy like him?

Janice returned. "They need nurses. I can start as soon as they verify my credentials." She excitedly kissed him. Her excitement was contagious.

Although Sarah had never met them, she recognized Andrew's parents from a family picture at his home as they entered the hospital room. They both immediately went to Andrew's bedside. He was still sedated. His face was covered in bandages from glass extraction as was the visible parts of his arms. Andrew's mother put her hand on his, careful not to disturb the bandage wrapped hand. The father, Jake, was first to look up and smile at Sarah with a nod.

After assessing her son's condition, Mary turned and walked to an apprehensive standing Sarah. "We've heard so much about you from Andrew, what a terrible way to meet." Mary's quick hug and knowledge Andrew had spoken often of her surprised Sarah.

"What do you know about his condition?" Jake asked.

"He has a concussion but no evidence of brain damage, his shoulder will need surgery and the glass cuts are superficial said the doctor."

"Please join us," Jake asked Sarah. With Mary and Sarah on one side of the bed and Jake on the other, Jake placed his hand on Andrew's left, reached for Sarah's hand as did Mary. Mary's hand touched Andrew's right hand and they prayed.

When they finished, the doctor who had been waiting in the doorway entered. "Good report from the MRI. I'm taking him off the sedative. We expect him to wake shortly, and the shoulder relocation surgery will be scheduled for tomorrow."

"I'm taking all you said as good news," observed Jake.

"That would be correct," answered the doctor.

Sitting near Sarah, Mary said, "Thank you so much for being here. We want to learn all about you."

"Andrew hasn't told me much about you. And I didn't know he talked to you about me," Sarah answered.

"He's been telling us about you for months. How you have the same interests, beliefs," and she added with a chuckle, "and both have this thing about ice cream."

"He also told us how attractive you are. Son got that right," Jake added.

Sarah felt herself blush, she had to wonder what she looked like, makeup hastily applied, after being rousted in the middle of the night. Was he only being polite?

The three sat in chairs near the window getting to know each other for an hour before they were interrupted. "May I be part of this conversation?" All three moved to the bed. Mary knew from the way her son looked at Sarah first they would become a pair. A mother could tell.

"You're awake, God wouldn't take our best church greeter," said Pastor Ken as he entered the room. Greeting Andrew's parents, whom he knew, he continued, "You've obviously met Sarah. Andrew and she are so… well I'll leave it there, let us pray."

Well into the evening, Mary insisted Sarah go home. "You've been here half the night and must be exhausted. Jake and I will stay another hour and go to the farm."

She looked at Andrew, "Go Sarah, thank you for being here."

Picking up the white plastic bag from the cabinet she started to leave. "Aren't you forgetting something?" he asked.

She was familiar with the look on his face and stepped beside the bed. As she leaned down, he propped himself up on one elbow and kissed her. Somewhat embarrassed, she left the room without looking at his parents.

With Sarah safely out of earshot, Mary said, "Son, you better not let this one go. She just seems so right for you compared to… oh, I won't go into that. What are your plans?"

"I'm going to ask her to marry me at the next appropriate time."

Jake added, "Don't tarry, son. We'd love to come back here this winter and bring our go-to-a-wedding clothes regardless of the cold."

Home after calling Beverly and telling her she wouldn't be at the library in the morning, Sarah collapsed on her bed. Beside the lack of sleep, the stress of meeting Andrew's parents and realization that the man she wanted to spend the rest of her life with had a narrow escape, had drained her of energy.

Sarah woke at 4 a.m. after a deep sleep. After a stretch at the edge of the bed, she found herself rejuvenated mentally and physically. Although she knew Andrew would fully recover, before getting out of bed, she wished – or prayed, depending upon your perspective – that Andrew would soon overcome his ordeal.

After a shower, she sought her makeup kit. Remembering it was in the bag she had left on the kitchen table; she retrieved it along with the prior day's clothes. Also in the bag was a container David left from Andrew's truck which she had forgotten. Thinking Andrew might want something from his truck, she opened the box.

Should she feel hesitancy going through what might be considered his personal items? No, she thought, they were…, after all they had discussed including their desire for children, she was acting for his interest. Given her emotional investment in him, if he harbored something negative, she deserved to know.

A small bottle of mouthwash, a bag of dental floss picks, cough lozenges, bank deposit slips, and a small address book. The address book contained email addresses, and telephone numbers of what appeared to be business contacts. Andrew was organized, she made a mental note to hard copy her phone address book in case her phone died as Andrew had copied his. She noticed that Melanie, the ice cream girl, was not among his contacts.

At the bottom of the container was something wrapped in a man's handkerchief. It was a small jewelry box, the size that would hold a ring. She opened it before thinking. It was an engagement ring. She knew she should put it back and forget she had seen it, but how could she?

What or who was it for and why was it there?, she considered. Three possibilities came to mind. It was the engagement ring returned from his former fiancée which he kept. Two, he had kept the ring intending to give it to someone else in the future, Sarah maybe, or three it was another engagement ring he planned to give her.

She preferred the third explanation be correct, but would she feel offended if an earlier fiancée had worn it? Why would she? If he chose to give it to her, it would be affirmation that she was the one for him. He would not change hearts if he chose another to marry.

Sarah slid it on her finger, it fit well, no it fit perfectly. She left it on her finger as she dressed admiring it in the bathroom mirror. She hoped to be at his room before his parents arrived. She started to pull the ring from her finger, then thought through possible scenarios.

Curiosity would nearly kill her wondering what his intent was with the ring. If he saw her wearing it and hadn't planned to give it to her, she should know sooner than later. If he had planned to give it to her, wearing it would be her acceptance of his yet-to-come proposal. *These were modern times, why should a woman wait patiently for a man to propose a future?* She would accept his proposal before he offered it. He might be timid; she would be bold.

Two weeks Janice and Clark had been in an extended stay hotel in Casper. Janice liked her job at the hospital more by the day. She was not likely to leave the area and Clark felt comfortable as he explored the town.

Clark researched law firms around town while studying online for the Wyoming bar exam in the hotel room. His hunt discovered a single attorney practice with a 65-year-old lawyer named Allen Hollister who specialized in property filings. A search of property filings in the county recorder's office revealed the attorney must have a heavy workload as many filings came from his practice.

When he sought an appointment with Hollister, the firm's receptionist said it would be two days before the attorney had an opening. A good sign thought Clark. He was early for the appointment. In the reception area he discovered that the receptionist was also the attorney's secretary. It was a two person office. With a couple questions, he determined that she was not a paralegal.

"What can I do for you?" asked Hollister. Quickly surveying the office, it was apparent that either he was inundated with work or very unorganized, both good for Clark.

"It is what I may do for you. I'm an attorney from Iowa, studying for the bar exam here. I wish to practice in Casper. My partner and I have decided to stay in Casper."

"Partner and you?"

"My girlfriend."

"Do you have any connection in Casper?"

"No, my girlfriend is a nurse at the hospital. And I should tell you upfront that I have a third great grandfather buried somewhere around here after being hanged for murder."

"Not proud of all my ancestors did either. Have you ever been charged with a felony or are there any warrants out for you?"

"No sir."

"Where did you go to law school?"

"Georgetown."

"I won't hold that against you," he snapped, then leaned back in his old wood office chair and studied Clark. "I've never had an appetite for taking anyone on, but my wife has been pestering me to slow down. You hit me at the right time. I'll give you a chance. Work here as a paralegal and in a month or when you pass the bar, we'll discuss other possibilities."

"Great, when do you want me to start?"

Hollister scooted one of three eighteen inch high stacks of documents on his desk toward Clark. "Start now, see what you can make of these. There is an open office across the hall."

"Yes, sir."

"We'll talk about compensation and a confidentiality agreement for you to sign later. I can't have you stealing any clients if it doesn't work out for us.

Before closing, Clark had organized the stack by client and task into folders and tossed a number of duplicates. He had also written and signed a confidentiality agreement. Hollister scanned the confidentiality agreement and accepted it simply saying, "Good, this saved me some time. Be in here before 9 tomorrow."

Although he certainly received no accolades from Hollister, Clark felt pride in what he had done. He would be effective here. Already it felt more at home than the overstructured large firm in Des Moines.

Janice heard of a house for rent from another nurse. They checked out of the extended stay hotel and moved in. After ignoring his mother's many calls and texts, Clark texted her.

> *Must make life for myself, have traveled to a western state*
> *which will be my future. Love you Mom.*

Sarah entered Andrew's hospital room before 7 a.m. and was surprised that Mary and Jake were already there. She casually slid her left hand in a jacket pocket. After greeting Sarah, Jake continued bemoaning the deer problem in Iowa.

"If you live here, you have a 1 in 68 chance of hitting a deer this year. That is over twice the national average. And they won't loosen hunting laws in this state, crazy I tell you. Are they more interested in deer or citizen safety?"

"Enough," interjected Mary, "We can't do anything about it and Andrew is going to be fine, aren't you Andrew?"

Andrew was locked in eye contact with Sarah and didn't hear his mother.

"Aren't you, Andrew?"

"Yes, mom."

"I want to hear all about what you do as library director," Mary said as she sat beside Sarah. Sarah gave her a brief description of her job. Twice she noticed Mary glance at her hand now awkwardly confined to her jacket. Sarah tried unsuccessfully to use the non-ring fingers on her left hand to slide it off.

"I'll be back in a minute, rest room calls," Sarah said as she left the room.

Andrew's mother turned toward him. "Why are you hiding something from us?"

"What are you talking about?" he asked.

"I saw an engagement ring on her finger before she tried to discreetly tuck her left hand in her jacket."

He didn't answer but humped his good shoulder upward in puzzlement.

"Jake, let's go to breakfast and let them sort this out."

"They left?" Sarah asked as she entered the room.

"They went to breakfast," he answered while turning to get a good look at her left hand.

"They noticed, didn't they?"

He started to say something, but she hushed him by laying a finger across his mouth and sitting on the edge of the bed. She reached in her jacket pocket and from her hand made into a fist held it over his and released its contents.

"Do you have something you wish to give me?"

He inspected the ring and recognized it as the one in the truck he'd bought for her. How she ended up with it he did not know. That would be to find out later.

"Sarah Conners, would you do me the honor of wearing this to symbolize our intention to be married?"

She answered by holding out her left hand with fingers spread. Once it was on her finger, she said, "I've been wondering what took you so long. The answer is yes."

After sealing their agreement with a kiss, she continued, "I do owe you an explanation. And likely an apology. The ring box was with your things David brought from the truck. I thought something important you would want might be among them. I couldn't help myself when I saw the box. I shouldn't have jumped to the conclusion you intended to give it to me. I'm sorry your mother saw it on me."

"I bought the ring two months ago and I've been looking for the right time to give it to you. I should thank you."

"Thank me for what, for snooping through your things?"

"No, for relieving me of the worry and difficulty deciding how, when and where I was going to give it to you."

They heard a knock on the open door, turned and saw Mary and Jake standing in the doorway. "We don't mean to interrupt the two of you," said Jake.

"Mom and Dad, we have an announcement to make."

CHAPTER 20

Mary nearly screamed, "I knew it, I knew it," as she grabbed Sarah in a bear hug. Jake reached out his hand to Andrew, "Good choice, son."

As Mary was inspecting Sarah's ring, Andrew attempted to clear up his mother's early ring sighting with a half truth, "I think we decided a few weeks ago, but hadn't officially announced it yet and wanted to both be on board announcing it."

"How many people know?" asked Mary.

"You are the first to know," answered Sarah which caused Andrew's mother to stand straighter in pride.

"When are you thinking?" asked Jake.

"Sarah and I need to discuss the date more, but" he turned to Sarah and announced, "it will not be long. Not one of those the year after next once we know each other better wedding plans. Perhaps you'll need to come back to Iowa with your go-to-wedding clothes as soon as the harvest is in and before the snow flies."

Pastor Ken stepped in the door, "What is all the commotion about?"

"Preacher, we have a job for you," Mary said as she led Pastor Ken to Sarah's ringed finger.

"I can't say it is the biggest shock I've had, congratulations all around. Let's say a prayer for this soon to be married couple."

After the pastor left, Jake asked, "Have you two heard of this new company that takes a DNA sample and figures out your ancestry? I think it is called Background USA. Wouldn't it be neat to know that before you have children?"

"Jake, that is none of our business," Mary scolded him.

"Dad, why don't you take the test, if you are curious?"

"I'm old school, you two aren't, you need to get with the present and use all the fancy new technologies."

"We'll give it some thought," answered Sarah hoping to drop the subject.

"The doctor says you'll be out of here tomorrow. Is there anything we can do? Andrew's mother asked him.

"No, once we talk to the pastor we'll set a date for the wedding and let you know."

"How many people do you see inviting?"

Sarah answered the question before Andrew had a chance. "It will be a small affair, not over a dozen people invited, maybe in the church vestibule, but we want you here for it." Andrew was pleased knowing that Sarah had spent time thinking about the wedding.

Jake added, "We'll be here. Mary said we'd stay if you need us, but she didn't tell you tomorrow evening we are in the pickle ball couples finals of the Mesquite senior league."

"That sounds like fun," Sarah said. "Andrew and I will need to get involved in some physical activity."

Jake slipped out the door desperately trying to hide a chuckle at his interpretation of Sarah's remark. Once he was back, they exchanged hugs and goodbyes.

Walking toward their rental car, Mary scolded Jake. "What is the matter with you letting your mind drift. Sometimes, you still act like a schoolboy. I hope they didn't catch the cause of you leaving the room.

"Don't be a prude, Mary; let's be happy for them and hope for grand-children soon."

At church, Andrew had his arm in a sling, otherwise he was healed. Word had quickly spread amongst the congregation of the engagement. A steady stream of people congratulated the couple to be and gave them suggestions and asked questions. How many bridesmaids do you intend to have? What are you colors? In this church only get married on Friday, too many have divorced here after marrying on Saturday. Are you moving to the farm? Is the congregation invited? How many from your family will be here? It went on and on.

After church, Andrew could tell Sarah was glum. "What's wrong?"

"A couple of things people asked. I don't have any family to invite. That is one of the reasons I want a small wedding. I wouldn't have any idea who to ask to walk me down the aisle."

"What is the other reason?"

"How many bridesmaids? I'm not close to many people here and wouldn't know who to ask."

"We will need a best man and maid of honor to witness the marriage certificate."

"I'll ask Beverly to be maid of honor, but she is all, no more."

Andrew countered, "I'll ask David. If you want a small wedding that is what we will have. I've no desire to make a spectacle of what is between God and us. People can go elsewhere for entertainment."

In Casper, matrimony was moving much faster than in Iowa. Janice and Clark stood before the justice of the peace with Allen Hollister and a nurse friend of Janice at their sides as witnesses. A dozen people had squeezed into the Justice's chambers. The groom's parents, Andrea and Gerald, stood in wonder as the perfunctory words were spoken, "Do you Janice…" Figuratively, Andrea's tongue was swollen and sore from biting words of discord. What could her son know about this woman after less than two months together? Gerald found himself to be proud of his son for making his own life on his own terms. Clark was finally out from under the wings of the woman who threw his father out of the house.

Only two days prior had the parents received notice of the upcoming marriage. The conversations Andrea had with her son since he moved centered on how happy he was. She was not. She had lobbied teachers throughout his school years for her son. Gave special favors to a little league coach to play Clark when he was clumsy. Used her alumni influence to pressure Georgetown into accepting him when his SAT score was below their threshold. And she convinced an ideological soulmate to bring him into a prestigious law firm.

For all her efforts, he took off with a fly-by-the-seat-of-your-pants nurse to a backwater location, now forcing Andrea to give them her blessing. He teamed with a hoe dunk attorney doing boring document work and said he was happy and motivated. Her time would have been better spent crocheting than attempting make a good life for her son.

Seated together on last minute flights to Cheyenne through Minneapolis, Gerald heard it all. Prudence had taught him through the years to ignore her. What he caught of her rantings made Gerald appreciative that he no longer was subject to them daily.

Gerald gave the couple an expensive kitchen knife set for a wedding gift. Andrea gave a fancy ornate wine bottle opener, the kind you sat on a wine table. Clark had to explain to Janice what it was. She drank only beer. He had quit drinking.

"Mom, Dad, get in the car with us. I want to take you someplace special," Clark said at the end of the ceremony and small reception.

"Where are you taking us? Hopefully not to a two-step dance hall. My shoes would not be comfortable, and I have no partner."

"No mom, this place has more meaning than that."

They pulled into a large cemetery, drove through a winding road into what obviously was an old section. Clark led them out of the car toward an old limestone marker with no inscription on the back side. All read the inscription when they walked to the front side.

James Adams
Born 1825 – convicted of murder
Hanged April 11, 1851

Both parents stood in shock until Clark said, "This is my great, great uncle's resting place."

"Is this some kind of a joke?" asked Andrea.

"No, he is part of our history."

"Son, you have not only lost your mind but now you dabble in morbid games."

"There is a point to it mother. What damage Uncle James did to the community by killing a leading banker, I intend to rectify by helping property owners."

"Frontier justice hanged many innocent men. Who knows, guilt from his money greed may have caused the banker to shoot himself and they had to find a scapegoat. Even if Uncle James did it, you have no responsibility for what this man may have done."

"There you go, no one is guilty of anything, unless their ideology is incorrect, right. If we bear no responsibility, why do you lobby for whiplash ideas and policies to rectify what slights your ancestors may have been involved in?

"Get me out of here Gerald," Andrea hissed at Clark's father.

The smile on Gerald's face told Andrea no help from him would be coming. She turned and walked across the cemetery. At the exit, they picked her up. Gerald decided to stay another day and Andrea was dropped off at the airport.

Sarah and Andrew sat across the desk from Pastor Ken. They intended to find a date on the pastor's calendar for the wedding.

"I always wish to have a conversation with prospective marriage partners before I commit to performing the service. Since you both are well past adolescence and I know both of you, we can manage that now instead of in a series of meetings."

In an attempt to add levity, Andrew said, "I suppose a high divorce rate of people you marry is comparable to a low batting average."

"Yes, something like that, but this is serious."

"Andrew was just joking," Sarah said.

"I know he was. If you look at the causes of marriage failure, the primary causes are money problems, disagreement over children or the desire for children, where the couple will make a home and adultery.

Let's take it backward. I know you were previously engaged, Andrew. Have you had serious relationships Sarah?"

"I also was engaged at one time. We were not compatible for a number of reasons."

"That is positive for a good marriage. It gives a person perspective and causes you to appreciate a good marriage partner more," observed the pastor.

"Have you discussed where you will live and whether someday you may wish to move? What if you are offered a library directorship in Omaha, Sarah, will you consider the job or stay with your farmer husband?"

Sarah answered quickly, "I like living in this community. As a child I moved from Chicago to a suburb, then to Des Moines and now here. I've moved enough."

Andrew added, "We are going to live in the farmhouse after a major remodeling. Until it is finished we'll live in her apartment. Her lease doesn't expire until the end of the year when the remodeling will be done. Since Sarah will not need to buy a house, she is putting up twenty thousand for remodeling and I'm matching it."

"Who is deciding on the remodeling theme?"

"I'm leaving that to Sarah. I offered to attempt getting Magnolia's Joanna and Chip up from Texas to do it, but Sarah doesn't like their style."

"He's kidding again," Sarah elbowed him.

"I know him. Have you discussed family?" the pastor moved on.

"Yes," they responded together, looked at each other, then Andrew backed off and let Sarah answer, "We want children, ideally two, possibly more, all depending upon how difficult they are to manage given his genes."

Pastor Ken didn't comment but looked at Andrew for his answer. "We are in agreement about children."

"The last critical factor is money. Tell me if I am wrong. You are both established, Andrew with the farm, Sarah a good job, and you seem to have no problem doing major remodeling. I know Andrew is not a gambler or heavy drinker. Do you see any major financial issues in the future?"

Sarah answered the question that wasn't asked, "I have a glass of wine occasionally, and went to a casino once. The constant ding dings drove me nuts and I lost half a paycheck, that's enough."

"Let me look at my calendar and find a date. Would you prefer a Friday or Saturday?"

"Someone told us to stay away from Saturdays," Sarah remarked.

"That is superstition," Pastor Ken replied.

Andrew asked, "I should have the crop out by mid-November. How about the Friday before Thanksgiving?"

"That'll work," said Pastor Ken as he made a note on his calendar.

Later that evening the couple met with a contractor who would do the farmhouse remodeling. The focus was the kitchen and master bath. Choices were made for kitchen cabinets, floor and granite countertop, Andrew defaulted to Sarah's wishes until it came to a pink marble floor she wanted in the bathroom.

Once the contractor calculated cost of their choices, he estimated the job would be five grand over the forty estimated.

"The crop looks good this year, I'll cover the difference," Andrew said.

"Okay, then I'll spend five on new landscaping next spring," Sarah added.

A down payment was given to the contractor and he agreed to start a week hence.

When he left Andrew said, "I'm glad that is all decided. I hope you're not disappointed about not having a sissy floor in the bathroom."

"No big deal. Have you thought anymore about your dad's suggestion that we do the Background USA ancestry thing?"

"I've thought about it but have been leery. I don't like submitting my DNA to a company or the government. But since we must submit blood tests for a marriage license, I guess if they are of a mind to control us by using our DNA, they'll have it anyway. How about you?"

"Clark wanted me to do it and I refused. I'm of different mind now. You know your ancestors led wagon trains to California. Legend in my family was we had an ancestor on a wagon train. Wouldn't it be interesting to know if they traveled the same trail, or unlikely as it may be, were on the same train?"

"What if you find out I have many adulterers in my family, and it is in my DNA? Will you dump me then?"

"I'd be incentivized to keep you so interested in me you wouldn't look elsewhere. And, of course, I'd keep an eagle eye on you." Sarah answered as she held two fingers to her eye then pointed them at him.

He grabbed her and kissed her, then said, "You better be heading home. Any later and more deer will be out. Be cautious and watch your speed."

Sarah considered the legal speed limit a suggestion. As usual, she was driving some miles per hour over it until she came to the river bottom where Andrew and the buck collided. Andrew's admonition came to her mind, and she braked a few seconds before a doe crossed the highway immediately in front of her. No doubt someone was looking out for her.

Before going to bed, Andrew opened the Background USA website, entered Sarah and his information, and ordered two DNA kits with his credit card to be delivered to their respective addresses.

CHAPTER 21

It was a hectic day for Andrew. The corn harvesting combine had broken down in the morning, and it was noon before it was pulling ears from the plants and shelling kernels from cobs again. If all went well, thousands of bushels and millions of yellow corn kernels would all be in storage bins within a week. Andrew hadn't gone to bed before midnight two nights in a row and he was up well before the sun. He was hesitant calling Sarah after midnight.

She knew he was busy, and they hadn't talked for two days. Although he was busy, he knew it would soon change. He missed talking to her. In two weeks, they would be married.

It was nearly midnight when he called her. "Sorry to call so late, but I wanted to hear your voice."

"Well?"

"Well, what?"

"What do you think about it?"

"I've been thinking a lot about our wedding and trip, you?"

"I'm not asking about that," she asked surprised.

Puzzled, he answered, "You'll need to fill me in on what you are referring."

"You haven't read your mail?"

"Not for days, why?"

"Go read your mail. You should have something from Background USA, then call me back."

At the mailbox, Andrew found a three-day handful of mail. As usual, he sorted it over the waste basket. *Junk, junk, junk, bill, bill, junk, ah… a letter from Background USA.*

It suddenly struck him. *Why did Sarah ask about his Background USA report? Why did she seem upset by it? She wouldn't know what was in his report as he wouldn't know what was in hers. When they submitted their samples, they each used their own address. If something were terrible in his report—like he was 40% Neanderthal or had a rapist for an ancestor – she wouldn't know it. She might be upset about hers, but of his she could not know.*

He anxiously opened the letter. Based on the DNA sample it said his ancestry was 51% British, 35% German, some Russian, Italian, and less than 1% of others. The only surprise was his British ancestry was higher than he thought and the German lower. Nothing to be concerned about, but then again if there was cause for concern how would Sarah know?

There were many pages in the report with detailed background on the ethnic groups in his DNA. Next came a statement that 196 people had submitted DNA which identified them as being related to him. The first pages listed three first cousins with name and known addresses. He knew them and was only surprised that one whom he knew to be timid had taken the test. A quick scan of following pages showed the report listed people through sixth cousins of which there were 122.

He read the names and addresses of eight second cousins, three he did not know. The list of third cousins was longer— fifteen, only two of which he knew. The list of fourth cousins was forty-eight on four pages. Halfway down the third page he stopped in disbelief. It couldn't be, but there it was in front of him.

Sarah answered on the second ring to hear Andrew say, "Hi, cousin."

"Funny eh? I couldn't believe it and read it multiple times. Do you think it is a mistake?"

"No, I don't, kissing cousin. I know for a fact some cousins it listed are really cousins."

"This isn't funny. What do we do?"

"What do you mean?" asked bewildered Andrew.

"Cousins aren't allowed to marry."

"Baloney, that's first cousins. We are fourth cousins. Beside interests, beliefs, and ice creams tastes, we share some blood. The discovery is great."

"Are you sure about the law?"

"Absolutely, you always lament your lack of family. Guess what, you now have a large family, including my father."

"What about children? I want children."

"I know enough from Ag Genetics that fourth cousins have virtually no more chance of creating handicap offspring than non-cousins. This is great news. We are closer than I dreamed of, and we can explore our family history together."

"You gave me a different perspective on it. And if you are right, I see it is positive as you said. But can we check with the pastor and make sure he has no problem marrying cousins?"

"You mean fourth cousins. Let's meet him in the morning and allay your concerns."

"Good night fiancée-cousin."

"Good night husband-to-be, cousin."

Andrew called Pastor Ken at eight a.m. the next morning and asked to meet at the church at nine. The pastor was in his office when they arrived. He was concerned about the urgency of their request and said, "I hope you are here to change the date of the wedding."

"No, we're not," answered Andrew. They could tell that was not the answer the pastor wanted to hear."

"Is there a problem with the date?" Sarah asked.

"No, do the two of you have a problem and desire counseling?"

"Not at all, we have a question. Do you have a problem marrying fourth cousins?

"Is that what you are concerned about? You threw me for a loop, usually when couples want to see me immediately for something other than changing the date, they are having problems. I've never married fourth cousins that I know of. But in a small town, I expect I probably have."

"Do you feel better now?" Andrew asked Sarah.

"Yes I do, perhaps we should move the date up. No, just kidding Pastor."

Beverly, library board president, was at the library when Sarah arrived.

"I saw your car at the church. Last minutes plans with the pastor?"

"Well, kind of."

"Tell me all about it, I am your maid of honor after all."

"Andrew and I discovered we will be more than husband and wife. We are fourth cousins. His second great grandfather, Daniel, and my second great grandmother, Jennie Viola, were siblings."

"That is amazing. Does it bother you?"

"At first yes, I thought it would prevent us from being married, but now no. It is just a shock to learn when you thought you had no family that you have dozens of cousins. Andrew seems to be quite excited by it."

"I assume the invitation list is now expanded."

"The wedding will remain small."

Beverly prodded, "Are you sure? The wedding would be a great chance to meet your new relatives."

"Another time, for the wedding a dozen is it."

Beverly let it pass. "The reason I stopped – we've put off getting your dress and something for me to wear too long. Let's go to Des Moines tomorrow."

"No, I've decided to get something here. The shop around the corner has wedding dresses. We'll go tomorrow and find something suitable. You told me you spent twenty-five hundred on your daughter's dress. We will have a dozen guests – that's five hundred a piece for a dress they will not remember, nor will Andrew care. I'm sure all will prefer money spent on prime rib at the reception instead of a wedding dress. I can find an adequate dress here for a few hundred."

Beverly had to bite her tongue. She had promised and would not spoil the surprise. "Why wait until tomorrow? The library can do without us for a couple hours. Let's head to the shop now."

As Sarah looked at a single rack of wedding dresses, Beverly looked at the bridesmaid dress rack. "You don't need to buy a dress, I'm sure you have something to wear," Sarah told her.

"Hush, what color would you want me to wear?" she said sifting through the rack.

"Your choice."

Sarah ended up trying on three dresses ranging from in price from $250 to $750. "I like the last one best," said Beverly.

"With only twelve guests, that one will amount to over sixty dollars per guest," countered Sarah.

"They are not paying for it. I appreciate your frugality running the library and budget, but this is your wedding."

The store owner injected, "You should know that a thousand dollar deposit has been made on any dress you pick out."

"Who would? Andrew?" a shocked Sarah wondered aloud. "That wouldn't be appropriate for the groom."

"No, Jake Augustine said you were a great niece."

Sarah chose the last dress and told the owner to refund Jake the difference.

The next day unbeknownst to Sarah, Beverly met Andrew for lunch. If Sarah wanted her wedding guests limited to a dozen, that's what she would get. However, no promises had been made on the reception. Andrew and Beverly had different plans following the wedding.

"Sarah and I have learned something about family, shared family, that is."

"Yes, she told me about it yesterday. She is in shock."

"Well, what we learned will add to our wedding reception list. Background USA gave addresses of all our cousins that have submitted DNA. I'm inviting all that live in Iowa and asking them to invite other cousins they know of who are not on Background's list."

"Added to the church congregation, library employees, and other locals, how many can we expect?"

"I think we should plan on a couple hundred."

"I believe to be safe we should plan on three hundred," guessed Beverly.

"In that case I better hit the grocery store for more beef and pork," observed Andrew.

"And more buns, salads the church women will bring. By the way, Amanda's daughter, Lyric, who put together that great medley of songs at the church Christmas party last year, is starting a DJ business. I asked her to come. I hope that is okay with you."

"Sure, why not? Let's make a real reception of it, but I hope no one expects a top dancing performance by Sarah and me. Obviously, we will not have taken lessons before the wedding as most couples do."

Early evening on the day before the wedding, Sarah stopped at the farmhouse to survey how the remodeling was going. The contractor assured them he would be finished in a week. They planned to spend their wedding night at Sarah's apartment and leave on a trip the next morning. When back, they would move her things into the farmhouse.

"Everything is coming together. It will look great when they are finished. I better be going now," Sarah said as she started to her car then added, "You did remember to get reservations for twelve at Stonehenge Restaurant tomorrow night for dinner after the wedding?"

"Of course, I did," he lied. "What is the hurry leaving? Stay for a while and we'll work on our trip plans."

"You may see me tomorrow at 4 p.m. in the church vestibule. You had better be there waiting."

"Okay, okay, I get it. May I put this suitcase in your car, so I'll have clothes at your place tomorrow?"

She reached for his suitcase and said, "Know that if you buzz my door tomorrow, I will not answer." Then she was out the door before he could kiss her goodbye.

"You're mean!" he hollered at her as she slid his suitcase in the backseat.

"Just don't be late tomorrow. If you aren't at the church, I'll come looking for you," she retaliated.

"Promise?" he responded as she shut her car door.

On her wedding day, her door did buzz mid-morning. She was relieved finding it was Beverly.

"With the wedding at four, I'll pick you up at noon, we'll have a quiet lunch and go to the church afterwards."

"Lunch sounds fine, but we can dress here and be at the church by four."

Beverly stammered some before replying, "It's tradition in our church for the bride to get ready at the church. Tradition says the bride is not to be seen before the ceremony. With the parking lot across the street from the church, you will be seen crossing the street."

"That seems a feeble reason to get ready away from where I am comfortable."

"Please for me, I've never been a bridesmaid, and if we got ready somewhere other than the church, it would be like going to a prom rather than a wedding."

"All right, for you I will."

It was two o'clock when Sarah and Beverly dressed in jeans entered the church carrying garment bags and accessories. Pastor Ken and his wife, Ginger, were waiting. Sarah noticed the stairs to the basement auditorium and cafeteria were blocked with a sign which read, *Closed for Family Reunion*.

"Who is having a family reunion tonight?" Sarah asked.

"I don't recall who the church ladies said," lied Ginger.

Ginger led the ladies to a sitting room adjoining the ladies' powder room. "You will have privacy here. If you need anything let me know. I'll be in the Pastor's office."

Although people had been told to not congregate outside the church before 4:30, it was assumed some would be waiting outside the church at four. The non-stained portions of windows in the vestibule were covered. If a question arose, it would be claimed that direct sun at that time of day, interfered with Pastor Ken reading the vows.

"I'm not sure why we came this early," inquired Sarah.

"A bride should not be alone before she is married, solitude allows the mind to diverge in needless directions. I brought your library employee evaluations, let's go over them." The time went quicker that Sarah anticipated. It was soon thirty minutes to vow time. Time to get into the white dress. It finally struck her that doing so was a once in a lifetime experience.

Five minutes from their vestibule entry, Ginger knocked and entered with a marriage certificate signed by all but Beverly and Sarah. "It's nice to get this perfunctory thing out of the way first," said Ginger.

"Once we sign this we are legally married, ceremony or not, right?" asked Sarah.

"In the state's eyes, not God's," replied Ginger.

Suddenly, thoughts went through Sarah's head. *What if the pastor asked if anyone had just cause for the marriage not to take place? What if Clark showed up?* It was all crazy she knew; pastors didn't ask that today and she hadn't heard from Clark since he was carted off to jail. Beverly rescued Sarah from crazy thoughts, "It is time."

Sarah and Beverly walked into the vestibule together. Pastor Ken, Andrew, and David stood waiting. Andrew's smile stood out. At that moment, Sarah remembered the door to the vestibule was the first time she had seen Andrew as a greeter. How appropriate that it was near. His parents both nodded at her as she took her place beside their son.

Just as Pastor Ken started to say, "We are all gathered," he was interrupted.

The front door flew open, and someone asked, "Am I late?"

Before Sarah realized the voice was not Clark's, she flinched, causing Andrew to soothe her with a hand on her back.

Ginger responded, "This is a private ceremony; please come back another time." She locked the door and nodded to her husband.

The ceremony was a blur to Sarah. They considered writing their own vows but didn't. They answered the questions as asked, were soon declared husband and wife, and sealed all with a kiss.

"I'm not sure whether to call you cousin, niece or daughter-in-law," offered Jake.

"She is our daughter-in-law first," stated Mary.

"You shouldn't have bought this dress."

"It was our pleasure," answered Mary with a hug.

The dozen at the wedding milled around swapping congratulations until Sarah asked someone for the time. "Andrew, we better head to my place and change clothes so we won't be late for our dinner restaurant reservation."

She didn't notice that all but Andrew and Pastor Ken had already slipped outdoors. The pastor held the door open, and Andrew walked Sarah into a church yard filled with people. Sarah was stunned as a cheer rose from the crowd.

"You didn't make the reservation, did you?" she asked Andrew.

"I did not. I promised you a small ceremony and delivered. I made no promises about after the ceremony."

The reception in the church dining room lasted three hours. Sarah couldn't remember how many approached her with, "Hello, I'm Cousin Diane, Linda, Carol, Bill, Dennis, Mary, and others. Suddenly she had not only a spouse, but a large extended family.

For Sarah, it was so overwhelming, any embarrassment on the dance floor was inconsequential.

Late next morning, the newlyweds left for California in a rented car. Their trip had been carefully planned. They would follow the Oregon trail as much as roads permitted and fly back. Five markers along the trail they would check out including Oregon Trail museums in Scottsbluff, Nebraska and Casper, Wyoming. It was the path their mutual third great grandfather and family took five times. In addition to their marriage the trip would cement their shared ancestry.

After six hours on the road Andrew pulled off Interstate 80 in Kearny, Nebraska and into a hotel. "I thought we were headed to North Platte tonight." Sarah asked. His look told her he had other ideas.

"We have more to do on our honeymoon than exploring the Oregon trail."

CHAPTER 22

At the complimentary hotel breakfast, Andrew told his bride, "I thought it was appropriate that we stopped in Ft. Kearny last evening. That was where any wagon train from Iowa would have joined the greater Oregon Trail coming up from Kansas City and St Joseph."

"We are married. You don't need excuses for checking into a hotel early. What are our plans today?"

"We'll stop at a small Oregon Trail exhibition hall in North Platte where we'll leave I-80 for Scotts Bluff, to the first real museum on our trip."

At the small North Platte exhibit hall, Sarah picked up a list of food items that had been commonly required by a wagon train captain for anyone in his caravan with two adults and one child. At lunch they went over the list.

- 200 pounds of flour
- 30 pounds of pilot bread (otherwise known as hardtack)
- 2 pounds of saleratus (baking soda)
- 10 pounds of salt
- Half a bushel of corn meal
- Half a bushel of parched and ground corn
- 25 pounds of sugar
- 10 pounds of rice
- 75 pounds of bacon
- 5 pounds of coffee

- 2 pounds of tea
- Half a bushel of dried beans
- 1 bushel of dried fruit

"I can't imagine two hundred pounds of flour. It makes me feel that we are traveling dangerously without anything to eat. A box of chocolates, and butterscotch hard candy is it in the car," observed Sarah.

As Andrew fueled the car at a truck stop, Sarah returned to the car from the convenience store with a half dozen bananas and donuts. "I know it is silly on a three hour drive, but the provisions will make me feel better." They left I-80 on Highway 26 staying as close to the original trail as possible. The Scotts Bluff National Monument and Oregon Trail Museum were their destination.

The museum was impressive. Particularly interesting was a huge mural from a screen shot of the cable series '1883', the prequel to the popular *Yellowstone* series. It depicted a view of the plains littered with furniture – everything from pianos, armoires, oversized wooden headboards to dining room tables. A narrative entitled '*Was this the way it was?*' about the mural could be accessed on headphones provided for visitors. Sarah and Andrew were fascinated by the narrative.

"*Contrary to popular myths, wagon train captains knew hardships would arise on the journey and did not allow overloaded wagons to begin. For a fee they led pioneers west but were adverse to trouble. The train captain held the power of a ship's captain. You followed their rules or were given your fee back and abandoned. The following is likely an outline of the protocols a captain would impose.*"

The narrator introduced a voice actor playing captain. The captain's voice was particularly real to Sarah and Andrew as he had a German accent.

"*Welcome all to our journey to California. You have the list of food supplies required on the trip. I will inspect all the wagons to make sure you are adequately supplied and carry no unnecessary weight. If either does not meet the requirements, neither you nor your fee will be accepted.*

Your wagon will be inspected to determine whether it is capable of making the journey as will your oxen, mules, or horses. Each wagon is required to have a firearm. I will take your word that you know how to use it. It will be necessary in acquiring game to supplement your supplies. Do not expect your neighbor to feed you. Proficiency with a firearm will also be necessary if we run into bandits or unfriendly Indians.

You will follow my instructions and participate in night patrols and other tasks as I require. You will not lag behind the caravan. Any thievery will result in your expulsion as will fighting or drunkenness. Unless you are familiar with the trail, traveling on your own will not be a healthy experience.

I will enforce the rules. Allowing someone to delay our progress because of a rule violation will increase the odds of not making it over the winter passes before snow arrives, which would doom us all.

If you agree to the rules I have outlined, you will sign our agreement and pay your fee. We leave at daylight."

"It sounds like a captain was stern with passengers on the train," Sarah observed.

Andrew answered, "Why wouldn't he be? His job was to get them across the country in one piece leaving as few graves as possible. Beside the human aspect of it, if his trains had a high rate of death, who would want to go with him on the next one? Hollywood makes the story fit the narrative people want to hear. One of the biggest misrepresentations is hats turned up at the edges, the cowboy hat. In practice, hat brims were flat to serve their purpose protecting the wearer from the sun. Hollywood had the edges turned up to prevent the actor's face from being covered with shadow."

The next morning the couple headed for Casper, Wyoming and the National Historic Trails Interpretive Center, the largest museum on their route they planned to see. Their research showed it was operated by the Federal Bureau of Land Management (FBLM) of the U.S. Department of Interior. The museum was represented as being a public-private partnership between the bureau, the National Historic Trails Center Foundation, and the City of Casper.

To their surprise they found that the museum was primarily administered, scripted, and run by a vogue woke mentality from Washington. The displays were elaborate but had a somber aura to them. In short, the museum was depressive, and it was hard to miss the agency's continuous highlighting of their active stewardship of public lands.

Toward the end of the tour, the entrance to an auditorium had a marquee reading 'Perspective on Pioneer Settlement. The FBLM offered the public a rotating group of American history PHDs to give perspectives on westward continental settlement. Three professors at a time rotated presentations while on sabbaticals from universities.

Dr. Adrian Thomas was the 3:00 p.m. presenter. She was a nonbinary thirty-something who wore black loose-fitting pants and jacket over a white shirt while in class, on the street or presenting at the museum. "They" was considered the most controversial of the presenters, although all the presenters gave enlightening perspectives on westward settlement.

Sarah followed Andrew toward the front of the auditorium. They took a seat in the second row. Unaware of the sound system quality, slightly hearing impaired Andrew did not want to miss the message.

Dr. Thomas entered from the left side of the stage and seated themself on a high stool that stood alone on the otherwise barren stage. Later the imagery stuck in the couple's mind. No clutter of ideas, but only one accepted perspective.

> "Good afternoon all. It is wonderful that you have shown enough interest in the settlement of this continent to attend. I will put the Western expansion into a forward looking perspective.
>
> Most all of us grew up believing in myths. As children we believed in Santa Claus, the tooth fairy and so forth. The myths served a purpose to give us a simplistic, positive

outlook in our formative years. But as we matured, we learned otherwise.

For a century Western expansion has been celebrated as a *'Manifest Destiny'* like it was bestowed upon us by an omniscient power. Today society has matured enough to put it in perspective.

What were the results of western expansion of invading white people from another continent? Let me quickly outline the results of this expansion, then I will provide detail about each tragic result.

Western expansion by Europeans caused the near extinction of many co-species, most notably the buffalo and wolf. Native inhabitants who had preserved the pristine land had their lands stolen and those not killed were herded into reservations as if they were cattle. Great untouched grasslands were plowed and subjected to erosion. Beautiful mountains were mined for minerals and fossil fuels which destroyed the environment. Rugged individualism ran amok, jeopardizing the less gifted. The predominance of a superstitious unfounded belief system locked many whose genes were outside the norm into imposed tyranny. The slavery of people of color for the purpose of capitalistic pursuits continued unabated for over two centuries after white people placed a foot on this land.

The greatest effect of these combined injustices was the establishment of an unjust nation that sought to impose on the world its distorted values. Now let me digress and explain the consequences of each of these outlined injustices…"

Sarah bumped Andrew's elbow. "I've had enough, have you?"

"Absolutely," he answered and stood. They made their way to the aisle past another couple.

They had taken a few steps down the aisle toward the exit door when Dr. Thomas said, "Unfortunately, some people are closed-minded, blinded by tradition, and since they are incapable of supporting their beliefs, they refuse to consider other viewpoints and run in fear when confronted."

Andrew stopped and turned. Dr. Thomas's eyes were on him leaving no doubt to whom they were referring. He projected his voice toward they, "Say what you wish. However, the bottom line is those who threaten to leave what they consider a vile, nasty country never do. And people from all corners of the world seek a way to come to this country. The ultimate means of voting is with your feet, as we are doing now."

A couple who had sat near them clapped and others joined. Dr. Thomas, unaccustomed to challenges in the classroom, retorted, "That is a warped capitalistic view as evidenced by his use of the term *bottom line.*"

Others began to stand and leave. "You are proving me correct about the prevalence of closed minds in this society," he/she harped at the dwindling audience.

"Someone leaving responded, "I can't believe my tax money pays for your bullshit."

On the way to check in at a hotel Sarah and Andrew agreed they had seen enough museums. "Let's forget the episode back there and not let it taint our honeymoon," Andrew stated. "We'll dwell on the route and the experiences our ancestors must have had. I just wish we could find the lost trip log of our ancestor's trip which would guide us."

"Let's do something to cast Dr. Thomas aside, perhaps ice cream or pizza," suggested Sarah. She asked the clerk as they checked in, "Where is the best pizza parlor in Casper?"

Allen Hollister had lightened his workload and pleased his wife. He now did not go to the law office on Monday or Saturday and limited his stay to eight hours when he did. Clark Adams was the right fit in the office. He passed the bar on the first attempt and was seamlessly taking over Hollister's accounts. Hollister had told Clark eventually they'd work on a deal for him to take over the office.

For Clark, the difference in his life was like driving your own car or riding in the back without a say in where it was going. The longer Janice worked at the hospital the more apparent it was to her that her early premonition about the hospital was a gift from above.

Janice and Clark habitually ate at their favorite pizza place once a week. Shortly after Clark was seated, he noticed a familiar looking face two booths distant. The more he looked, the more convinced he became that the woman couldn't be a look-alike of Sarah.

"Remember, I told you I was previously engaged," Clark said to Janice. "Unbelievably, that woman is here. I want to introduce you and need to apologize to her for my past behavior."

Cautiously, Clark approached the booth in which Sarah and Andrew sat and recognized Andrew as the farmer he'd sparred with. "Sarah, I want to introduce you to my wife, Janice."

Sarah was shocked beyond words. Andrew finally answered for her, ignored Clark, and said to Janice, "Glad to meet you." Then he turned to Clark, "Amazing running into you here."

Clark noticed the ring on Sarah's finger, "Are the two of you...?"

Sarah answered his question, "Yes, we are married. We are following the Oregon Trail that our common ancestors traveled. Why are you here?"

"I'm here because we live here and commonly come to this restaurant, no stalking by me. I just want to extend my apologies to both of you for my behavior in what I consider a prior life."

Andrew surprised Sarah by saying, "Please join us, we want to hear about how you came to move here."

"And I wish to hear about the two of you having common ancestors," added Clark as Janice and he took the booth seat across from Sarah and Andrew.

The conversation started somewhat guarded but as it continued, it became more relaxed as one couple learned of Janice and Clark's move to Casper, and the other couple learned of Sarah and Andrew's discovery of common ancestors and marriage.

Andrew related their experience at the FBLM museum. Clark said he'd heard of similar complaints about the slant of the museum.

Pizza eaten, and the waitress with two credit cards to split the bill, Clark asked, "Isn't your name *Augustine?*"

With Andrew's nod, Clark revealed, "I'm doing property work for an elderly lady who is selling her house and moving into an assisted living facility. She was previously married to a man named *Augustine* and said she holds historical family memorabilia and doesn't know what to do with it. I know it is unlikely that there is a connection, but who knows— with Sarah and you finding ancestry?"

"I'd love to meet her," Andrew said.

"I'll text you her contact information tomorrow."

As they stood to leave, Andrew reached his hand out to Clark, "I'm glad we met under a different circumstance than before. I'm happy to let all in the past slide away."

"As am I," Clark responded. Andrew gave Janice a polite hug. Not to toss cold water on the reconciliation, Sarah welcomed Clark's hug and wished him well.

With contact information from Clark, Andrew contacted Mrs. Shelby at nine the next morning. At ten, Sarah and Andrew were at her house.

"Sorry for the mess. I'm getting ready to move as I'm sure Clark told you. I'm a widow now for the second time. Guess I've not been easy on husbands. I don't know what to do with this box of family items of my first husband. We had no children. I don't know if he and you have any common ancestors, but you are more apt to have a use for it than me."

They asked a number of questions about her first husband and what she knew of his family. She knew little. Andrew could tell much laid within the box, but this was not the place to scour it. They thanked her and left.

At the hotel, married cousins opened the box. Andrew was digging through it when Sarah held a picture she lifted from the box and exclaimed, "Oh, my God!"

The picture was of a large somber looking pioneer family. On the back, it identified the parents as Dorothy and Albert Augustine, their third great grandparents, of wagon train fame. On the back it listed them by name.

Back row: Jennie, John, Mary, Frank, Mike, Dorothy (Dora)
Front row: Daniel, Joshua, Albert and Dorothy, mother

"Amazing that we are looking at our ancestor who came through Baltimore at two years of age, took wagon trains across the country, tried to settle in Missouri, got run out, and helped a slave escape. I wonder what he looked like when he was younger."

Then Andrew looked further, "Oh, my goodness, near each other on the left is your great, great grandmother Jennie and my great, great grandfather Daniel!" exclaimed Andrew.

"So, there is Jennie who married the son of a truck farmer in Illinois and died at 24." Sarah couldn't take her eyes off her ancestor. "Do you think I look like her?"

"Andrew looked closely at Sarah, then at the picture of Jennie. Although he couldn't, he answered her, "I believe I can see resemblance."

Next they found a listing of the couple's 13 children with birth and death dates. Andrew noted that it completed the missing information from Background USA.

Children	Born	Passed
William	October 5, 1847	Nov. 14, 1847
Nancy Jane	Feb. 8, 1849	Oct. 29, 1851
Mary Josephine	May 21, 1851	adult age
Daniel B.	June 18, 1853	July 24,1935
Hannah Sophia	Dec. 28, 1854	June 6, 1856
Michael G	Nov. 6, 1856	Aug, 1940
Albert Joshua	Nov. 18, 1858	adult age
Frank Tobias	Dec. 27, 1860	May 24, 1892
Sonora Melvina	Nov. 1, 1862	Aug. 25, 1864
John Henry	June 27, 1864	adult age
Dorothy Mayette	May 14, 1866	adult age
Eliza Arthur	Apr. 18, 1868	Aug. 31, 1874
Jennie Viola	Apr. 1, 1870	Sept 14, 1894

Studying the list of children, Sarah observed, "Notice the nearly perfect two year separation of children's birthdates. Family planning existed long before contraceptives."

It was a few minutes later that Andrew pulled a rubber band tied bundle of handwritten notes wrapped in paper from the box. On the wrapping paper was written Wagon Train Logbook of 1855.

CHAPTER 23

The newlywed couple followed the Oregon Trail as closely as possible; Sarah and Andrew took turns driving. As one drove, the other read the wagon train log. It took more than one reading before they were able to get a feel for the historical event.

Andrew knew that Captain Albert could not write English. The log was a third person day-by-day recap of the trip written by an unidentified passenger on the 153-day journey. It was not easy reading. Reading the poor handwriting was a challenge. Spelling was horrendous. Camped was continuously spelled *campt*. Punctuation was sketchy or non-existent. But the flavor and syntax of the time gave it a realness that could not be forged.

They attempted to find in the log the approximate location they were on the trail, but it was difficult. Most present day towns didn't exist. Some rivers had been renamed, and landmarks were seldom identified. It would take research to match the log with the present road route which was too difficult on a cellphone. Nevertheless, they found the log fascinating. They concentrated on a segment of the log they believed to be around their location.

Aug 6. Mon. morning.

On again. 6 miles to river. No grass. Then 11 miles to Willow springs to right of road. In this slough Bed water alkalie. In 7 miles, we strike the Big muddy, large body of grass & campt, but ½ miles good springs, no wood & no game, few Indians. Made 24 miles.

Aug. 7th. Tuesday morning.

Started early. Some grass for 6 or 7 miles, then no more until you reach the sink wich is 20 miles, here we campt. There is two trading posts here, one on each side of slough. Her is forks of road. One to Carson & the right to Truckee. Made 27 miles.

Aug. 8th. Wed. morning.

All night, some of us on a bust. The frenchman that is with us in particular & about 1 o'clock we take the Truckee route. Traveled all night and next day till noon. Reach truckee fine stream, 100 feet wide, some cotton wood on the river. The Desert stony & rough good part of the way. No water nor grass except for the boiling springs we passed at midnight.

August 9th.

After daylight in crossing a alkali slough one of my oxen came unyoked, had quite a time. Charles Rickersen & Mr. Abel & John Johnson had a quarrel on the Desert & C. Rickerson left the train. We crossed the river & campt for the rest of the day. Made 45 miles. Made an estimate of dead stock lately from 1 hundred miles until you reach here & it is 8 to the mile.

10th August. Friday morning.

Started on. Crossed the river 3 times in going 8 miles. We go up the river & the roughest old roads we have had for some time. Shot at one wolf & killed one hare & campt at 5th crossing. Making 9 miles.

Fort Bridger in southwestern Wyoming was the location where the California Trail split from the Oregon Trail. As planned, they took the California Trail as the pioneers did in the log.

Andrew asked, "On one of our first dates you posed the question of whether I would choose to go forward or backward in time if given the choice. I chose backward, you agreed. Let me ask you… where in time and place would you choose to go?"

"That's an easy question to answer. I'd go to Iowa and join Captain Albert Augustine's wagon train as an anonymous passenger. You?"

"Yeh, I guess we would be on the same train. You are right— hypothetically, we couldn't disclose to him that we were his descendants or interfere with the past. I know it is all moot as it is impossible to travel in time, but fun to think about nevertheless."

In California, the couple exited the trail at Soda Springs and headed to Nevada City, about 50 miles north of the famous Sutter's' Mill. They did not know where Albert and family started the successful second gold mining settlement general store. However, they did know the first general store was in the Nevada City area located 60 miles northeast of Sacramento because Albert, Dorothy, and their oldest daughter, Nancy, were listed as residents of Nevada City on the 1850 census report.

In route, Sarah researched the town and found it had a population of three thousand. It was originally called *Ustumah*, then *Deer Creek Dry Diggings*, and later *Nevada* before *City* was added to the name in 1864 to avoid confusion with a nearby state.

"Tell me what else you learned about the town," Andrew asked while driving.

"European-Americans first settled Nevada City in 1849 during the California Gold Rush. In 1850–51, Nevada City was the state's most important mining town, and Nevada County the state's leading gold-mining county. According to the census the population bounced up and down in the nineteenth century, some decades plummeting 40%."

"Any more details on mining there or in nearby settlements?"

Sarah searched more websites. "Wikipedia for one is true to their nature, hardly mentioning mining as today that is a politically incorrect activity, but the site details the number of opposite-sex and same sex-married couples as they do the unmarried couples of both persuasions in the town."

"No surprise there. They have their agenda," Andrew commented.

Unlike their find in Carson City, they found no evidence of their ancestors in Nevada City. Neither did their search for outlying former mining camps in the county find where Albert established a general store. Although they struck out in California, finding the log made the trip a success.

The newlyweds' flights back from Sacramento through Denver then Des Moines were on time. David was waiting for them at DSM.

"Good trip?" he asked.

"In more ways than I could have imagined," Andrew answered, squeezing Sarah, and showing David a copy of the wagon train log they had discovered. At a California Kinkos, he had made two copies and mailed one to the farm for safety.

They found the farmhouse renovations finished and meeting their expectations. After a different bed every night on the trip, they looked forward to becoming accustomed to the same bedroom. It would be the second and last night they would spend on Andrew's bed. The first time was before marriage, and they were clothed.

Before they started moving Sarah's furniture, they stopped at a local furniture store and purchased a queen-sized mattress. Andrew would have bought any of a few headboards they looked at, but none were to Sarah's liking. They would do without a headboard until the right one was found.

In the three days that remained of Sarah's time off, they moved furniture... and moved furniture. Andrew was sure all possible configurations of furniture were tried. Unlike many men, Andrew enjoyed the decoration trials. Sarah sometimes took his suggestions and often they made a game of it getting to know which buttons to push on the other.

Twice after Sarah returned to the library, they shopped other furniture stores, buying a few pieces but not finding a headboard that fit the décor or created the ambiance Sarah sought.

Winter was colder than normal. Twice Sarah had been snowed in and unable to get to the library. She had never experienced being stranded by weather conditions. She found it not an unpleasant event as Andrew and her made the most of it.

Back home from a day at the library after the roads had been cleared, Sarah received a call from Andrew at the farm shop. "Hi, Honey, good day at the library?"

"All is well there. I spent most of the day training a new hire."

"I just wanted to let you know, I'm in the middle of repairing a tractor and I may be late for supper."

"Don't worry about it, your dinner and I'll be here."

Sarah decided she would take dinner to the shop. She fixed two Styrofoam plates of crockpot-cooked pork, carrots and cabbage and walked to the shop. It would be a chance to see what kept him busy in the winter. Andrew was happy to see her and happier yet with what she had brought. They ate in the shop loft which was used for coffee time breaks.

With the shop warmer than she expected, she stayed in the loft and looked down on him as he continued work on a farm tractor. She had no idea what he was doing. It was as foreign to her as the Dewey decimal system would be to him. At a toolbox, he couldn't find a tool he needed.

"I'm going to the storage room to find a special tool I need," he told her.

Sarah followed him. It was another space on the farm she had never been seen. As he searched for a tool, she surveyed the room. Something caught her eye leaning against a wall. It was an old ornate bed headboard, rusted to the point that coppered colored rust scales were peeling off.

"Where did you get this headboard?" she asked.

"From the soil," Andrew answered. "Actually a few years ago we were running a soil tillage chisel over an old farmstead site. One of the chisel shanks caught the headboard. Evidently, it had been buried and frost eventually heaved it enough for a shank to catch it. Don't know why I didn't toss the old rusty thing."

Sarah continued to inspect the antique. "Can this be cleaned up?"

"I guess, but why?"

"It would make a perfect headboard for our bed."

Andrew replied, "Our mattress is queen-sized, and this appears to be for a full-sized bed."

"It could be made to work. Can it be sandpapered and cleaned up?"

"I suppose I could sandblast it. Are you sure?"

"Absolutely, it is perfect."

They shuffled stored farm machinery parts around to get the headboard out. It was heavy and all the two could do to move it. The headboard was made of inch diameter steel formed in semicircle with legs extended. The joints of eight-inch spaced balusters were each encapsulated with an ornate leaf-like decorated cast iron piece the size of a small fist.

"Are you sure about this?" Andrew asked.

"This will be gorgeous. If you can get it cleaned up. I will paint it. You can't buy anything like it."

Hesitantly, Andrew told her. "My grandmother once told me something that was likely a myth. Supposedly, Ralph, one of our ancestors, bought a fancy headboard for his wife, Thelma, as an anniversary gift. The family considered them a little *different* as grandmother would say. The next day she fell out of a rowboat while they were fishing in the river. The current was so strong they never found her body. He was so distraught over her loss he disappeared after her funeral and was never found. It was if they had disappeared from the earth. Some family believed the headboard was jinxed and rumor has it they discarded the headboard."

"What was *different* about them?" Asked Sarah.

"She never said, but once I heard her refer to them having mystical qualities."

"That is a strange story. Do you think this is the headboard?" Sarah asked.

"I don't know. Given that Grandmother had no details and no one else seemed to know anything about it, I suspect it was a figment of her imagination. She was old at the time."

"I'm not superstitious, are you?"

"No, not at all, but I thought you should know."

"Okay, now I know, can you get it cleaned up for me?"

"Yes, I'll do it, it's just that I thought you should know," said Andrew feeling better that he had told her.

Later in the week Andrew told Sarah, "I finished cleaning the headboard. The sandblaster and some elbow grease made it look much better than I expected."

"Saturday, I'm going to paint it white, and all the cast iron gussets gold with sparkly metallic chips. I've already purchased the paint."

Sarah fixed breakfast for Andrew, said she wasn't hungry, and left for the shop Saturday morning anxious to paint the headboard. Later, Andrew went to check to see how she was doing. She wasn't in the shop. About the time he was going to look for her, she stepped in the back door of the shop.

"You look pale, are you okay?" he asked.

"Yes, just a little nausea."

"Do you think you've caught something?"

"It depends upon what you mean by caught."

"I don't follow you?" he inquired further.

"I've got a doctor's appointment Monday morning, but I suspect I know what it is."

He finally caught the drift. "You mean you may be…"

"Yes, I'd say it is likely and we'll know for sure Monday."

Andrew grabbed her and picked her up before he thought better of it. "Sorry, I need to be more careful with you now."

"I'm glad you are as excited as I am."

"Go to the house, I'll finish painting this headboard. You shouldn't breathe paint fumes."

"Ridiculous, let's do it together."

Both knew they shouldn't be premature with planning but the discussion while they painted centered on the prospect. *What gender will it be? How long should we wait before we tell anyone? When might the baby be due?*

It was well after dark that Andrew used a furniture cart to move the headboard to the bedroom.

"You do have a good eye for these things. It looks great. I'm sorry I relayed that story about the death and disappearance of relatives. It is probably just a story of her imagination. Even if true this headboard is likely not that headboard. But by chance if it is the headboard in Grandmother's story, it couldn't have anything to do with what may or may not have happened to them."

"Forget it, I haven't given it a thought," Sarah assured him.

Sarah hadn't told Andrew that the first Walgreen's kit gave a positive reading until a second confirmed it. She wanted some question left just in case the first test was a false positive. By Monday afternoon the doctor had confirmed the tests. She was in a family way.

When she arrived home, no champagne awaited her. But a bowl of fresh homemade cherry pecan ice cream did.

"How long? When does the doctor expect the baby?" Andrew asked.

"She thinks I'm two to two and a half months along, so that would put the due date in September."

When will they be able to determine whether it is a boy or girl?"

"My next appointment is in April; they will be able to tell then."

Sleep for Sarah had not been coming easy. This night she slept well until 3 a.m. Perhaps making Andrew aware of her condition eased her mind or maybe the headboard, which finished the house remodeling and decorating, brought her peace of mind.

At 3, a vibration woke her, it seemed to be coming from the headboard, but couldn't be she knew. The source she ignored as the hum calmed her back to sleep.

CHAPTER 24

More than once, Andrew had visited his third great grandfather, Albert Augustine's, grave in Wymore Cemetery, Monroe Township, Mahaska County, Iowa. It was only a few miles from the farmstead. He knew that family members had chipped in and replaced a smaller limestone headstone on the wagon train caption's grave with a larger red granite headstone sometime in the 1930s.

It was an unusually cold early March day, the morning after their bedroom had been completed with the restored headboard, when Sarah asked, "When are you going to take me to see Grandpa Albert's grave?"

"On the first nice day, we'll go there."

"Please, I really wish to see his grave today," she asked in a voice he would not disappoint. He didn't understand her urgency, but she was carrying his child.

Bald eagles were becoming more common in Iowa, but the couple were shocked when the magnificent bird swooped down and flew parallel to them as they neared the cemetery on a crushed limestone gravel road. Neither had seen such a view of the bird's white tail as it seemed to lead them until they turned toward the cemetery.

The truck crunched on six inches of snow as they pulled off the road onto a parking strip beside the cemetery entrance. The entrance was framed by arching steel framework identifying it as Wymore Cemetery.

From Andrew's prior description, Sarah soon identified the red granite headstone even before Andrew could point it out. It stood six feet tall, with a distinctive two foot diameter perfectly polished globe sitting on top.

"I've never seen a headstone like it," she observed.

They stood two rows back from the headstone studying it at a distance. At the distance only the family name, Augustine, could be read on the stone. It was as if permission was required to step closer.

The wind suddenly picked up lifting newly fallen snow from greening grass. The flakes were whipped around other stones then swirled around the red granite stone as if the flakes were water in a stream. A reflection on the granite globe showed the truck lights behind them blink. They turned. The truck rocked with a wind gust. Andrew wondered, *had he accidentally compressed the key fob in his pocket?*

"Thank you for bringing me here," said Sarah. "Perhaps on a nicer day we can walk to the stone."

When April arrived, Sarah was beginning to show such that her clothes would not conceal her condition to anyone observant. It was time to announce her pregnancy. As expected, Andrew's parents were overjoyed. With both parties on a speakerphone, Andrew could hear his father whooping. Mary gave all kinds of warnings – don't do this or that, exercise – but not too much. It went on and on. She volunteered to come at any time. Given her mother hen advice by phone, neither Sarah nor Andrew would ask her to come unless absolutely necessary.

"September, you say," Beverly reacted. "That is a great month to give birth. Your contract stipulates six weeks maternity leave. And frankly, if it runs over that, no one here will notice or care. When should we plan a baby shower?"

"I'll know more about the due date the 19th of the month at my doctor appointment. Let's think about summer," Sarah answered.

"Many people are gone on vacation or attend the state fair in August. I'll talk to Ginger at church, but let's plan it in July. Have you bought any maternity clothes?"

"Not yet, but I've about reached the limit of my regular clothes."

"I know a great shop in Des Moines. Let me take you there this week," offered Beverly.

The shop was in a strip mall, not one of those chain stores. Sarah had no real idea of what she wanted. Beverly was relishing the role of her shopping consultant. Looking through a rack of summer maternity dresses, Sarah saw someone she knew.

The woman was headed for the checkout her hands filled with maternity clothes as Sarah approached her. "Andrea, I'm surprised to see you here."

Andrea was startled, laid her handful on the counter and eyed Sarah up and down. "Well, I see you've come a long way."

"Yes, I hope all is well with Clark and you," Sarah responded while her eyes assessed at least a dozen outfits Andrea had laid on the counter.

"Well, you should know Clark's wife is expecting and I'm providing for them. That child will have every advantage his grandmother can offer."

"I'm sure the child will. Andrew and I met Janice in Casper. She seemed like a nice person. Tell Clark hi," then Sarah turned and continued shopping, leaving Andrea in shock.

"Who was that?" Beverly asked.

"Just someone from my past who I prefer to forget," she answered.

"It's good to put the past behind us," Beverly said. "We can't change it so why dwell on it."

"I suppose that is so. What, are you a philosopher now?" Sarah asked as she sifted through a rack of clothes.

"Look at this, I love it!" Sarah said to Beverly. She held a long denim dress that buttoned up the front. It ballooned in the midsection, but a wide belt allowed it to be constricted until more fabric was needed.

"It looks kind of pioneer," observed Beverly when Sarah modeled it.

"Nothing wrong with that, although pioneers didn't have denim. I'm buying it."

Sarah and Andrew lay in bed the evening of the 18th of April. "Tomorrow we'll learn whether our first child will be a boy or girl. For which are you praying?" Sarah asked Andrew.

"I'm praying for a healthy baby whichever God chooses to give us. Whichever gender our first is, I'll pray for the other next time."

"What makes you think there will be a next time?"

"Don't be ornery, we agreed on that a long time ago."

"I know, just kidding," she answered, glad she was able to return one of his many teases.

After a few hours of sound sleep, they both were awakened by a vibration. The room shook. "What is happening? Sarah asked.

Fully awake, they realized that the headboard was vibrating. Andrew's first thought was he would need to attach it to the wall, then he realized more was behind the vibration than a loose headboard. Both Sarah and Andrew raised their hands and gripped the headboard in an effort to steady it. Within seconds, the vibration was gone. The couple looked at each other as if they had experienced the same dream.

Without talking, Andrew got out of bed and opened a window blind. The sun had not risen, but light was beginning to encompass the eastern sky. He pulled on a pair of wrangler jeans and a flannel shirt. Sarah put on the denim dress she had purchased with Beverly. Although Andrew had not seen the dress, he didn't comment.

Both were in a daze of sorts; they did not speak. It was like they were somewhere else, not in latitude and longitude but in another dimension.

In the truck, they headed toward Wymore Cemetery. Their movements were involuntary as if orchestrated from elsewhere following an unknown script. Strangely, neither had any questions or inclinations to fear where they were going. Out of the truck, quietly they approached the granite headstone of their third great grandfather. It was a cool April morning; the last hurrah of winter was in the air.

Unlike their first visit to the cemetery, this time they walked up to the headstone and read ancestor Albert's birth and death information on one side of the stone and grandmother Dorothy's on the other side.

A verse was carved in the granite.

Amiable and beloved parents farewell not on this perishing
stone, but in the book of life, and the hearts of thy afflicted
friends is thy worth recorded.

While facing the headstone with their backs to the east, the sun broke the horizon and immersed the headstone in yellow light. A warm breeze from behind them engulfed the couple erasing their chill. In unison, they each laid a hand on the polished ball which topped the granite headstone. It was pleasantly warm.

Suddenly all started to rotate, and they felt weightless. The last vision they had of Wymore Cemetery was from above, rows of tombstones and a lone truck parked with both doors open. It was like the satellite view of an address you access online, only not on a flat screen but in three dimension.

When the rotation stopped, they found themselves seated close on a wood bench and bouncing over rough terrain. *Weird, in the truck,* they first thought, but Andrew sat on the right, not the left side. *Was she driving?* He wondered. *Had the rotation altered his sense of right and left?* He looked down expecting to see a steering wheel on the wrong side of the truck but found leather reins in his hand. The reins led to four oxen in front of them. Again, their seat bounced as a wagon wheel moved in and out of a chuck hole on the trail. Sarah turned and saw barrels and wooden boxes inside a covered wagon behind the seat.

Andrew suddenly realized that customarily the man with the reins sat on the right, not the left as in a vehicle. It fit but were they actually in a wagon pulled by animals. The bewildered look seen on each other's face said that their spouse was experiencing the same... what?

CHAPTER 25

As Sarah and Andrew contemplated their situation silently looking at each other, they didn't notice a man on horseback approaching them. "Welcome to my train," the man said startling them.

The man was dressed in black clothing wearing a broad straight brimmed hat. In a Western movie he would have passed as a traveling preacher. The couple starred at him in shock.

"Are you all right? You look pale" he asked.

"Yes... I think so," Andrew answered. The man was younger but definitely resembled the patriarch in the old family portrait they found in Casper.

"A few days in the sun will correct your color," he observed.

Andrew said, "I take it you are Captain Augustine."

"Oh, you know my name – that is unusual; Ralph seldom tells his recruits my name. And you are?"

Andrew stuttered, looked at Sarah, then said, "Conners, Sarah and Andrew Conners."

"I hope your hesitation in giving your name doesn't mean you are here to escape trouble. I tolerate no trouble in my caravan."

"No, sir, we mean no trouble," said Sarah.

How about past trouble? Are you here to escape the law?"

"No local law agency or the FBI is looking for us," answered Andrew.

"What is the FBI?" asked a bewildered Albert.

"What is the date?" asked Andrew ignoring the captain's question.

"It's April 19, a good day to get started."

"No, I mean the year," Andrew added. Sensing confusion in Albert, he added, "Sarah and I were arguing about it. We don't keep a calendar."

"The year of our Lord, 1855. Oh, I see Ralph coming now. He'll inspect your wagon and if all is as required we'll soon be on our way."

Albert added to Sarah, "When we camp for the night, come to the second wagon. My wife, Dorothy, will give you tips on cooking and life on the trail."

Albert started to turn his well-used bay mare, then turned back. "I've seen a variety of garments on the trail, but I've not seen pants and a dress made from blue canvas. Where did you get those?"

Sarah hesitated, then lied, "I made them."

"Looks very practical, perhaps it will catch on. We can always use a good seamstress on the journey. By the way, are you…?

"Yes, I'm in a family way."

"As required, we have a doctor with us if you need him," Albert said as he rode off. *It took all kinds,* he thought, *these newcomers were industrious but mighty strange, not knowing the date and having to think about their name.*

Ralph rode up. "I loaded your supplies before you arrived, so I know your wagon is in order. You've started to make the adjustment I see," nodding at Albert riding away. "Only discuss your situation and how you came to be here with me."

"Who are you? We've so many questions," stated Sarah.

"That is natural. Tonight, I'll answer as many as I can. It was an adjustment for me also. I'm glad you liked the headboard."

"But…?"

As his horse trotted off, he answered, "Tonight, tonight, we'll talk."

Andrew remained on the wagon seat driving while Sarah tried to keep her balance on the rough terrain inside the wagon surveying what was there. She opened a number of wooden containers and returned to the seat with a report. "I'd say 200 pounds of flour, 25 or sugar, and 75 of bacon are about what is back there as was on the list we saw on our honeymoon at the museum in North Platte."

In mid-May, traveling through what they believed was to become western Nebraska, Andrew helped rescue a team and wagon stuck in quicksand. A log chain was broken in the process. The next evening, they camped without wood or water after encountering a hailstorm. It was said they made 25 miles that day.

Measuring distances traveled was achieved by multiplying the revolutions of a wagon wheel by the circumference of the wheel. Among other inventions, it was Benjamin Franklin who invented the odometer when he was postmaster general in order to calculate the distance between cities. In 1847 William Clayton, a Mormon pioneer, improved the invention and called it a roadometer.

As most families, they slept under the wagon. Sleeping in the wagon required unloading it. A blanket on the ground and sheets around the wagon for privacy was their bedroom. One morning they were startled to find two prairie lizards had spent the night with them.

In June, Andrew assumed they were somewhere in what was to become Wyoming. About noon, 18 Indians blocked their path. The Indians spread blankets, which was a message they expected gifts. Bread, flour, meat, and sugar were given them. Then everyone, including captain Albert, took a whiff from a pipe of peace, and they moved on. It was said they made 18 miles that day. The next day they stayed camped at a place with lush grass. It would be an opportunity for the livestock to fill on grass. Grass would be sparse on much of the trip they were told. Everyone rested, and the men had a shooting match. Andrew thought his Winchester model 94 at home, wherever that was, was an antique but not compared to the long, heavy rifle found in his wagon.

On a day in July, they came to hot springs, then a creek of cool and fresh water. There laid an Indian who had been killed for stealing horses. Someone remarked that hell must not be more than a mile from where they were. That night the guard was doubled.

The next day 75 to 80 Indians came down mountainside ravines. The caravan was put in battle array. Leaving 25 men with the women and wagons, the rest of the men made a charge at them. One shot fired by the Indians passed over them without hurting anyone. The Indians backed off, then followed the caravan at a distance the rest of the forenoon with no trouble.

In early August they traveled at night. The desert floor was stony and rough with no water or grass. A Frenchman left the train thinking he could find a more favorable route. After crossing an alkali slough, one of Andrew's oxen came unhitched. It was quite an ordeal getting restarted. After camping, they killed a wolf and a few hares. They estimated that they had seen eight dead livestock per mile in the last hundred miles.

Sarah was nearly eight months along. The train doctor was routinely checking her. He said she was big for her stage. Neighbors lent extra blankets for her to sit on during the rough trip. She laid in the wagon when it became particularly rough.

It was the 18th of August near Soda Springs; Ralph rode up to the wagon. "The train is headed for Petaluma near Santa Rosa and the ocean. It is another month's ride; Sarah should not go further. I'll lead you to my cabin on the mountainside, only a day's ride halfway to Nevada City."

As they started to leave the train, Albert rode up. "I was glad to have you along this far on our trip. Wish you God's speed and take care of your wife. By the way, what was your name again?"

"Collins, it is Collins sir." Andrew sensed skepticism in the captain's look.

Captain Augustine was sure he answered Conners when first asked. But they were off the train now and hadn't caused any trouble. Whatever they hid, it was not his problem.

In route to the mountain cabin, Andrew asked Ralph, "If you have a cabin here, why did you go to Iowa only to return?"

"I was sent to assist in your transition." The questions his answer raised were numerous.

Sarah asked a simple one, "Do you live alone in the cabin?"

"Oh, no, my wife Thelma is there. She has some experience in birthing. You will be fine."

It was hardly a trail they meandered through heading toward Ralph's cabin. Often, they stopped while Andrew and Ralph cleared a path for the wagon to squeeze through. The mountains and canyons in the Sierra Nevada were formed by granitic rocks, a by-product of a geologic process known as subduction. They were headed toward a sheer red granite cliff rising far above the tree line. Closer, Sarah could see a cabin close to the rock wall with a distinctive upside down Y crack pointing toward the heavens.

Thelma greeted them on their arrival. She was obviously expecting them. "How was your trip?"

"It was wonderful, but I'm glad we'll be off the wagon now," Sarah answered.

"Come with me. We have a smaller cabin in back. I've fixed it up for you."

It was small, not over twelve feet square. On one wall a fireplace, near another a table and across from the fireplace a double bed. Sarah recognized something, "Oh, I can't believe it, the headboard is like ours, no it is exactly like ours."

"I'm glad you like it," Thelma said assuming Sarah liked hers.

The next few weeks were peaceful. Thelma and Ralph couldn't have been better neighbors. Often Andrew and Ralph went hunting while Thelma helped Sarah sew baby clothes.

Often both Sarah and Andrew asked what would become of them. What would they do to earn a living? Where would they permanently live? How would they provide for their baby?

Thelma and Ralph brushed off their questions with a version of, "Don't worry about it. You will be taken care of." Years later, Sarah and Andrew would look back and not understand why they had such little concern about the answers to their questions.

One morning Andrew was up early, unable to sleep. He went for a walk. The morning had heavy cloud cover. When he headed back to the granite wall which the cabins sat near, he was bedazzled. It was as if the cabins had disappeared. Nothing stood next to the upside down Y crack in the granite. Convinced that he had taken a wrong turn, he looked around. The sun suddenly came out. When he looked over his shoulder, the cabins were there. Embarrassed and convinced that it was the mountain air affecting his sense of direction, he never told anyone.

It was the middle of September. Ralph suggested Andrew and he ride into Nevada City for a few supplies. It would be an all day trip. Andrew was skeptical about leaving Sarah for the day. Ralph insisted. They left at daylight and didn't expect to be back until dusk. While taking a break enroute, Ralph pulled a hand carved wood racoon and duck from his saddle bag and handed them to Andrew. Each were small, only four inches; easy to slide in his pocket.

"They're for the babies," Ralph told him.

Andrew thanked him but missed Ralph's use of a plural.

It was mid-morning when labor pains struck Sarah. The men returned before the sun was down and were putting supplies in Thelma and Ralph's cabin when Andrew heard something. "What is that?" he asked, concerned that it was a wild animal.

"Step outside and listen closely," Ralph said.

It was the cry of a baby from the other cabin. Andrew ran, opened the door to find Sarah holding a newborn. He leapt to her side and looked at the baby. A kiss for Sarah was interrupted by a baby cry behind him. He turned to see Thelma holding another baby.

"We got our wish – a boy and a girl," Sarah joyfully answered his question before he could ask.

"Shall we use the names we picked early on the trip?" asked Andrew.

Ralph walked in the cabin. Sarah looked at him and said, "I want to introduce you to Steven and Annette."

The newborn babies were more peaceful than expected that night. Sarah and Andrew slept with the babies between them. It was approaching dawn when the headboard shook. In the dark, neither could see the other. But both steadied the headboard with a hand. The room started to spin. Sarah reached for the babies, but they were gone. She tried to warn Andrew, but she couldn't speak.

The haze and spin slowly dissipated. They felt a warm breeze blowing from behind them. Each were on a side of a red granite headstone immersed in sunshine with a hand on the topping polished globe. Sarah looked down and saw that her belly protruded as it did months earlier or was it the day before. Where and when were they? They wondered until the realization struck them that they were at Wymore Cemetery in Iowa.

They found Andrew's truck doors open as they had left them. Sarah felt rumbling in her belly, it was the first she'd felt – that is the first movement she felt in Iowa. Andrew checked his cellphone in the truck. It showed 7:15 a.m. April 19, 2022. He turned it toward Sarah.

At a loss for words, neither said anything until Andrew pulled in the farmstead driveway. Sarah then reminded him, "We've a 10:00 appointment with my doctor."

At the medical clinic, the doctor and nurse set up a sonogram to check the baby. The doctor asked, "Do you wish to know which sex the baby is?"

"I already know I have two, a boy and a girl, Steven and Annette," Sarah answered very matter-of-factly.

The doctor turned to Andrew, "Your wife seems very sure about that."

"She is," he answered.

Sarah turned and saw Andrew holding Ralph's gift of two whittled animal carvings. The carvings were not imagination. The question that would haunt them was why and by whom did they experience the impossible.

WAGON TRAIN LOG BOOK

Captain Albert Augustine

April 19, 1855

to

September 19, 1855

THROUGH:

Fort Atkinson to Platte River

Chimney Rock

Fort Laramie (North Plate River)

Independence Rock

Snake River to Boise on

South to Humbolt River

Sola Springs, Idaho

Miles

Traveled as recorded -2200 miles

Oskaloosa, IA-Petaluma, CA (Map Quest) – 1866 miles

Travel Time

Time as recorded- 5 months or 153 days

Road Travel- Oskaloosa, IA – Petaluma, CA (Map Quest)— 25 hrs., 48 min

Flight Time- Des Moines - San Francisco (layover in Denver)— 5 hrs., 26 min

Log writer unknown.

Note: This log is of the fourth wagon train trip by Albert Augustine from Iowa to California or Oregon; trips were made in 1849, 1851, 1853, 1855 and 1856. On the 1849 trip he was a passenger rather than captain. For purpose of easier reading, some punctuation was added to the copy. However, original wordings, grammar and spellings were preserved as nearly as possible.

A journal of our travels across the plains in the year eighteen hundred and fifty five. (1855)

April 19

We left Albert Augustine's 2 miles west of Oskaloosa in Mahaska County Iowa. Went to Belfountain first day. Incampt. John Doughman & Anna, his wife, fell in with us at Bellfountain. Made 12 miles.

April 20

Passed on through Knoxville & went on four mile est of town. Struck tent making 16 miles.

April 21

Thence westward & campt 8 miles east of Indianola in Marion County makin so many miles.

April 22

On again and passed through Indianola & brought up at John Johnson's in Madison County making so many miles.

April 23

Struck tent and reloaded.

April 24

Remained here.

April 25

Ditto.

April 26

Ditto.

April 27 Friday.

Ditto.

<u>April 28 Saturday.</u>

We have a good shooting match today. Fine sport. Our cattle in good plight. We organized or rather registered our names which are as follows—I will give our proper names as well as nicknames, beginning with:

Albert Augustine, he being Kap. Of our train we call him "pappy"

Tobias Augustine, him we call "san tyanne"

John Johnson, his name "Doolittle"

L. S. Comstock was called "Skyheels"

Converse Wing was "Broadhorns"

Samuel Newell was called "Lazarus"

John Doughman was called "Friday"

Pat Delaney was called "Boston"

James Fullerton was called "Moses"

<u>April 29, Sunday 1855</u>

<u>April 30</u>

We start for the bluffs. Passed through Winterset, the county site of Madison County and traveled on to middle river 15 miles from Winterset & campt. We guarded our stock last night for the first time.

<u>May 1</u>

Theodore Case left us this morning, then we started on our journey and padded on to Snake Hollow & campt. It rained all night & still raining this morning.

<u>May 2</u>

Quite cool. We traveled all day and brought up on Notaway Creek in Adair County. Our company has killed one duck & one prairie hen.

May 3

We left Notaway Creek. Took dinner on West Notaway Creek and got on of A. Augustine's carriage horses mired. Then on and campt that night ½ mile to right of read at or near Bear Grove.

May 4

On again and passed through Lewistown, the county seat of Cass County. Then on to Indiantown. West Ivaniston, it in Potawatamie County; then crossed Nishnabotna Creek; then Indian Creek at noontime; the on and campt on Walnut Creek on west side of creek.

May 5 Saturday morn.

Left Walnut Creek and passed through Wheelers Grove, and took dinner on Jordan Creek John Johnson traded horses here, then went on to West Nishnabota Creek :& campt on west side, went fishing- caught 4 or 5 small fish.

May 6 Sunday morning.

Cloudy. On and crossed silver creek took dinner one mile West of silver creek, then crossed Key creek and campt on Camp Creek 5 miles east of Kanesville.

May 7

We passed on through Kanesville & campt on east side of Missouri river making 234 miles in all. We saw some of the Omahan Indians for the first. Grass plenty. We have not fed any corn since we left Winterset.

May 8

Crossed over the river & passed through Omahan City, and compt on Heaven Creek a little west of town making 1 ½ miles. Here we initiated three other into our band, as follow:

Merrit Norton was called "Badger"

Wm. Ables was called "Grissley"
John Wright, "Curly"

May 9

We traveled 22 miles and campt on Pappe Creek. Quite an excitement in camp last night with a bay mare pulling hook by the halter. Made 22 miles.

May 10

Thursday. Crossed Elkhorn River. Took dinner on west side of Eld and that night well in with quite a train & campt on the river Platte. Saw some Paddnus Indian. Making 18 miles today.

May 11

Friday morning. Started on again took dinner at the round Grove & campt on the Platte again & made 20 miles.

May 12 Saturday morning.

We have again organized in to a company of 50 men & have 268 head of cattle. We crossed shell creek took dinner a little west. It is raining a little. Campt again on Platte River & caught 2 cat fish weighing 4 lbs each, making 15 miles.

May 13 Sunday morning.

Started on again and took dinner on Louss (Loup?) fork of Platte & campt on east side of ford making 10 miles.

May 14 Monday morning.

forded Loupe Fork. Tobiases team stuck fast in the quick sand and broke one long chain but got through, then traveled about four miles and took dinner and on again & campt on Loup fork. Made 16 miles.

May 15

Traveled all day making 16 miles.

A WAGON TRAIN LEGACY

May 16 Wed.

We traveled about 7 miles then went about 18 miles & campt without wood or water. Today we had quite a hail storm & we saw some of the prairie lizards for the first. They are a singular thing being about 1 1/2 to 3 inches long and very Expert. Making 25 miles.

May 17 Thursday morn.

On again. Took dinner where there was a little water. To the right of road & campt on Prarie Creek. No wood, we used weeds for cooking. Making 20 miles.

May 18 Fri. morn.

Left Prarie Creek traveled about 14 miles through the rain and struck tent at 2 p.m. on the head waters of Prarie Creek. Albert's Bull (dog) had 9 pups. Albert scolded John Doughman for whipping his horses and gave his team in charge of Sam Newell. Making 14 miles today.

May 19 Saturday.

Before starting 2 of A. Augustine's horses took the back track. The train started on we took dinner on east side of Wood River, a tributary of Platte. After dinner we crossed Wood River and traveled about 8 miles & struck tent without wood or water except what we had with us. A. Augustine & T Augustine and another hand started on pursuit of the horses, but are not in camp yet. Made 15 miles.

May 20

We started on & took dinner in the Platte Valley & campt that night on or near the river, the horse hunters came into camp this evening but no horses, we have given them up for lost. John W. Johnson killed & brought in an antelope this evening. We had some for supper, Making about 20 miles this day. The first company we organized with left us today and we fell back to another company. We are now with Allison from Marion Co. Iowa.

May 21

On again. Took dinner on a slough to left of road and ampt on Elna creek to left of road. No wood handy. The company killed 2 buffaloes and wounded two others. We also had two stampedes last night of 700 cattle and 70 head of tem were found the next day. Made 18 miles.

May 22

Started on this morning. Took dinner on the plains without wood or water. Crossed Buffalo Creekand campt to the left of the road where there was a little water. Used buffalo chips to cook. Made about 20 miles.

May 23 Wednesday.

Morning saw seven large wolves. Then started, took dinner near the Platte. Split with our company again and campt alone, us five wagons. Our split on account of fast traveling. Made 18 miles today.

May 24 Thursday.

Started on again. Fell in with another small company and crossed Skunk Creek and Cassion Creek and campt on black mud creek. Had a tremendous rain and hail storm. We are now with Captain John Grissly from Missouri. Made 14 miles.

May 26 Saturday.

Started this morning quite cool and raind a little today. Took dinner near the river. The road miserable muddy and campt on small Goose creek. The Indians stole 2 horses last night from a company $\frac{1}{2}$ mile below us from Missouri. Made 18 miles.

May 27 Sunday.

About 30 of the Siouse Indians came to us and company just below with about 15 American horses and sold them or gave them up for some flour and sugar and other little things. This morning we leave goose creek and cross Duck Weed Creek and a little farther and crossed Rattlesnake Creek. Campt a little below Crooked Creek. Made 16 miles.

May 28, 1855 Monday morning.

Left Crooked Creek about 10 o'clock. Crossed Camp Creek first thence onward and camped on Watch Creed. T. Augustine killed an antelope today. We saw 10 buffalo. Killed on hare. Made 16 miles.

May 29

We left Watch creek and crossed Castle Creek and campt. Making 18 miles today.

May 30 Wednesday.

Started again. And crossed small branch and took dinner on the north bank of North Platte. Saw one antelope. Campt that night on Platte. Good grass. One mile and half left of road. We have had no wood since we left Wood river. We use buffalo chips for cooking all the time. Made 18 miles.

May 31, 1855 Thursday morning.

Started again and took dinner on Crab Creek and passed Cobble hills and campt at the ancient Bluff ruins. Making 25 miles today.

June 1, 1855 Friday morn.

We left ancient Bluff ruins, having the shape and form of old ruins appearing done by hands, invarious shapes, sizes, and forms. We took dinner on the bank of the river. W. Doughman kill a hare. J. Fullerton killed one. T. Augustine shot at an antelope but missed, then we campt on the river bank. Making 20 miles today.

June 2

Started in the morn. Took dinner without wood or water and that night campt on the river again, right apposite chimney rock it being on the south side of river. Saw one hare and two antelope. Making 15 miles today.

June 3 Sunday morning.

Left chimney rock and saw 10 antelopes. Took dinner on the bank of the river forked Scotts Bluffs and campt on Spring Creek 4 miles west of Bluffs, making 25 miles.

June 4

We left Spring Creek traveled until on o'clock, took dinner on the river bank then started on and about the middle of the afternoon and J. Doughman and wife dissolved partnership. We went on and campt on the river again. Some wood and scattering timber along the river. Made 18 miles.

June 5 Tuesday morning.

On again. Passed some French traders and took dinner on the river mouth. Killed one hare and saw a few of the Siouse Indians and campt on the river bank. Wood plenty, make 16 miles.

June 6 Wednesday morning.

Raining a little but started on went 3 miles, or opposite Fort Laramie, then went 2 miles above and took dinner grass not good, went 1 1/2 miles above and campt, wrote letters, and took them over to the fort. Made 6 1/2 miles.

June 7 Thurs. morn.

Started on and struck into the Black Hills on north side of North

Platte. Country very rough and covered with pine and cedar timber. We traveled about 16 miles and campt on river bank. That night we organized a company, 67 men and strong.

June 8 Fri. morn.

Started on and passed the Twin Springs and Spring Creek. Saw some Indians and crossed Indian creek, went 3 miles and made for the river, campt in sight of Laramie peak. Snow on the peak continually. It rained this evening. 18 miles.

June 9 Sat. morn.

Started on Traveled about 5 miles crossed Deep Creek. About noon 18 indians seated themselves in the road before us. Our train made a halt, they spread their blankets to receive presents for the privilege of the traveling through their country. We gave them some bread, flour, meat, fruit, salt, sugar and etc. Then we took a whiff all around at the pipe of peace, then drove on and campt on the river again. Game scarce, saw on antelope today. Five of the same Indians came to us this evening, took supper, and left. Made 18 miles.

June 10 Sunday morn.

We rolled westward 5 miles & crossed Cotton Wood Creek, then went 10 miles further, took late dinner. Then passed purgatory gate & campt on the river again. Made 20 miles.

June 11 Mon. Morn.

On again, traveled a few miles & commenced climbing the ragged peaks, then kept the backbone ridge and after passing the ridge we made for the river bottom & campt at 1 o'clock, washed some clothing, and rested ourselves. It rained & showered this eve. Grass very poor, inadequate. 12 miles today.

June 12 Tues. morn.

Started on again and we left the Black Hills yesterday & we took dinner on the Platte River today. A little below the White sand Mound & campt on the river again. Grass a little tonight. We caught 3 young antelope today & saw 7 Indians the eve. Made 18 miles.

June 13 Wed.

Westward again, we took dinner on the river today to left of toad, considerable of timber roads very heavy, struck tent on the river again. Grass good. John Doughman left our train here & joined Montgomery train of Missouri. Chas. Rickerson and A. M. White were of our company, they disagreed on religious matters & dissolved partnership. John W. Johnson took Rickerson in with him. Made 18 miles.

June 14 Thur. Morn.

We traveled about 8 miles & came to the bridge where the Morman route crosses over on the North side of North Platte. We passed the bridge about 2 miles & campt for one of our company to get the tyre set on his wagon. There was 10 of the Araprahoes Indians here today & traded some but late this eve. There was some 30 odd more came into camp. They had their letter of recommendation, as friendly Indians. We gave them some presents. They handed their pipes of peace around and sang for us, got on to ponies and rode off after dark. Made 11 miles today.

June 15 Fri. morn.

Got late start on account of our cattle getting scattered, perhaps were driven off by Indians the evening before. They were in 3 different gangs, apart of them was 8 miles off, another 10 miles off, and the rest not so far. The Indians brought in about 70 head and we paid them for it, then we campt on Alkalie Creek, grass good, we left the Platte River today for good, made 16 miles.

June 16 Sat. Morn.

Left camp this morn. Took dinner on a small branch and went on to Willow Springs and campt at 2 o'clock. Making 15 miles.

June 17 Sunday.

Started on and went mile to Prospect Hill then 8 miles to Grease Wood Creek, took dinner then to Independence Rock and campt, trading post on east side. Made 21 miles.

June 18 Mon.

The Independence rock is rather a singular rock it is the valley of sweet water all alone and it's length is 500 paces and breadth 300 paces and height 300 feet, names inscribed there on from one end to the other. We then started on our journey and crossed sweet water and came to Devils Gate, which is another curiosity of the wide west. It is where the sweet water passes through a narrow cut in the solid rock of perpendicular walls of some 300 feet at the foot of a big mountain. We then passed a trading post on our left hand and took dinner on sweet water. Grass good. Went on a few miles and campt on sweet water again. We split with our company today. We left our names on Independence Rock. Made 15 miles.

June 19th Tues.

We started again and took a left hand road and came to the river at noon. Took dinner. There was 15 California packers all coming back to Missouri. We then left our company and campt alone, our 7 wagons and 12 men. Company divided on account of grass being scarce in the mountains. We leave our names and dates on the rocks here to the right of the road. We saw a few antelope today. Wood and water comes together. 18 miles.

June 20 Wendesday.

We started onward again and crossed the river twice in the narrows and want about 8 miles and crosst again. Took dinner at 10 o'clock then traveled 15 miles further and campt on Sweet Water again. A shower this evening, grass good. Our company has divided into 5 different companies and we are foremost, making 25 miles.

June 21. Thurs. morn.

Crossed the river early, went a short distance and crossed it twice more & climb the mountain. We passed today where there was digging & washing gold on Sweet Water. We climbed the mountain and passed Stoney Basin went a little further and struck tent on Strawberry Creed. No grass whence it rained and hail today. Made 22 miles.

June 22nd.

Started on, went 2 miles & crossed Willow Creek went 6 miles further & took dinner on Sweet Water again. Left there at 1 o'clock & went the south pass, then to the Pacific springs & no grass & then on to Pacific Creek & campt, no wood. Pat Delany lost $10 this morning. We saw 9 antelopes today & some sage hens. Made 25 miles.

June 23rd.

Started late this morning on account of John W. Johnson being quite sick. We left Pacific Creek and traveled on to Dry Sandy, no grass, alkalie water, and nothing but wild sage to cook with. We are now past the summit or south pass. Perpetual snow on the mountain here and cool of morning & evening. Tobias Augustine killed an antelope while we were striking tent. Made 9 miles.

June 24th. Sunday.

John Johnson little better. We started on 6 miles to juction of roads, there took right hand, went 4 miles to little sandy, and took dinner here. Grass fine. Left here at 1 o'clock & passed bluffs no. 1 & 2, then 4 miles to Big Sandy. Good grass, fine stream of water & campt. Killed on sage hen. Making 16 miles.

June 25th–June 26th. Tuesday.

Stayed here until 2 o'clock p.m. then started into the desert of 45 miles. We passed Clay Mound. 200 feet high, in four miles, crossed Alkali Creed. Keep your stock from this. Six miles to summit of hill. Six miles to Dry Creed. 3 miles to basin no. 2 three miles and seven miles to long steep hill. On this desert we traveled all night. Took breakfast at daybreak on the 26th. Then six miles to steep dangerous hill. Mr. Barker has one of his wagons upset here, no great damage done, then 5 miles to Green River, best ferry we crossed over and campt 2 miles below the ferry on the west side of the river. Grass good. Indians deep the ferry, some of the Snakes, one Cherodee, one Delaware, and the rest half breeds. Some scattering timber on Green River very rapid stream. Made 45 miles since yesterday noon.

June 27th. Wednesday

Had a late start. Took down the river a short distance, then went up a bluff, came into bottom again and crossed a small creek four miles from the place of starting, climb the bluff again, then in 6 miles came to Lost River. Kept up the east side 2 miles then crossed the river twice and campt about 1 o'clock. Made 12 miles.

June 28th.

Thursday. Started again went six miles to Bird Creek then 9 miles to Red sand Creek and 1 miles to pine grove took dinner. Here grass and water good. Then 5 miles O'Hara's creek, a very mountainous road. To a small creed one mile then 3 miles to Crow creek here campt early. Myself and 2 other young fellows took a tramp after some snow. Brought some to camp in my handkerchief get into camp at midnight but one of the boys lye out all night. Making about 20 miles.

June 29. Friday.

Started on the road very rough. Went 11 miles to Hains fork took dinner then climbed the mountains, very dangerous 2 miles to summit, then to quaking Asp grove no water, passed on to fir and pine grove, good water and grass here. We campt hers, saw a Grissly Bear. Made 25 miles.

June 30. Saturday.

About of us took a gun each went after fame Elk and Grissly Bear but did not succeed. Then we started through the grove and the flies bothered our cattle very much for the first time. Here we have a hill to ascend and descend very rough to Stoney Creek being six miles. In 3 miles you will strike Bear River Valley. The Fort Bridger road intersects road fine to grass creek. 4 miles. Grass plenty but water not good thus to Smiths fork which is 3 miles, we then turn down to the left and campt. A. Augustine bought a pony here. Made 16 miles.

July 1. Sunday morning.

Started on. Did not go between the Bluffs but crossed Smiths fork on a bridge. Paid 25 cts. Each wagon. A. Augustine boutht another pony. Mr. John W. Johnson got one & in 2 miles a bad slough, in three miles more a small creek but no grass, in 4 miles more a cold & beautiful spring to left of road, good grass. Here campt. All hands went fishing & caught any amount of spotted trout, an excellent fish. Took them out of Bear River. Tobe Augustine is very sick of the mountain fever, no weed very handy. Made 11 miles.

July 2. Mon. morning.

Started on again. Came to Smith's Fork. A mile to pleasant spring then 3 miles to Brookarts Creek. Now a long and tedious assent to summit of mountains & the descent is 3 miles. The most of the way very rough- be cautious how you go down. In 3 miles we strike Bear River again. Here campt, grass good, went fishing. Caught some fine trout. Made 18 miles today.

July 3.

On again & came to Creek which is 4 miles, some grass, then in 4 miles Beautiful Branch & 1 miles to swift water, then in 4 miles a branch, grass & wood, then in 3 miles Indian creek. We crossed 2 Branches of it near together & campt here. Some of the Shoshones came & traded with us. Made 15 miles.

July 4. Wed. Morning.

We started on this morning. Went 3 miles to a small branch of good water & grass. Crossed on & came to an excellent spring to left of road but went on 1/2 mile & took dinner. Good grass then crossed Black Mud Creek in 8 miles, the water in this creek is not good in summer, then crossed o to the Soda or Bar Springs nine miles, struck tent on a little east. The Soda Springs are the greatest curiosity on the route. They are a short distance east of the Ft. Hall & California roads & are scattered over perhaps 40 acres of ground. They do not, like the most of the springs run out of sides of hills, but boil directly up from a level & contain a gas & has an acid taste & when exposed to the sun or air it passes but a short distance before it takes formation of a crust or solid of scarlet hue, so that the continual boiling of some of these for a time will create a stone to the height of 15 to 25 feet some from 10 to 30 feet in diameter at the base & 2 to 5 ft. at the top. After arriving at a uniform height the water has ceased to flow from several of them but bursting out in other places. There is a French trading post here now and a number of the Shoshone Indians. Making 21 miles today.

July 5 Thurs. morning.

Started a 8 o'clock, went 6 miles to junction of Fort Hall road, the left hand is Brophnf (spelling?) Cutoff. We take the left hand to go a short distance where there is other curiosities in the formation of cavaties, chasms, underground & the air is completely filled with grasshoppers, then 8 miles to foot of mountains. No water nor grass, then 7 miles to Cady's Creek. Campt. Good grass. Made 21 miles.

July 6 Friday morning.

Left Cady's Creek & went 6 miles to Shoshone Creek. Grass & camping place. Then 3 miles to Jenison river, then 4 miles to a swamp, then 2 miles to a branch of hanach river, low and flat rolling country. Grass good. Made 19 miles.

July 7 Sat. morning

We left Pancach River, the road is now hilly ascending and secending to a branch of good water where we campt to rest ourselves & cattle. Good spring 3 rods east of road. Made 9 miles today.

July 8th. Sun. morning.

Started on our way and crossed a branch in 5 miles, then 3 miles to a small creek. No grass, then 6 miles to a spring & campt on east side below. Made 15 miles.

July 9th. Mon. morn.

Left spring run & went 9 miles to steep descent, very rough. Had to hold our wagons from turning over, then 16 miles to spring and branch. Some grass. Made 28 miles.

July 10. Tues morn.

Lost one of our best cows, the first that had died. At this spring, we found a Frenchman & wife that had been left by their partner. He left them on the night of the 7th and took their horse and one ox, which left them but one ox. A Augustine took them and plunder in. Started on went 9 miles to a little water to left of road, then 3 miles to summit then 1 mile to descent to an excellent spring to left of road & campt making 14 miles.

July 11 Wed. morn.

Started onward again. Went 5 miles to small branch. Good grass, then 5 miles to head of sinking Creek, then to first ford & campt. Good grass. Made 11 miles.

July 12. Thurs. morn.

Left ford #1 of sinking creek, went 4 miles to ford no. 2 & crossed over & traveled 12 miles to east branch of Raft River then 3 miles to middle branch of R. River. No water in it now, then 5 miles to west Branch of R. River & campt. Good grass & wood. Made 23 miles.

July 13. Friday morning.

We tarry here today. Do some washing, gathered some currants & gooseberries & caught some fish & have a shooting match & our Frenchman caught some crawfish & had them cooked.

July 14. Sat. – July 15 Sun.

A. Augustine had a pony stolen this morning before daylight, spent no time in hunting for it but passed on to Pyramid Circle which is another singular place, a beautiful little valley in the shape of a circle with rocks shaped in the form of a pyramid & other curious forms too tedious to mention. Then 1 mile to junction of Salt Lake & California roads, then three miles to creek but dry now. 4 miles to Flint Springs. 2 miles to Steep creek & old road & another creek in 3 miles, then Goose Creek in 3 miles. Went down a short distance & campt opposite a high craggy mountain. Making 25 miles.

July 16. My birthday.

We had a stampede of some cattle that campt near us this morning, then started up goose creek 6 miles to another small creek then 2 miles to another small Branch then went on left hand side of goose creek 8 miles to Record Bluffs to left of road & struck tent on right side of road. Splendid grass & meat, making 16 miles. We had another shooting match this evening.

July 17. Tues. morn.

Left Record Bluffs went 4 miles to east end of canyon, 5 miles then to Stone Hill, then 9 miles to thousand spring valley. No grass. Then down the Valley 6 miles & campt to left of road by springs. Used ships to cook. Made 25 miles.

July 18. Wed. Morn.

We drove our cattle to yoke them & we missed Old Dick, my near tongue ox belonging to A. Augustine. Five men of us followed the ox and three yardians (Indians?) by their tracks 14 miles but by their short turning on rocky places we lost their tracks & being short of water we was obliged to make for the train, which was on the way. Then went 7 miles to small creek & then 8 miles to Spring Creed. Made 15 miles.

July 19. Thurs. morning.

We caught some fish out of these springs. We then started on & after going a few miles, we came to the hot springs then a short distance to a creek of hot water. A few steps parallel of this was cool & fresh. We also found a dead Indian here that had been killed for staling horses. Some one of the boys remarked that Hell was not more than a mile from this place. We had not gone far until 2 packers were attacked & robbed of some of their things. We made a halt until another small train would take up with us. While here we were running bulls for fight, but we turned to left of road & campt in open valley. Had couble guard out tonight, not molested. Made 18 miles.

July 20. Friday morning.

Started again, passed Hope Springs, then one mile to mouth of canyon. There about 75 to 80 Indians came down the ravines & mountain sides with most hideous yells. We stopt the train, got in battle array with 25 men leaving the teams in charge of the women. We make a charge on them but they retreated & fled into the mountains. They fired one gun & its contents passed over one of our teams, but hurt no person. They followed after us a good part of the forenoon, but not very near. We traveled on a short distance on a left hand road & took dinner at a spring to left of road. Good grass, road by some large springs. Grass appearing good. Made 15 miles.

July 21. Sat. morning.

We started on & came to where right hand road came & presently struck into Deception Valley, then 5 miles to head Branch of Humbolt River, passed down the river 6 miles & campt. Our cattle all sick, gave them the last bacon we had. Made 18 miles today.

July 22. Sunday morning.

On again, we traveled about 6 miles to another tributary of Humbolt & campt on the west side. Grass not good, wood plenty. Some went hunting, others fishing. Killed some grouse. Made 6 miles today.

July 23. Monday morning.

Made an early start, traveled till mountain. Dinner on the north side of Humbolt. Roads good, & grass plenty, we campt above the west Branch on the north side of the Humbolt, grass & willow wood. 7 of the Pyutes Indians came to us this evening. Making 22 miles.

July 24. Tues. morning

Started on & crossed the west branch & kept the valley, took dinner at 12 o'clock, caught some fish, on again till night, campt. Saw good many Indians, good grass, game scarce. Made 23 miles.

July 25. Wed. morning

Started on, went 8 miles & came to junction of roads. The right goes over the mountains. The left hand crosses the river & strikes the canyon & campt. Caught fish. We passed the Hot Springs this morning. Right opposite the springs 4 of one head team took fright at some dogs & hare, ran about ¹/₂ mil but hurt nothing but on ox a little. Made 18 miles today.

July 26. Thursday morning.

On again, went 4 miles said to Poison water. Crossed another creek close by, then came to an ascent of 3 miles & rough descent, spring, & branch in making this discent. Charles Richrson got a little behind the train & had his pockets rifled by the Indians. Struck Humbolt & campt. Made 23 miles. This evening, 2 young men fell in with us that had stolen 2 horses from a train just behind. But the Indians took their horses & blankets from them left them on foot & alone. 33 miles.

July 27. Friday morning.

Crossed over on the south side of river & traveled until 11 o'clock & campt at a beautiful place, wood & grass. Caught some fine fish. Made 6 miles.

July 28th. Saturday morning.

Started on this morning, went 6 miles, & cross over on north side of H. river. Took dinner on the bank, traveled on a short distance & crossed over on south side & campt opposite stony point. We guarded an Indian last night that say with us. Made 26 miles.

July 29th. Sun. morning.

Crossed back on north side & passed Stony Point, then on 10 miles, struck tent, nothing but Willows to burn, roads dusty, lots of Indians all along this river. Made 10 miles today.

July 30th. Monday morn.

Took an early start. Went on till 11 o'clock & watered our stock. At 12 o'clock, took a left hand road, rounded the hills, and came to Alkalie swamp. A little west of this, the grass is uncommon salty. Went on passed another hill to left & made for the river, & campt at 4 o'clock. Good grass, made 18 miles.

July 31st.

Tuesday morning. On again, followed the river till 12 o'clock, took dinner, then left the river, crossed a sand ridge, then turned to right & passed canyon, then 6 miles to river & campt. Made 20 miles today.

Aug. 1st, 1855. Wed. morning.

Started on again. Kept on north side. Roads sandy. Crossed Rush Creek & went 2 miles below & campt. Saw 18 Indians. We are yet with Capt. Grissby & McLaughlan from Missouri & 3 packers, making 30 men in all. Made 20 miles today.

<u>Aug. 2nd. Thursday morning.</u>

Left the river this morning, went 2 miles, struck heavy sand for 11 miles, made for the river and watered our stock. Had bad hill, went 2 miles further & campt. 10 Indians today. 15 miles.

<u>Aug. 3rd. Friday morning.</u>

Left the river & struck on high ground very sandy, came to steep bank in 5 miles—150 ft. perpendicular, then watering place, then barren for 14 miles without water or grass. About half the distance very rocky. Then made the river again & campt. 4 fugitives camp with us here. Roads very dusty. Made 23 miles.

<u>Aug 4th. Saturday morning.</u>

Started on & came to Bluffs right of road 7 miles, then 5 miles made the river. Kept the north side nearly all the way. Went 2 miles further & campt. Good grass on the rise all along. Made 14 miles.

<u>Aug. 5. Sunday morning.</u>

Started on, went 18 miles to Deep ravine watered and took dinner at 3 o'clock. Then on 8 miles, made of to river & campt. Made 28 miles. Today A. Augustine & family started on with horses to get through to truehee on account of bad water.

<u>Aug 6. Mon. morning.</u>

On again. 6 miles to river. No grass. Then 11 miles to Willow springs to right of road. In this slough Bed water alkalie. In 7 miles, we strike the Big muddy, large body of grass & campt, but ½ miles good springs, no wood & no game, few Indians. Made 24 miles.

Aug. 7th. Tuesday morning.

Started early. Some grass for 6 or 7 miles, then no more until you reach the sink wich is 20 miles, here we campt. There is two trading posts here, one on each side of slough. Her is forks of road. One to Carson & the right to Truckee. Made 27 miles.

Aug. 8th. Wed. morning.

All night, some of us on a bust. The frenchman that is with us in particular & about 1 o'clock we take the Truckee route. Traveled all night and next day till noon. Reach truckee fine stream, 100 feet wide, some cotton wood on the river. The Desert stony & rough good part of the way. No water nor grass except for the boiling springs we passed at midnight.

August 9th.

After daylight in crossing a alkali slough one of my oxen came unyoked, had quite a time. Charles Rickersen & Mr. Abel & John Johnson had a quarrel on the Desert & C. Rickerson left the train. We crossed the river & campt for the rest of the day. Made 45 miles. Made an estimate of dead stock lately from 1 hundred miles until you reach here & it is 8 to the mile.

10th Augst. Friday moring.

Started on. Crossed the river 3 times in going 8 miles. We go up the river & the roughest old roads we have had for some time. Shot at one wolf & killed one hare & campt at 5th crossing. Making 9 miles.

11 Aug. Sat. morning.

Crossed the river first thing. Rough roads. One place for a few rods, the most dangerous we have had. We crossed the river 5 times in going to little meadow which is 7 miles. Here we have had since we left the states. Made 7 miles today.

Aug. 12th. Sunday morning.

On again. First crossing of the river very deep. Roads somewhat rough. We crossed the river 3 times more in going 8 miles, then we campt. Grass and wood. Made 8 miles.

Aug. 13th. Monday morn.

On we go slowly westward & crossed the river 4 times in going 7 miles. Very rough until you reach the Big Meadow trading post here. We overtook A. Augustine & family today. All well & right. Merrit Morton left us for California this morning. Made 7 miles.

August 14th. Tues. morning.

Went 2 miles & crossed over on north side of river. Sand roads & kept on north side 15 miles & crossed on south side, went $^3/_4$ mile & crossed back again. Went a little below & campt. Not much grass & the roughest road ever went any place, this is the first grass since we left Big Meadow. Struck into heavy pine forest. Made 18 miles.

Aug. 15th

Tarry today with sick cattle. A. Augustine lost 1 ox and 1 cow; J. Johnson, one ox; Grissby, one ox & 1 cow. Cambels train with us they lost Bossen. (He) died suddenly.

Aug. 16th Thurs. morning.

Left Big Truckee River this morning & made into mountains, 3 miles very stoney & rough & 1 mile very steep ascent into Dog Spring Valley, one mile of good spring & campt. Fine tall pine timber. 2 of the boys went back to Truckee to find a steer & heifer belonging to A. Augustine but not found. Made 5 miles.

Aug. 17th. Friday morning.

We started on, turned to left & took up pine & fiere (fir ?) hollow.

Went 3 miles to summit then 3 miles down to a beautiful meadow & campt. Our boys went back again to find the lost cattle. Found the steer dead, but heifer, they found not. A. Augustine lost another of his best oxen today. We amuse ourselves by pitching yuates. Made 6 miles.

Aug. 18th. Saturday morning.

Our Frenchman & wife left us to come thru to Sacramento, and 2 of Grissby's boys & one wagon. We stay to recruit our cattle. It rained a little today. 8 Indians were here today, beggars.

Aug. 19th Sunday morning.

Started on, went 3 miles to a nice little valley. Grass & water, then took up mud spring valley, then down a rough Descent & into another valley 3 miles, then 2 miles to little truckee river & campt. Rained & hailed today. Made 8 miles.

Aug. 20th. Monday morning.

Crossed little truckee took up on south side. Roads very rough & short turning that are difficult to make. I broke my forward axletree on the summit of the Sierra Nevada. Went 1/2 mile past old carol (corral?) & campt on a Branch of good water. Albert Augustine lost another ox. Made 7 miles.

Aug. 21. Tues. morning.

Staid here & made an axletree & hunted some. Killed 4 grouse.

Aug. 22nd. Wed. morning.

Started on again. Went 2 miles to truckee lake to left of road. 1 mile further passed a shanty & ranch to right, then took a timbered hollow 9 miles and about as rough as you please, then turned to left & crossed a Brach to an open valley. Shant & hay prep. Campt. Made 12 miles.

Aug. 23rd. Thurs. morning.

Here we stay today. This is what is called Jackson's rancho. Some game here. ^ of the boys followed some bear tracks but did not overtake them. Killed three ground hogs. No more today.

Aug. 24th Frid. Morning.

Still here. Grass splendid. Killed one ground hog, some grouse, we have shooting match & pitch horse shoes.

Aug. 25th. Sat. morning.

Still here. Fine weather. No Indians to bother. Stand guard no more. Today, killed one hog, one pine squirrel & one grouse.

Aug. 26th. Sunday morning.

We gathered up our stock & about 1 o'clock we started on & passed Jackson's ranch, went 4 miles to foot of Jackson's Hill, then 1 mile to good camping place. Struck tent. We crossed the head of the middle Yuba this afternoon. A. Augustine's youngest boy was standing up I carriage & caught hold of a limb & pulled himself out of the carriage, the hind wheel passing over him but lucky, no serious injury. Roads till rough. Made 5 miles.

Aug. 27th. Mon. morning.

Took the mountains again. Went miles to summit then 4 miles to water place to right of road, and shanty by it, then 6 miles to Nebraska City in the canyon to right of road & then 2 miles further & campt in a hollow where there is a spring & Branch & the hull of a house but no grass. Some of us went back to town in the evening & went into a tunnel 5 hundred feet underground. Made 15 miles today.

Aug. 28. Tues. morning.

On again, 2 miles to Galloway's Ranch, then 4 miles to Forest

City to right of road & Orleans Flatt to let of road, then 8 miles to watering place. No grass, then 3 miles to Bopes tavern in Plum Valley. Here campt. No grass. Digging after gold all around here. Made 18 miles.

Aug. 29th. Wed. morning.

Went one mile & John Johnson's wagon upset but no damage done. Then 2 miles further to watering place on left hand side & 1 miles to Franklin House on left hand side & 1 mile to Grissley fort, then 1 mile to fork of road. The right goes Marysville, then 1 mile & campt where house burned down. Not much grass settled all along. Made 8 miles.

Aug. 30th 1855. Thursday.

On again 4 miles to Junction House. There took right hand road again. Went 2 miles to Wisconsin House, right hand road again, 2 miles to Willow Creek House, then 2 miles to Foster's bar. Crossed over north Yuba, then terrible time climbing the hill. Went on 4 miles to Greenville & campt. No grass. Made 15 miles.

August 31. Friday morning.

Left Greenville & past the Oregon house. Climb the hill 1 1/2 miles to summit & campt that night at the Cregans House. Making 7 miles.

Sept 1st. Saturday morning.

Started on & passed the Tennessee House kept by R. Yinton, then passed Missouri House & campt at the Androse house at the foot of mountains to left of road. Made 12 miles.

Sept. 2nd. Sun. morning.

Left the Androse house. We are now in the feather river & Sacramento Valley, passed on to farmer house & then to Briggs

house & Bridge. Crossed Feather River above the mouth of Uba.
Passed through Uba City. Went one mile below & campt to left of
road. Made 14 miles.

3rd Sept. Mon. morning.

Two steam boats went down the river this morning. We then stated
on went to ten mile house, took dinner, winter, & grass. Then went
3 miles further & campt to right of road. Made 13 miles.

Sept. 4th. Tuesday morning.

Traveled to 7 miles through Tulas to Sacramento River, ferried
over & took dinner then went 12 miles to Cooke Creek, there campt.
Not much grass. Passed some good farms today. Had sport shooting
squirrels. Also saw some wild oats. Made 19 miles today.

Sept. 5th. Wednesday.

Went about 5 miles & turned our stock on the wild oats to feed.
There is thousands of acres of oats then on again 10 miles to Putah
Creek & campt. Capt. Grissby's son came to us this evening. Made
15 miles today.

Sept. 6th Thursday.

On our journey again. The country a little rolling & came to
junction of roads, then to Wilson's tavern. A small Branch and
little village here, then 2 miles to small valley & lade. Telegraph
line to Nappa City. Campt by this lake. Made 16 miles.

Sept. 7th. Friday morning.

Left the lade & came to suisus valley. Passed through, took right
hand road passed a canyon, then came to suscal house. Here campt
on creek. Made 16 miles.

Sept. 8th. Saturday morning.

Left the Suscal house & came to Nappa Valley. Here Miss Kise *left us & also the Grissbys. Took up Nappa Valley, passed on a short distance & came to Bridge. Crossed over & passed through Nappa City. Here took left hand road to Petaluma. Left the valley & came on to creek. Crossed the main creek, went on to small branch & campt. Made 17 miles today.*

Sept. 9th, 1855. Sund.

Started on, went to Sanoma, then 1 mile to creek, took dinner, then on 4 miles & met Judge Churchman & family, then 2 miles to old Spums fort and campt on creek, just above the road on east side of creek. Made 15 miles.

Sept. 10. Mon. morning.

All hands to Petaluma, families here yet.

Sept. 11.

Here yet. Branded all the stock still here.

Sept. 12.

Here yet.

Sept. 13.

Here yet.

Sept. 14.

Ditto.

15 Sept.

Here yet.

Sept .16.

All right.

Sept. 17.

Ditto

Sept. 18.

Ditto

Sept. 19.

4 of us boys go to chopping wood. A. Augustine rent a ranch just above. Tobe moves to Petaluma. J. Johnson a little west of town.

Made in the USA
Monee, IL
23 May 2023

34000065R00164